I Am To Tell You This

And I Am To Tell You It Is Fiction

Jeremy Vaeni

Kynegion House

Kynegion House

First Edition: September 2020
Printed in the United States of America
ISBN: 978-0-9746854-3-4

"Joy In Repetition," written by Prince, released in 1990 by Paisley Park Records & Warner Bros. Records.

Find the author on the web: https://www.ourundoing.com

Cover Design: Jeremy Vaeni
Printed in USA

Special Thanks

Though it is not my intention to injure any of my friends, family, or people who put up with me, with guilt by association, I must thank the following people for making this book come alive:

John Randall for his tireless dedication to his art. This book does not work without you! Best. Illustrator. EVER.

Jeffrey Kripal for the amazing, humbling foreword and proofreading, neither of which I asked for, both of which I greedily accepted. Thank you.

Tyler Kokjohn for making his serious writing contribution knowing full well I'd turn it into a joke and probably harm his reputation in the process. (Oh, wait, you didn't know that? Eh, you'll be fine.) Also, for his editing input.

Carol Fong for her thoughtful input throughout and for putting up with a husband in writer mode. More importantly, for rescuing me from being the pathetic guy in this book! You are my heart, my bunny, a true partner, and I love you.

Elaine Randall for her fine editing suggestions.

Nancy & Bill Birnes for letting me keep the rights to my *UFO Magazine* articles. Also, for lighting the fuses of several projects, including my documentary, *No One's Watching: An Aliens Abductee's Story*, which figures heavily in this book for no apparent reason.

Also, thanks to Tiokasin Ghosthorse, George Hansen, Carl Jung, Jeff Kripal, Jiddu Krishnamurti, Dennis McKenna, Jeff Ritzmann, Whitley Strieber, Jacques Vallee and any other genius I'm forgetting, whose style, substance, and inspiration are glaringly obvious in these pages.

Foreword

What Jeremy Vaeni Can Teach Us

(After We Stop Laughing)

> "It's no exaggeration to say that I am science fiction: one part tentacle monster, three parts futurist, all too human. . . . the only fact we may discern about abductions is that something is happening that we cannot experience directly because we filter it through our own fiction, composed of stories, assumptions, and visualizations conjured in fear.
>
> - Jeremy Vaeni

Jeremy Vaeni is my teacher. I first met him in Hawaii the second week of December, 2016. He had generously invited a trio of us for a conference entitled "The Living Mysteries Symposium." The science fiction writer and alien visionary Whitley Strieber, the ethnopharmacologist and psychedelic explorer Dennis McKenna, and I were the head-liners. Okay, Whitley and Dennis were the head-liners. I am not sure what I was doing there, but I was there, for sure, I suppose mostly talking about Whitley.

But still.

4.

My first encounter on the island was appropriately a bit strange. The frick'n sky was glowing orange. It was night. I was tired. I just got off what seemed like an infinite plane ride. For some reason that was not entirely clear to me, Dennis was driving us toward the glow in the sky, up a mountain no less, which seemed, to me anyway, like a rather dubious idea. Then we got there, to a parking lot of a restaurant perched above an active volcanic crater. The orange glow in the sky, it turned out, was a reflection on the clouds of the bubbling red lava in the crater. "Geezus. This place is nuts," I thought to myself. "And pretty awesome." Jeremy tells me that the volcano exploded in 2018. I am not surprised. It looked pretty bubbly in 2016.

The three of us told Jeremy not to do this, I mean, try to hold this conference. We knew it was expensive to fly us all half-way across the Pacific, and that he would likely lose money on the event. He did it anyway. Jeremy was like that: generous, kind, and supportive. It was a great deal of fun, and I really enjoyed my first and only visit to Hawaii, which ended with a five-day road trip around the Big Island with Dennis McKenna at the wheel of a mini-van with our mutual Houston friends Jerry and Linda Patchen. I have since associated Jeremy with a kind of laid-back wisdom or grace, a slowly exploding island of flowing lava and dubious real estate investments (have you ever seen what cooled black lava will do to a piece of land, much less a house?), and a McKennaesque tour of the Big Island.

Not bad.

But I have also read Jeremy Vaeni, and here my associations become something else, as I read him in a long line of nondual and idealist visionaries, none of whom, I must add, sounded anything like Jeremy Vaeni. Except for Bill Hicks. Hicks, not unlike Jeremy, was an American mystic posing as a comedian. Jeremy reminds me of Bill Hicks, who could get very metaphysical on his otherwise raunchy stage and just blurt out things, like how we are all the temporary imaginings of a single immortal consciousness. He also had some pretty elaborate UFO encounters. Not exactly your typical stand-up, but oh so Jeremy Vaenish. Or maybe Jeremy is Bill Hicksish. Same thing.

Back to this book. There are four motifs I most associate with Jeremy's writing: (1) human deification (Jeremy is God, or better, God has manifested through Jeremy); (2) bizarre energy effects in the spine, brain, and physical environment, which were somehow connected to human sexuality; (3) apparent alien abduction, which was somehow connected to human sexuality; and (4) humor, which is definitely connected to human sexuality. Jeremy thinks I am obsessed with sex. This is what we call projection.

I often confess to my graduate students that there is a reason I am a Freudian and not a Marxist. It is this: I have never met a funny Marxist, and I have met plenty of very funny Freudians (Freud himself is another matter). I also often tell anyone who will listen to me that there is a simple rule for whether or not to trust a particular spiritual message: humor. If people can laugh at their own sincere beliefs, there is every reason to trust them; if they cannot, beware. Humor, after all, is a kind of humble transcendence or reflexivity. One cannot laugh at something one has not stepped beyond, or at least imagined beyond. One instead becomes deadly serious, stuck, and dangerous.

The thing about Jeremy Vaeni is that he can and will laugh at just about anything, even things you definitely don't want him to laugh about. Which might mean that Jeremy is truly trustworthy. But it might also mean that Jeremy's humor is functioning sometimes as a kind of defense mechanism (to keep him from taking seriously what actually happened to him—hey, it's not so easy being God, especially when you are writing an email to your mom, which he has also done, or tried to do[1]). But Jeremy is perfectly aware of the defense mechanism thingy, and he often says the same. No one seems to take him seriously. Jeremy Vaeni doesn't even take Jeremy Vaeni seriously.

But I do. Do you want to know why I so admire Jeremy, why I listen and read him, and why he is my teacher? Because he makes me laugh and then think again about that laughter. Laughter is not just a defense mechanism here. It is also what he is trying to get us to see, or to be. Jeremy is my teacher because he makes me think that maybe all those previous deified human beings in the history of religions took themselves way too seriously, didn't have to die like that, and certainly didn't have to be tortured by their unfunny, much too serious contemporaries and then get gory theologies

---

[1] Unsent email draft made public in blog post, "How Not To Tell Your Mom You've Solved Aliens And Are God," on www.jayvay.com.

wrapped around their unfunniness. It's really sort of morbid, if you think about it. And unnecessary.

Jeremy is also my teacher because he knows what he is saying is so unbelievably serious that he has to hide behind the laughter to endure it and then to say it in a way that also unsays it. It, of course, will largely escape most of Jeremy's readers ("the five of us left who read," anyway, as he puts it in one of his gazillion great one-liners). "It," after all, is not an "it." It's more of a No-Thing, a Oneness that includes to transcend, an uncanny Other that is also oneself, or Oneself, a oneness of multidimensional being, as the Mystery Voice puts it toward the end of the book as the laughter subsides.

But maybe the laughter doesn't really end. Maybe the comedy routine is more than it seems. This is my deepest hunch. What we finally have in these pages is a paradoxical place between fact and fiction, levity and levitation, a kind of metaphysical science fiction that is always unwriting itself.

Or just laughing at itself.

Laugh out loud, then, but do not be deceived by your laughter. You are laughing at yourself, which means you are not really you anymore, even if you are also still you.

Jeffrey J. Kripal
Houston, Texas
26 August 2020

8.

06/24/2004

Dear L:

I apologize that I am reckless with the tenses in this recital, but such is the rawness of a dream and the laziness of this writer.

This morning I was having a long, involved, semi-sexual dream about various imaginary women who all represented my ex-girlfriend. It essentially was a breakup dream. When I walked out of it and closed the door I found myself in the hallway of an apartment building. The walls were painted glossy brown and the hand railing was a darker, un-glossed brown.

I walked down the stairs as a blonde couple in their late twenties/early thirties walked up. The staircase was narrow, typical of New York apartment buildings, and there was a brown-haired bearded fellow of the same age range sitting in our way. The couple and I struggled to get by. When we finally passed, I realized I was asleep and that this was a dream. At first I couldn't wait to leave the building and see what I could do in this dream world, but then I thought, No. Let these people know you're awake.

I've woken into dreams before. In those instances I'd let the dream characters know I was awake. They would inevitably pretend to not understand what I was talking about but I'd keep badgering them until they'd cave. Their attitude would change immediately from dumbfounded commoners into seething fury. It always goes this terrifying way. It feels as if these dream characters are just the façade for some demonic force, some human-hating guardians whose job it is to keep the dreamer from seeing what lies beyond the sleep state.

I gently grabbed the blonde man at the elbow and said, "I'm asleep." He looked taken aback. I repeated myself—I'm asleep—and the bearded man stood up. Suddenly, the two blondes and the brunette are friends with each other, sarcastic friends taunting me. They walk toward me backing me against a wall.

The color scheme remains the same but the scenery changes in that we're now on the top floor of this apartment building. The hallway is no longer a narrow staircase but a large rectangular room, the center of which is a rectangular stairwell protected by those same brown wooden guardrails. This hole is the majority of the room. The long walls are lined with doors, presumably to apartments, and I cannot yet see what is at the end opposite me.

I feel intimidated by the trio crowding me, yet bold nonetheless. I refuse to let fear stop this again, as it has in the past. I ask them—but primarily the blonde man who seems to be the leader—if they are real people or characters in my head. Do they exist independently of me? This is a nagging question

I'd never asked before. Usually I end up asking about alien abductions—like are they real and have they really happened to me. That's when things turn especially sour as if I'm a petty human asking stupid questions that don't involve me. They would sooner destroy me than answer the question. I asked a different one this time; for the first time, it didn't dawn on me to ask about abductions.

When I ask them if they're real they joke with each other, toying with the question. It's the type of disdain I'm used to from pissed-off dream characters. But I persist, asking them for a genuine answer: "Just tell me yes or no. Are you real? Are you real?!"

I feel stronger, less and less scared. There are others, now, coming through the doors and down the long walkways toward us on either side of the open center stairwell. I desperately try to force a confession from the blonde man. "It's simple," I explain. "Are you real? Just say yes or say no."

He ashamedly avoids my gaze. "No," he mutters, his head bobbing around, his eyes looking for any object that isn't me.

"What?" I say shocked. I was absolutely sure he would tell me they were beings alive unto themselves. "You mean you're not real? You're a part of me?"

He stopped fidgeting and looked me dead in the eye. "Yes. We are aspects of yourself."

The encroaching mob is rowdy. Some of the men start

swinging fists at each other. I can see that this trio is now allied with me. They are friends who will fight with me if I ask. I don't want to fight; I want to question him more about the nature of consciousness. The problem is, there's this old high school adversary aiming to pummel me. I knock him to the floor. Everyone is rioting. I think he's knocked out but he wraps his legs around my left leg. I realize that no one dies in a dream. You think they're down and out but they get back up like the living dead.

I look to the blonde guy who is also fending off brawlers. His facial expression tells me he's sorry; he, too, wishes we could have talked more. I feel a tad perturbed by this but knowing that I'm dreaming, I'm aware that I can do anything I want.

My tad perturbed turns to blind rage. I pick up the high school bully and throw him down the stairwell, letting loose a primal scream as I act. I watch his limp body bounce off of handrails as he plummets into the abyss. He's dead. I know it. Everyone there knows it. It's that movie scene where everyone stops what they're doing and stares at the madman.

The stunned people get out of my way as I pass, surveying the scene. I walk to the other end of the floor. On that other side there are round tables with gentlemen and flappers playing poker. It looks like a mixed up scene from the Old West.

Two women wearing short puffy black skirts bend over, revealing their black thong underwear to me. I think sardonically, Nice vaginal walls, and would have said this except I wasn't sure if "vaginal walls" was a real term. I thought I might be confusing vaginal walls with a song Prince wrote called, "Sugar Walls." I didn't want to look stupid since all eyes were on me, so instead I barked out, "Nice vaginas. Way to go. Why don't you wear clothes?" I felt mean and dumb and offensive—the key ingredients of arrogance.

I scanned the gamblers who showed their cards absentmindedly. Then, at a table to my right, I found her. Hiding. "She" was a woman who also attacked me during the brawl. I mean it didn't happen at the time of the fight but I now had snippets of memory of her trying to hurt me. I jogged over to her like a lunatic, lifted her above my head, ran back to the stairwell, and tossed her to her death, one floor below. To my dismay her spine cracked on the rail, then her carcass slunk to the floor. I wanted her to fall the other way, into the abyss. It was anticlimactic, but oh well. At least she was dead.

A piece of me felt sick for fighting and killing but I suppressed it. Everyone went back about their business, gambling and what not. There was a disjointed moment when automobile traffic appeared and would stop to let me walk by, but that didn't last.

Suddenly, an older military man, maybe in his late fifties, strutted in through the swinging saloon double doors to my right. I watched the stride of his long black boots. My vision swept up his black and blue uniform to his face like a movie entrance. Clearly he was a general in some type of army. His uniform looked like something out of the Civil War.

He started barking at the blonde guy about the piss-poor job he'd done as leader. Apparently the older general had left the blonde in charge while he was away. The blonde man argued that, no, in fact, people were happy gambling and fighting and being free. I barely paid attention to their quarrel. I was observing the card sharks and the whores.

I stopped ignoring the young blonde and the old general. I pieced together that if this is all me, and the general was in charge and he suppressed this, then I was suppressing it. I reflected on my fixation with these women wearing revealing thongs and how I ended that one woman with such vengeance. It made sense to kill the high school bully who refused to die just to attack me—but the woman? I had only flashbacks of her attacking me, flashbacks of an event that never took place. And I murdered her for it.

Christ, what was I?

I then had an abstract vision of my brain. The depths of my consciousness were bubbling up; subconscious merged with conscious. I saw that there need not be this divide between the unconscious and the conscious mind—they are one. We divide them ourselves and this is a monumental mistake.

The general and the blonde had drawn short swords and were going to duel for control. I now had a long sword in my hand, more like a fencing sword. I whipped it between them and forbade them to fight. I told the general that I liked this place much better since he left. I sided with the blonde's handling of things.

The general didn't care what I thought. I was nothing to him, a peon. He swatted my sword away and the fight was on. I could have stopped it, could have done anything I wanted. I chose to let the duel play out.

The blonde sliced his short sword all the way inside the general's left cheek. It was a cartoonish, gruesome display. The general maneuvered out of the painful hold. I thought he was finished but he kept fighting. It was a short fight, though, and a surprising finish. The two leaders clashed swords and bumped chests dramatically. In one swift motion, the general drew a tiny dagger and thrust it into the back of the blonde.

He cheated! The general cheated!

The blonde dropped slowly to his knees and then dead to the floor. The general had won back control. I was finished here and so I walked away through a door opposite this bedlam. The door opened out into a desert town. I had a sense that it was Mexico. There were white villas and an old white church against a red sand backdrop. I walked up to a cove and snooped inside. I saw a dead man in a hammock. His body was wrapped in a white blanket but I could see his face: dirty, hardened, and unshaven. He had the look of an average man who had coped with the harshness of desert life.

The deceased's family brought his cadaver outside to the open desert. We stood around it in mourning. Two men unwrapped the body but it was gone. This hollow husk of a torso covered by clothing spilled out onto the sand. Everyone gasped at the remains.

Two men arrived carrying a Tibetan monk who sat cross-legged on a cot-like platform. The monk was bald and dressed in flowing white garb and open-toed sandals. He wore a naïve smile that masked his spiritual greatness. I gained the impression that everyone here was Native American, Mexican, or Tibetan, except for this white guy standing to my left, and me.

The monk opened his robe and this long white snake slithered out. The snake had lengthy, pointy bristles jutting off the sides of its body. The snake slithered over the hollow torso. Like a magician, the monk produced a twin snake from his right sleeve. The two snakes writhed over the husk of what I thought was author Carlos Castaneda. Their quick movements had the effect of particlizing the remains. I could see the particles zipping around, bouncing off each other, humming with energy.

An old woman in the crowd told me it wasn't Carlos but a Mexican friend of his who had ascended to a higher plane of existence. Given the image of the corpse transmuting into vibrant energy, the old woman's words, and the spiritual cliché characters around me, I realized all at once that this is what is happening to me in real life.

One after the other, the snakes slid off the body to the

ground. They slithered between our feet. The other white guy was afraid they might bite us because we were barefooted. I told him, "No, I don't think they are here to hurt us. And besides it's just a movie anyway."

The snakes brushed up against my skin. They felt rough and real. I was alert but they slithered off into the red desert, no harm done.

The funeral ended. I walked toward a home out from which my ex-girlfriend was stepping. Physically, it wasn't her, though; it was one of the girls from the first dream who had represented her. I kissed her hello and could not remember why we'd broken up. It slowly came back to me that the meaning of this entire display was the reason why. We parted ways again.

I was sad and scared when I bumped into you, L. You asked me what was wrong and I told you everything. I broke into tears. You hugged me close but loose.

I knew this was about my ascension, but I didn't feel ready for it. What does that word "ascension" even mean anyway?

You held me in your arms and let me cry. I told you that this is what my life is. I was clutching a small box that had instructions on it. I was crying and talking and trying to read at the same time. The words were too blurry; I couldn't make them out. We remained this way until I woke up.

* * *

17.

Now that I am awake and reciting this, I wonder if I will ever dream the same old unconscious way again. Fortunately, I don't have to wait long to find out.

I feel different, L. Stronger. Sadder, though. I know this is attachment speaking but like all selfish newborns...

...I don't want to go.

18.

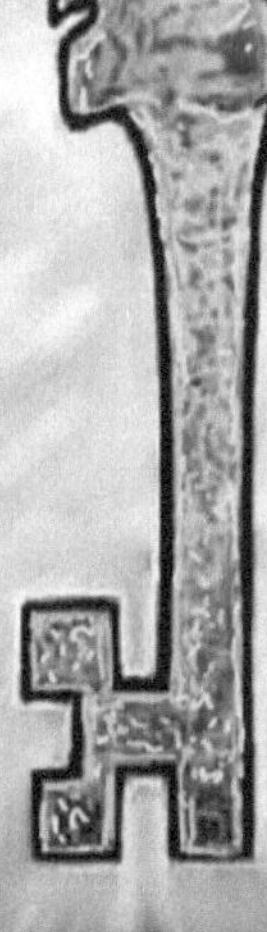

19.

"Joy In Repetition"

Song by Prince,
who changed his name to a symbol,
then changed his name back to Prince.

20.

When We Last Left Our Hero....

"So what do you think?"

Crouching Beavis, Hidden Butthead turned away from the unwieldy loose pages clutched in her kung fu grip. She turned away from me, preferring the intensity of Hulk Hogan's hulked-up eyes. Or maybe it was Michael Moore's dumpy everyman physique she was staring at. Since moving to Queens I had diversified my poster collection to include movies and WWE superstars. Michael Jackson still clung to my bedroom walls, but now he finally had something he'd been in desperate need of his entire life: friends.

Pregnant pause achieved, she turned to me, face plastered in shell-shocked confusion, like a child finding out Santa isn't real. Her nude body, glowing with after-sex, was slinked across my bed, hands holding the latest draft of the Nickelodeon chapter from my book, *I Know Why The Aliens Don't Land!* This is the chapter about my short stint at the children's cable network; this is the chapter ending in her.

She had pleaded with me to let her read it. I didn't want to. For one, we had just spent the night making "love" or whatever the first of a two-week marathon fuckfest is called. For two, I was certain the moment she read her ingeniously racist pseudonym, *Crouching Beavis, Hidden Butthead*, my China doll would have a porcelain heart attack. I thought the moment she read my account of her antics, she would freak out, cry, run naked in the streets. Okay, maybe not that last one, but you get the point. I thought she would be, in a word, *upset*. When she finally made eye contact and her lips pursed and words breathed out, I was thrown.

"You think I'm getting fat?" she deadpanned.

I was thrown. Did I say that already? Yeah. Thrown.

"What?"

"You said I'm getting fat."

Oh, shit! That's right! There's this through line about how her boyfriend keeps telling her she's getting fat and I keep defending her. Then, at the very end, when she screws me over, I write, "But fuck it. She's getting fat." This is the type of insensitivity readers have come to expect—nay, *demand*—of me.

Anyone with a sense of irony could see what I was doing. I mean it's an obvious joke. I explained it to her anyway. I backpedaled right out of that Shogun bamboo trap (which wasn't hard because she was nowhere near getting fat), then asked about the racist pseudonym. Didn't *that* bother her?

"No, I thought that was funny."

"So, you're not upset?"

"No, why would I be? These are your feelings about what happened. I think it's pretty accurate."

"Wow," I said, letting out a nervous tremor. "I thought you'd be pissed. I mean I can't believe it. That's so mature of you!"

"It's not like anything you said was wrong. I would be

pissed if I didn't do those things. But I did. God, was I really that mean?"

"Yeah. Why did you do it?"

For those who did not read the prequel to this book, we're talking about why she... No, fuck you. Read the prequel. I can't grow fatter off your money without your money.

"I don't know," she continued, after I interrupted to chastise the first-time reader. "I still don't know. I guess I didn't think it would affect you the way it did. I didn't know how sensitive you were."

Most bullies are, dear.

"So, you don't mind if I print this?" I had to keep reiterating because I couldn't fathom how being publicly outed as a jackass was on anyone's wish list, especially now that we had literally kissed and made up.

"No, I don't mind," she said. "But if you write another book, I don't want to be in it."

"Okay," I said.

"I'm serious. Promise me you won't write anything else about me. I don't want to read about this in the sequel," she said firmly.

"What sequel? I haven't even printed *this* book yet."

"Promise!"

"I did! I do! I swear to God I will not write anything about you ever again."

From His Ashes, A New Hero Rises

How does one begin a sequel 17 years in the making? Pretty fucking brilliantly, by my estimation. As you read, I started off all deep and mysterious and personal, then dove right into a hilarious, if risqué, bit of misogyny that is both a callback to the prequel and a way to solidify my sexual prowess. You know, just in case readers of *I Know Why The Aliens Don't Land!* thought I was still a virgin 17 years later?

It's not about my insecurity, by the way, it's about seducing you. All of you. Even the #metoo movement. Is that still a thing? Hashtags, I mean. Clearly, men are still abusing women to assert dominance. Or at least I am.

Plus, opening with sex is the only way I could hold Jeff Kripal's attention. I really needed that Foreword. Mahalo, Jeff.

Sorry if that last quip was too inside baseball. I promise the rest of this won't be. In fact, you won't have to have read *I Know Why The Aliens Don't Land!* to enjoy this book. Odds are, you won't enjoy this book either way, but we'll get to that throughout these pages. For now, let's get the newest Jeremy Vaeni fans up to speed on his (aka my) absolutely ridiculous life.

What a whirlwind life has been since publishing that little book with a big name back in 2003. For you, too, I bet. Life is a whirlwind, you know? It must be. I've said it twice now. That and other truly deep, helpful thoughts will be forthcoming in this meaty tome. For me—and let's stick with the protagonist here, since it's my book—for me, the calm before the storm hit in my East Village apartment in Manhattan, before I published the prequel. Toward the end of finishing the last draft, a mysterious universal energy liars claim to master called, *kundalini*, came alive in me. I wrote a thorough accounting of how and why in *Urgency.*[2], so I won't go into it here except to explain that it is an impersonal force of will that comes active when our own personal will goes dormant. It moves the body into strange postures and contortions we observe in Buddhist and Hindu statues, including, sometimes, tongue waggling. Cute, right?

It also does yoga, Tai Chi, Whirling Dervish twirls, basic stretches, activates dormant psychic capabilities, chakras—oh, all sorts of expensive New Age workshopping I used to make fun of. But it's free. And if you don't become mesmerized by all of these powerful "new" awakenings happening in you, to you, as you—and if you don't cower in fear that you're going psycho—you might just get to that point where you realize what you're witnessing: intelligent energy that both is and is not you at the same time.

Because that's not insane enough there are also other personas in the body who are and are not you. You become

---

[2] Vaeni, Jeremy. *Urgency.*: Kynegion House, 2011.

kinda like conjoined sextuplets who display differing masterful skill sets, but without all the noisy jibber-jabber and bragging I imagine they would torture you with if they were actual people.

It's funny how those of the New Age persuasion like to talk about all objects being one energy manifesting as separate things, as if that fact overrides the multiplicity of objects. Both aspects are facts, right? And they are necessary, as is the third basic aspect of existence we tend to overlook: interconnection. All things are interconnecting precisely because they are the forms manifesting "within" one formless Being.

The big picture of reality boils down to a single hyphenated word: No-Thing. No-Thing, roughly speaking, is pure consciousness self-realizing as all things by simply being. Pure consciousness is, as you might suspect, pure intelligence. What this pure intelligence is purely doing is purely being. Being what? Being all things.

Succinctly put, Being, with a capital B, is being. And that's everything. Or No-Thing.

Is that succinct or obscure? I have a hard time with that when it comes to this. In any event, what multiplicity within oneness looks like from our measly human vantage point is the universe exploding from light. Light that is the functioning visual of consciousness per se.

Words. Am I right? Here come more....

Often, when we think of the universe we picture stars and planets, but really all the contents of the universe are the universe. And those contents are both interconnecting and distinct. If you've heard a smiley Youtube guru or two talk about us being waves on an ocean or being like manifestations of appearances on one body of water?—That. That is what we are talking about.

So, the universe is the appearance of multiples within oneness.[3] And kundalini works kinda the same way, if backwards.[4] To see what this means, let's change the body of water in our clichéd Youtube guru's analogy from an ocean to a stream. Think of kundalini as a flowing stream composed of raindrops. In our analogy, the droplets are spirits, archetypes, and whatever other formless awarenesses exist, and you are the pool of water in which they coalesce. They are all flowing into and through you. They are, therefore, also you.

So anyone who talks about kundalini as an energy that they turn on and off to activate chakras and all that as part of a meditation exercise or yoga regimen are talking about a different stream, are bragging about their own falsely autonomous stream, are pissing in the pool. Which, come to think of it, would be like a snake mistaking pissing in its own mouth for eating its tail. Welcome to post-modern eternal energy.

Anyway, long story short? That's me. Not the pissing in my mouth part, but the kundalini aliveness. Because, you know, thinking I was an alien abductee was getting too passé.

---

[3] Objects within objects exploding alive from the doings of one energy.

[4] Living energy exploding from the undoings of objects, namely thoughts, within objects, less-psychotically referred to as, "people."

Anyone can write *that* sequel. *Look at me! I was abducted... more!*

Predictably, all of the truly spectacular kundalini stuff I experienced didn't unfold until long after I wrote, *I Know Why The Aliens Don't Land!*, which is why I left out any mention. It began as an energy that rolled my head around my neck like a basic neck exercise when I rested my sense of self. I didn't know what the hell to do with that, so I stuck with aliens.

In 2004, the kundalini worked its process and I became God. Not *that* god; *that* god doesn't exist. What god does exist was worth its own book, I thought, hence I wrote *Urgency.*

Actually, just go read *Urgency.* You'll like it. I don't hide in toxic masculinity or talk about pee-pee snakes. It's reader-friendly. You'll like it.

Getting back to this book, many people, I'm now convincing you, have been anticipating this sequel for so long that it's hard to live up to the hype I just created. Maybe that is why I am steering you to a different book. And maybe that is why I put off finishing this one for over a decade. I kept putting it off and putting it off. Well, no more. This book deserves to see the light of day. "Daylight," I calls it. Unless you'd rather read *Urgency.*—I'm telling you, you'll like it.

Never mind. Where was I? "Daylight," I calls it. Morning sun peeks through curtains right now. Prepare. Prepare to wakey-wakey, tired one. You deserve it. I deserve it. This book deserves it. I said that already. I'm stalling. No more. Here comes the sequel. Like you paid for. Like you were promised.

To quote the greatest of cinematic heroes, Ash Williams,

"Like in the deal."

29.

Coughs Out Himself In Dust

But first, I want to talk about ants.

You know ants are amazing insects. All insects are amazing in their own right, but ants especially because I know more about them. This provides me an opportunity to look intelligent on a wide range of topics when what I am is limited to ants. But that's our secret.

Ants, too, have a secret. Well, it's no secret to them. To us, they don't look like formidable intelligences that could even hold secrets. Fifty times their natural body weight? Sure. Like the average Walmart shopper, they could hold that. But not secrets. No, sir. Secrets are for people and other highly intelligent animals. So here's the secret they don't have....

Ants: They're Just Like You And Me

Humans have been scrutinizing and interpreting ant behaviors for centuries. Parallels between these industrious social insects and the human condition have served for centuries as traditional cautionary tales for children. Aesop's fable *The Grasshopper and The Ant* celebrates the virtues of hard work and foresight while including a memorable example of the inevitable fate of idlers. A more distilled admonishment may be found in the Bible, Proverbs 6:6 - "Go to the ant, O sluggard, Observe her ways and be wise."

Simple in so many ways, as is the case with humans, ants can play more than a single role. Anyone with a looted farm, garden or pantry may be inclined to view these opportunistic, active creatures not as virtuous role models of personal industry, but as brazen buccaneers.

Seeing Ourselves

Not withstanding some obvious differences, ant activities seem to correspond to human behaviors in several ways. Ants are social beings exhibiting complex patterns of cooperation, division of labor (specialization) and communication. Many are predatory, but leaf cutter ants, sometimes known as 'parasol ants', are insect versions of farmers and harvest plant leaves to cultivate the special fungus gardens that sustain them. Other ants ranch nectar-producing aphids, tending to them constantly and taking care to protect them from predators.

Ant colonies are the living embodiment of a superorganism in which individuals work as a selfless collective. While they have no independent existence outside the colony, ants are sensitive to their environments and because some of their behaviors are flexible in response to situational demands we should not dismiss them as pre-programmed zombies.

Ants Are Builders

The species most familiar to us construct complex, often large, living quarters harboring many thousands of individuals. Some of these colonies may be active for years or decades. Shelter is essential because ants go through complete (4-stage) metamorphosis and are completely helpless during every life cycle stage—egg, larval and pupal—other than the adult phase.

Ants Do Not Stay Where They 'Should'

Judging solely by raw physiologic potential, the ants might be predicted to have a rather restricted geographic range. Instead, like humans who are best physiologically adapted to more tropical conditions, the ants have spread out and dominate a huge portion of the terrestrial biosphere. Being able to create shelters has enabled ant species to colonize many permanently or periodically hostile environments. Species such as wood ants build mounded structures to maximize solar warming effects thereby enabling them to be active for longer portions of the year in colder climates. In addition, ants exhibit flexible behaviors that enable them to exploit favorable environmental niches. In cold regions ants excavate nests under rocks and stones that have their surfaces exposed to sunlight. Solar heating of the exposed rock surfaces will also warm the soil. The ants can bring their developing eggs and larvae to galleries lying just underneath the sunlight-warmed rock to take advantage of the favorable temperatures.

Some Ants Are Invasive

Beyond exhibiting a remarkable ability to adapt to many

environments, a few ant species, like humans, have truly gone global. The red fire ant (*Solenopsis invicta*) may have come in to the U. S. through the shipment of products between nations. The Argentine ant (*Linepithema humile*) and Raspberry crazy ants (*Nylanderia fulva*) have probably been inconspicuous hobos who traveled with us briefly and jumped off in new locations. Because ants are significant predators of other insects, when these invaders multiply unchecked they significantly alter the local ecology. We may regard them as insignificant little things, but when invasive ants decimate insect populations the consequential impacts echo up and down the entire food chain as birds and other consumers that prey on bugs and spiders suffer.

The record of invasive ants reveals that humans and some ant species travel and live well together. Pharaoh ants (*Monomorium pharaonis*) plagued a Harvard University laboratory for years before being eradicated. As we eye Mars and other locations as potentially terra-formable abodes, perhaps some ant species will journey right along with us to new solar system homes. Maybe in those instances we will make the deliberate decision to include them as our partners in an interplanetary terraforming tag team.

All Ants Are Not Created Equal

Ant societies have a caste system of workers and elites, or royalty. The activities of the colony revolve around service to the long-lived queen ant. Reproductive activities are essentially the sole privilege of the queen, male royals, drones, live only long enough to perform fertilization activities during a single mating episode. The worker ants, genetic kin to the queen, never reproduce.

Ants Are Aggressive

Ants compete with each other and attack others they recognize as different species or sometimes take aggressive actions against individuals of the same species identified as coming from other colonies. Ants also engage in clear and deliberate warfare against their neighbors. Warfare may be about capturing resources and territory, but a few raider species are parasitic slave-takers stealing the brood from other colonies to put them to work.

Successful, aggressive, resourceful and immoral, the ants obey only the dictates of their biology to seize what they need and modify the environment to suit their precise specifications. A dominating, irresistible force in the biosphere, but heedless of most of the universe our amazing analogues will never cease to fascinate us.

For authoritative information on ant taxonomy and biology – Bert Holldobler and E. O. Wilson. 1990. The Ants. Belnap Press.

***

Okay, okay, I didn't write that. Ya caught me. I'm not writing about ants, I've got shit to do. I recruited my friend,

Tyler Kokjohn, PhD. He's not a PhD in ants, but it still sounds impressive. Not as impressive as what I'm about to write. And, yes, I really am writing it this time, you can tell by my chronic overuse of commas. Quit buggin' me.

The point is, ants really are just like you and me in certain ways. We share complex behaviors and social structures. How is that possible when we are completely different organisms? How is that possible when an ant is minuscule in size compared to a person?

If size doesn't matter and composition of brain/body matter doesn't matter—if both exhibit the same or ridiculously similar complex behaviors and social structures —then is form following function? Do behaviors exist prior to physicality and whatever organic material is wrapped around them is just kinda like body art?

Are all living beings actions performing thingness disguised as things performing actions? Or are we all just glorified sleeve tattoos rippling down the arms of an invisible biker?

So many questions, so little universe.

35.

“Joy In Repetition”

Song off of the *Graffiti Bridge* soundtrack, sequel to the movie *Purple Rain*.

36.

The Dust Is On Its Own Journey

The shit thing about writing a sequel 17 years later, besides the fact that you have to write it, is that most anyone who is going to want to read it will have followed you around, keeping up with your life. Thanks to the miracle of the internet I can blog and podcast and sniff my own farts on social media. Between that and my last nonfiction book, the aforementioned, highly likable, *Urgency.*, which utilized the guts of what was originally going to be this book, there's not much the astute Jeremy Vaeni sycophant doesn't know about my high strangeness experiences or my penchant for getting blacklisted in ufology. I could rehash my swashbuckling adventures in a murky subculture and whine and make myself look like a hero, but does anyone really care about me calling obvious charlatans by their names (Steven Greer; Billy Meier; you, probably), or explaining why hypnosis is a terrible tool for memory retrieval for the umpteenth time (brilliant for behavior modification; garbage for remembering things)?

Do you wanna hear about how I became God that one time again? What about that?

After a while, isn't it all a snore?

It is. Unless you've got an obsessive fetish kinda thing for ufology, the paranormal, and mysticism. And honestly? I think that describes most of the audience for this stuff nowadays. Right, everybody?

Generally speaking, ufological obsessives are like super fans of a one-hit wonder. Dexys Midnight Runners are dying to play *The Celtic Soul Brothers* and *Dance Stance*, but all we want to hear is *Come On Eileen*. There are better competing theories for what's flying around in the skies and "abducting" people than aliens in spaceships. But aliens in spaceships sell, so ufologists, on the whole, give the masses what they want. And then young upstart podcasters bitch about it to look smart and offer nothing better because they are incapable and because Jeff Ritzmann and I already did the heavy lifting on that front with our classic podcast, Paratopia. I'm not bragging, mind you, I'm *humble* bragging. Our show was better than even that.

Why don't most people approach the unknown from divergent perspectives, you may ask?

To answer, please allow me to flip the script, as the kids used to say, and present a different book. A children's book. Something even you could understand. Forget the naughty words and tell-all bullshit. Forget your appetite for my insights, which you will likely just shit out on your blog, unattributed. Forget, even, if you can, forget your alien fetish. Let's not talk about fetishes. Let's talk about feet.

No? Not yet? A bridge too stretchy?

Fine. We won't flip the script. I'll bore me with what's left of the sequel I wrote 17 years ago until you cave, and we'll leave whatever I just said a confusing mess. For now.

Here, then, are the parts that didn't make it into *Urgency.*, for obvious reasons. Obvious to those who read it. Which you should. You'll like it.

Let's start in 2001, just after the 9/11 terrorist attacks, where Chapter 6 would have been. This clusterfuck ended before Crouching Beavis, Hidden Butthead and I reconnected. I wrote the first draft 18 years ago. Should hold up.

CYBER 6

I thought they spelled true fairytale love, her words on the screen. They broiled my belly and swam rainbow colors before my woozy eyes. They were intelligent words, humorous words. Not always kind words. They challenged me and taunted me and agreed that this exchange was unlike any previously experienced.

Her online name was "Wildcherry," after the soft drink, not the sexual connotation, and for a time she lived only in my imagination and my plastic radiating pixel box. I used to wonder why it is humans must sit nine feet away from the television, lest we go blind, but the computer screen is deemed safe two noses away. Now I had the answer and the answer was Wildcherry. She killed the pain and the poison.

We met in an MSN chatroom. Online. Like nerds. I had arrived late on the computer scene by many, many years, so this whole chatroom thing was a fresh addiction: Jeremy's new toy. But I still had my reservations. Clearly, whomever produced the words on the screen not born of my own fingertips must be a repugnant, lonely basement dweller. In short, a C.H.U.D..

And, in short, that tends to hold true. But not always true, *mostly* true. So when you find those special somebodies who get the joke that is their lives, you clutch them like a miser clutches diamonds and appreciate their shine. You, like they, assure yourself that this internet thing is for losers, *your* losers, your captive audience. You are better than the other names on the screen, you understand, because you rightly objectify the object in front of you. It is a bland little box with a screen, a clicker, and keyboard. It only feels the emotions you give it. You are its god, its troll king.

THEY don't understand this. THEY need this. THEY spin a worldwide web around themselves, believing they are living in the silken grace of a blessed life of cyber friends and cyber sex, when what you know is that the web being woven is a cocoon sarcophagus. Yet and still, the truth is, always is, in any given situation, neither you nor they know shit.

But just try telling me that. I was snapped out of my virtual head world when Wildcherry lifted the floodgate on a constant stream of jokes at my expense. She saw through my psychological firewalls and never let me get away with tormenting her the way I tormented so many other screen names. I was only trying to help them, of course, wake them up to the fact of their god power. Whatever flattery or insult one feels from words online is one's own projection. One needn't live in this regurgitation cycle, one need own it.

Wildcherry saw through that, too.

We needed to meet, needed to be with each other in the flesh, if only to know one another's eyes. No matter what the words on the screen tell you, eyes are the sole domain of honesty. Honestly. Ask any good serial killer.

"How old are you?" She asked this many hours into our conversation. This question usually pops up at the beginning of online chat, lest John Ashcroft and his Ashcroft puppets swoop down into Cyberia and haul away one's priestly pedophilic ass. The myth of Big Brother scares most eager addicts into writing, *A/S/L????* at the beginning of any exchange. Those letters stand for AGE, SEX, and LOCATION, with the question marks standing for DESPERATION. Wildcherry wasn't desperate even if she was and neither was I, neither was I.

I had turned twenty-eight on the third of September, mere days previous her question. "Oh shit! You're an old man!" she typed.

"Why? How old are you?"

"19."

Great. Jailbait. We traded diatribes on the significance of age. She's too young to drink but I don't drink, so no problem there. She comes across more maturely than most of my age-appropriate friends, so what does that say? I'm as goofy and immature as the next nineteen-year-old, so, fine-fine. She attends an all-girl's college in Massachusetts, which plunged her deep into celibacy, and I tend my virginity in New York, like Mr. Miyagi tends his favorite banzai tree.

Law-wise we were set. There were no ethical issues at

stake, but morally it felt wrong. Her age ended in *teen*, for Christ! Was I a dirty old man in liberal clothing? A basement dweller after all? A C.H.U.D.?

She decided for us that age was just a number—a favorite saying of the NAMBLA community—but I wasn't completely sold. She gave me her digits and for the first time I heard a voice from beyond the screen. That voice sounded sweet and funny and smart and adult. It sounded like all that the hands had typed.

We spoke for weeks on the phone late into the night. We argued and cooed and agreed and something in there felt like romance. She had a vacation break coming up in late October, but I warned her against visiting me. New York was suffering through the boldest attacks in the nation's history and, oh yeah: you might not want to come alone to one of the biggest cities on the planet to visit a male stranger living with three other strange males, and on Halloween no less. That might end in tragedy.

We hammered through these issues. She'd give her mother and her roommate my phone number. She would call them as soon as she got here to tell them she's alive. She would call her mom every day.

Her mom. Her MOM! She'd call her mom because she's nineteen. My tummy felt like I'd eaten bad Mexican, having harped on this age thing for too long.

One random night I asked, "Don't you even want to see what I look like before you come?"

"Oh yeah. I forgot about that part. I guess we should do

that."

We mailed photos to each other. Mine was from a year ago when I was looking kinda sharp and kinda young. She didn't have any recent pictures of herself, so she sent me a copy of her high school yearbook photo and a group shot, also from high school.

From high school—from HIGH SCHOOL!

I felt that Mexican bubbling up again.

Cherry In The Sky With Jacksons

Her Greyhound bus was late. No soul-dead Port Authority information booth corpse could tell me which bus arrived at what terminal and when. Gross incompetence is another reason to never visit New Yor—*Is that her?*

I squinted at any lone female arriving from whichever bus at whatever terminal. If she looked lost, my stomach tingled. Any single gal with a backpack or suitcase could be her. What else could I go by? The photos? A lot of physical changes take place between seventeen and nineteen. Just look at Britney Spears.

That reminds me, why am I beating myself up over this age thing when Britney friggen Spears was mass-marketed to males age 12-65 before she finished puberty? Can you name any of her songs?—Yeah. You can name *one* of them. It's the same song played a dozen times on all of her albums. She can afford this eternal repetitious karaoke. Nobody gives a shit about her shitty music because at most we want to fuck her in her smooth Pilates pooper. That and gymnastics are the extent of her tal—*Is that her? That girl with the long, blond hair and the confident stride? That girl whose eyes betray stride, darting around, searching for....*

"It's me," I whispered shyly.

"Oh my god, hi."

We hugged nervously and for the first time. I traded her an obligatory rose for her bags. She was not moved by the flower at her alter. This goddess was going to be tough to worship; it might take blood sacrifice. I assured my nerves I'd have almost a week to crack her bible code. I'm sorry, what am I talking about? I got lost in the trying to make this about something. Jesus, this is the slowest audible stumble toward first-time fucking since Dad's birds-and-bees chat.

***

If I seem callous now, it's a defense. Trust me when I tell you that on the inside I am mush. I am fish gut. I feel like I know less about Wildcherry now than I did then.

What did I know about her then? I knew a handful of her personality traits, as previously discussed. I knew the threat of sex was more real than real. *Real* to me meant that in my mind I'm either making sweet, sweet love to an incredibly fine woman, like a Prince song, or humping her brains out like a... um... like a Prince song. That's in my mind. In my body I'm watching TV or reading a book, or at a movie, or whatever it is we C.H.U.D.s do to drown the discrepancy.

Wildcherry made her plans to snatch me from my mind

obvious when she casually told me her mom makes her get a birth control shot in the arm in case she becomes sexually active like Bruce Banner becomes the Incredible Hulk. I knew that fact prior to her arrival. I knew she hadn't had sex since she broke up with her boyfriend back when. After Senior Prom, most likely. I knew she was from the state of Maine. Podunk, most likely. Put two and two (or two and nineteen) together and you get a disease-free chick on birth control. I mean odds are. You know... in my mind.

Even so, that was no guarantee I'd have sex with her, and certainly not without a condom. I was too old and too a virgin to skinny-dip in septic watering holes. No, I'd definitely have to have been in love to have sex or else why did I wait so long? I wanted the wait to have meaning, after all. And you say, "Self-imposed meaning." And I say, "All pedestrian meaning is self-imposed."

And now we've learned a little lesson together. Sleep with me.

***

One of my fears in any prospective sexual encounter is that because I'm an alien abductee, there might be some outside interference. Gray gingerbread men from elsewhere who prefer the druid tunics from *Spinal Tap* over the hazmat suits from *E.T.* have an alleged tendency to extract sperm and ova from their human subjects or victims or friends, depending on one's sense of relationship with them, possibly to make hybrid children; possibly, an egg salad sandwich. And so I've always got this tiny fear nagging me: What if my Herculean sperm fertilizes an egg and tiny thieves steal my lucky lady to airlift said zygote to their test tube orphanage?

In the past I never had a lucky lady to worry about, so it was hypothetical in every sense. But tonight? Tonight there was a lady. And she was lucky. She didn't know about any of this alien stuff. I begged the invisible sky doctors not to rudely awaken her with my bad luck.

***

During our first night together, we warmed to each other by playing the *getting to know you* game. She showed me her vitiligo, the pigment-eating skin disorder Michael Jackson had, and I showed her the wall-eating Michael Jackson poster collection I had. Her skin disorder actually appeared chic because it was spreading up her arms from her hands and looked like long white lace gloves. Plus, Michael Jackson.

I don't recall doing much of anything in the way of entertainment that first night. Well, except the fucking. There was lot's of that. Or... maybe not lot's. Fifteen seconds to be exact. I hovered above her nakedness, contemplating my virginity and do I really want to do this, when she grabbed my dick and shoved it inside her dirty blond nether mouth. Only way, way more romantic than that.

Anyway, I lay there staring at her and feeling this first feeling of being inside the very thing *Porky's* movies are made of. I thought about all the jokes I'd heard over the years of not being able to last the first time; you know, premature ejaculation? But I thought I could distance myself enough to actually last—like Sting claimed to do during tantric sex. I didn't know anything about tantric sex, so instead of meditating or going to my happy place or bathing in imaginary light, I concentrated on childhood.

My bedroom looked like a nightmare straight outta 1983. Besides a thousand eyes of Michael Jackson staring at us from every inch of the walls, I slept on an old mattress on the floor with my green bureau I'd had since I was a wee one acting as headboard. I looked over each and every sticker I'd collected on that thing: a standard cartoon frog, a Gamorean Guard from *Return of The Jedi*, some Slugger baseball stickers, *G.I. Joe* characters, about a thousand stickers of my name, some motorcycles from that movie *Tron*, a round green sticker screaming the words "Go For It!" —Oh they were all there, old friends, cheering me on, egging me toward my first pump.

I thrust inside her. She moaned my name, sunk her claws into the fat of my incredibly forgiving ass. *I need to be anywhere but here at this moment if I am going to—because you see this feels so good and—crap, no! No! NO!—*

"Yes! Yes!" she wailed. Or would have if I'd lasted even the liberal fifteen seconds I lied about four paragraphs up. Yeah, this was embarrassing. I was laughing. She was panting. I was apologizing. She was consoling. I was apologizing. She was hushing me. I was apologizing. She was taking my face in her hands, romancing my eyes with her eyes and telling me I was wonderful.

I was apologizing.

***

Day two with Wildcherry was a good time. We went sightseeing, did all the corny tourist shit I refused to do until I had guests. We made out in public a lot, which is something else I refused to do until now. I was among the many who hated watching couples slobber all over each other like pooches licking hello. I found out right quick those couples I hated didn't include me.

We were so in love it was unreal. You know it had to be that drastic kind of tug on the heart for her to overlook all that I have described and the describer describing it. Very real was my sense of relief that no other out of town/off-world guests crashed the party.

Abduction tragedy averted!

Go, Team Vaeni!

***

What should have been a lovely view of Manhattan from atop the Empire State Building was a nightmarish vision. There, through telescopic viewfinders, we watched the smoldering holes in the ground where the World Trade Center Towers stood only a month ago. We could see the smoke and the fires and the ash—the heat of it, the twisted evil results of a political web we could merely guess at. Having taken in that sight, we took to the other attraction of the skyscraper: the motion odyssey movie called *Sky Ride*.

Sky Ride is a whirlwind trip through the Big Apple via the big screen. The seats jerk and vibrate along with the onscreen action to achieve an immersive virtual reality feel. Our tour guides for this airborne journey? Why none other than James Doohan, as *Scotty* from the old *Star Trek*, and Yakov Smirnoff, as himself!

Wait. Is that Kevin Bacon's voiceover I hear?

It is?

Yeah! It doesn't get any more cheesetastic than this!

Whoop! There we are swooping around the Brooklyn Bridge! And, ooooooh!—Watch out for the Empire State Building!

Weeeee! This is fun!

Yakov's jokes are... well... he brought his A game to this project, let me tell ya! And Scotty, that fat, old drunk shoehorned into his tattered Trek uniform! Oh, man. He's so clumsy.

I wonder if we'll get out alive?

Speaking of which, there's the Twin Towers! WATCH OUT! We're going to crash! We're going to crash into the... into the... Jesus fucking Christ, into the... This is inappropriate. Who green lit keeping this? Can we get off now? I think we're all feeling a bit sick.

What's that, Yakov? In Russia, buildings crash into you?

You're right: What a country.

Beam me up.

Later That Night

Wildcherry and I are snoozing away the predawn hours on my floor mattress. I don't know what time it is but it must be between three and six because we got to sleep really late and it isn't light out yet.

Correction: it *is* light out. It's very light out. In fact, there's so much light pouring in through my bedroom windows that it wakes me. The quality of light is strange. It's bright yet dull. Foggy. Yeah, like sunlight diffusing evenly through a thick fog.

I prop myself up on my left arm and just stare at it. Wildcherry remains out cold, unmoved by the brightness. I hover over her and peel back a curtain. Yup, it sure is bright out. But if she's okay, I'm okay.

I collapse onto my back and find that there are now three beings standing over me to my right. Terrified, I scream, but no sound comes out.

The beings are short, not more than four feet tall. They are wearing brown tunics. Their skin tone is gray to the blue hue, not chalky white or deeply gray, and from what I can see of their hooded heads, they are bald. They have diminutive facial features, save for the eyes, which are huge black oval pools. If human eyes are the windows to the soul, these eyes are windows to the infinite depths of everything.

There is something else curious about them: they have a

playful nature. The one closest my face, at least, is smirking and exuding this childlike naivety. It is as if they want me to come play and yet I am horrified beyond the meaning of the term.

None of these beings speak a word to me. Wildcherry remains unconscious through all of this, as well as the next thing I know.

The next thing I know—and there is no transition here, it's literally just the very next moment—I am standing in a foreign room. I'm wearing the boxer shorts I went to sleep in. The room is long and open, not quite cavernous but the illusion of that given the lighting, or lack thereof.

About ten feet in front of me begins a row of tables, vertical to my sightline. I'm not sure how many tables there are, maybe five. They're lit from above by unseen sources. The fixtures, if indeed that's what they are, give off that same misty/foggy light that had flooded my bedroom. These are the only sources of illumination. Outside of the tables everything is dark and empty.

There are people lying on the tables. Humans. Strangers. Men and women. Naked. Immobile. Unconscious. One closest to me is a blond-haired woman, Caucasian, in her late forties or early fifties. A bunch of similar beings—maybe even the same ones who brought me here—stand around her. They are examining her in an inclusive way, letting me in on the situation, gesturing to me as if to say, "See? This is what we do for a living."

Standing there and observing this, I'm totally calm, the

antithesis of the terror that plagued me when they stood in my bedroom. 'Why am I seeing this?' I wonder silently.

A female voice answers in my head, "Because you've always wanted to remember an abduction." The voice is soothing and familiar. I know this woman. I *know* this woman. She is not human and I am not on Earth.

The telepathic voice and I have a lengthy discussion. I remember it long enough to jot it when I'm returned to my bed, but I don't. I let it go.

This wasn't a dream, this was real. But it couldn't be. What are the odds? That light in my window. Why didn't it wake the whole neighborhood? No, this was a dream.

No, it wasn't.

Vivid dream.

No, it wasn't.

Shut up and sleep.

Okay.

***

Next day, I brought Wildcherry to a taping of *Late Show With David Letterman.* It was the episode where guest Farrah Fawcett comes on blitzed out of her mind on either drugs or some mental derangement and lets the world know she's the grandmother of coo-coo. Yes, long before Bobby cracked out Whitney and Courtney found Love in a warm gun, there was Farrah. And now we all knew.

Letterman, a pro in any situation, turned her instability

into comedy gold. It was that or call for an on-the-spot intervention. He chose right. We all have stuff to do.

After the show, we dined in one o'them fancy-shmancy restaurants. I probably got a hot dog. It probably cost 15 bucks. Want relish? Add $1.50. I don't really remember what we ate, but I recall the conversation like it was tomorrow. Wildcherry admitted she was a week past due getting that birth control shot. Fucking glorious. This led to a wonderful, completely sensitive discussion about abortion. Me? I'm all for it. Her? Not so much.

"I can raise the baby myself. I don't need a man. My mother raised me by herself and I turned out just fine."

She went on to spew a bunch of male-hating filth: men are worthless; fathers are unnecessary; she wouldn't even tell the father if she got pregnant; blah-blah. Yup. She turned out juuuuust fine. No issues there. Not a one.

After the feeding, I marched us into the nearest pharmacy in search of a home pregnancy test. She protested, assuring me she couldn't get pregnant from skipping a week. I protested and said it's that or the coat hanger. Then half the readers tossed my book in the garbage and set it ablaze—No! Come back! I didn't say anything about a coat hanger, honest! That's crass and misogynistic and tone-deaf to the times we live in.

I'd never do that.

***

The rest of her stay was scorched by that molten discussion. It was incredible how over the course of not even a week we ran the gamut of emotional attachment from newlyweds to death.

“I knew this would happen,” Wildcherry admitted as she peeled herself from the mattress on our final morning. “My mom was right. I always do this.”

“Do what?” I asked.

“Lose interest.”

“Oh. Okay, great. Can I have my virginity back?”

By the time I saw her off on a bus, we were barely speaking. We had played happy couple at the Halloween party my roommates and I threw, but even that ended up in her barfing and passing out and us not existing anymore. Outside of two phone conversations, I never heard from her again.

Mine was a shockingly wonderful, horribly complicated way to lose one’s virginity. Personally, it was tragic. For the storyteller in me, though, it was perfection. If given the option I would not rewrite this ending for happily-ever-after. If I did I might not have gotten to plow (romantically speaking) Crouching Beavis, Hidden Butthead several months later. That two-week romp was equally priceless. But I promised her I’d never talk about it publicly, so I won’t. That would be crass and misogynistic and tone-deaf to the times we live in.

I’d never do that.

Intimate Connections At A Distance

54.

Okay, so you remember back near the beginning of the book when I said I had this kundalini energy alive in me? I neglected to mention that it wasn't alien-related. At least I think I neglected to mention—Lord knows I ain't proofreading this shit.

Prior to what I'm about to tell you, I had no direct link between that energy and aliens. After I'd initiated the energy coming alive by being pure silence back in my old East Village apartment, there was a night when I felt and heard an enormous crunch, followed by a boom high up in my nasal cavity. I felt it reverberate throughout my skull and suspected I was having an aneurysm and was about to die. It felt like it should have hurt, yet somehow I was anesthetized, so the episode felt numbed, as opposed to excruciating.

Instead of dying, this really bad sci-fi grid of Earth appeared in my mind's eye. It was a green 3-D model of our planet, like a computer simulation that someone was beaming into me. The model spun slowly, as Earth is prone to do, and without warning, a white mass, presumably ice or snow from the North, slid over the North American continent. The vision crackled and popped with an electricity I could see. I'm tellin' ya, it looked like a bad early 80s Atari graphic, but it did its job. I now feared some huge, natural catastrophe was going to wipe a lot of us out in my lifetime. I figured this was an alien transmission from an implant that had been shoved up my schnoz when I wasn't looking because that's the association alien abduction literature told me to make, but for all I know, a sentient dolphin beamed it into me using echolocation. Or kundalini, that rascal.

The second link between aliens and internal energy is much stronger. This happened in the deep AM of April 17, 2004. I was asleep in bed when the kundalini energy began tapping lines over my face with my hands.

When I shut up and let the energy do its thing, a lot of its thing is this tapping out lines and arcs all over my body. The patterns remind me of the lines native peoples from around Mamma Earth paint on their bodies. Ever wonder where they got the idea?

This night's tapping ended with my left hand pinching the bridge above my right nostril, as one would do to stop a nosebleed. The energy had never woken in me while I was asleep before (unless I slept through it) and had never done anything mundane, like pinch my nose. I didn't actually have a bloody nose, so in my tired stupor, I thought I was dreaming the whole thing.

The timing of what happened next is hazy. It could have been shortly after or maybe hours later. Not sure. But the next thing I remember happening is waking up because my bedroom was lit up. I thought the sun was rising and invading through my window across the room.

I should note here that when a roommate got married and moved out, I graduated to his much larger room and a bed frame. It was there, lying on my right side in my fancy new room, that I opened my eyes to find my wall missing. Where my wall with its posters and pictures should have been was this field of diffused white light. It was the same quality of dull light as I'd experienced that October night with Wildcherry three years prior, and it was, if nothing else, my wakeup call to stop ignoring that incident.

As I lay there staring confusedly into the void that had once been my wall, my nose began to bleed. It didn't bleed out, though. Instead, it trickled down my throat.

Nosebleeds are common to abductees and other forms of nerd, so I think I might have been visited by nerds that night —*aliens! Visited by aliens!*—and the kundalini must have had the foresight to cauterize my nose so that I wouldn't bleed all over the sheets. Per usual, I didn't bolt out of bed hysterically screaming or leap through the energy field into Narnia. At least I don't think I did. Huh.

I don't recall what happened next. In fact, I'd forgotten about the episode entirely until I climbed out of bed at a decent hour and scampered into the kitchen. There, I spoke at length with a subletting roommate named Brian. In the middle of our normal "Hi, how ya doin'?" conversation, my nose bled out the left nostril and onto my shirt. In with the red torrent rushed memory of the previous night, as described.

Welcome, Brian. I'm a bleeder.

The Sound of One Man Napping

Boy, that's a lot to unpack. It looks straightforward enough. Surfaces always do. But really, can it be coincidence that the very night I released myself from the burden of a fear over a decade in the making—that of aliens abducting me the moment I allowed love into my life—aliens showed up?

What, were they waiting on the other side of an invisible barrier to jump in and yell, "Surprise!" the moment I had sex?

Would you if you were an alien? Like, would you care about that at all? Would you pour your hard-earned tax money into building technology to traverse space, time, or dimensions just to mess with a semi-evolved chimp on some planet somewhere? Does that make sense?

This is the beauty of what we call *alien abductions*: they are not alien and likely aren't abducting anyone. And yet there they are. Can't deny that.

They do tend to obey a surface narrative, these beings, but are we writing it? Are we writing it to smother the subtext, the experience that is *really* happening, the communication that is *actually* taking place? Or are the aliens and abductees characters in a Trickster archetype's roleplaying game?

Thanks to authors like Philip K. Dick, movies like *The Matrix*, and plants like marijuana, people nowadays love to giggle nervously as they imagine we are all trapped in a video game or a technological simulation of some sort. But that is lazily confusing the metaphor for the actual.

Do you really think we're trapped in the toys we recently invented? Don't you see that we invented them as expressions of what we're missing inside?

It's ludicrous. As ludicrous as a coincidental, postcoital, alien abduction, featuring a dude paranoid that aliens will show up the moment he loses his virginity.

Perhaps I'm going too fast. Perhaps you've never pondered any of this deeply. Let's make an abrupt halt and define what we mean by *trickster*, *alien*, *interdimensional*, *space*, and *time.* Maybe that would be helpful for you to see how all of this alien stuff *doesn't* work.

We say, the many and the masses, that we know how abduction works. We know what it is. It's aliens. Abducting people. And yet it is not that and does not work that way and so we cannot say we know, we can only understand what we don't, which is everything we've thought thus far. This gets confusing when you start to talk around it, but if we key in on some of the main points, I promise it will all clear up and make sense. And likely still be wrong.

You wanted some depths with your shallows, didn't you? You wanted this book to take a turn away from my dick and into my brain where I'm thinking about the deeper meanings and machinations at work in impossible phenomena that have less to do with the mysteries of attraction and more to do with the attraction of mysteries. You wanted sense and you wanted this book to make it. Well, let's stop tickling your senses and start making sense. If not now, when? If. Not. Now. WHEN?!

But do take a nap first. This chapter was exhausting.

59.

Our New Hero Lumbers To A Forest

Back? Feeling refreshed? Cool. Let's get to the deep stuff you paid for. But first, let's talk about something else that's been on my mind lately. Let's talk about recording devices. Isn't it weird that they exist at all? I'm talking about records and tapes and CDs and USB drives and cloud storage. All of 'em. So many ways to record sound. And video, too, but let's keep it simple. Let's just stick with sound and keep in mind how weird it is that we can record anything at all.

Sound. Recording. Weird. Right?

And that's only the beginning of the weirdness. Think about how different each of these devices is. I mean what is a record to a tape to a USB drive to cloud storage? A compact disk looks like a mini record without the grooves, but there's no needle. There is no physical interface between CD and player. There's a laser light translating and transferring information, which basically makes the same sound as a record or a USB drive or a... a... a whatever a cloud is. And, right, tape. Almost forgot. Remember when tape was the future?

What, if anything, does physical variation, absolute difference, tell us about the hidden nature of objects and their actions?

It seems that the object is superfluous, doesn't it? The object is a representation of how we believe the world works. We invent according to how we perceive the world and then, *presto!* Out come devices made of completely different materials, none of which are human organs, but which nevertheless mimic exactly what you hear with ears and store in memory.

And no one questions this?

When we imagine and then conjure ways to record sound, some device comes out of us that is physically unique and yet bears the not-unique ability to reproduce sound that is, conveniently enough, exactly as our ears hear it and our brains record. If we lived in a society that focused on stones instead of plastics, would we invent stone recording devices? Does that only sound impossible because we never tried because it sounds impossible?

Also, we know we only hear a tiny portion of the sound spectrum. What are the odds we could stumble into inventing that which records and translates exactly our tiny portion?

All of these unquestioned, weird coincidences beg a mystery, the mystery of ants, the mystery of objects and organisms: Which came first, objects that perform actions or the actions themselves?

You want to say objects, right? But if the objects can be anything—a tape, a CD, a record, a USB drive, cloud storage, your ears and brain—and yet the action they are performing is singular—recording and playing back sound—then does it not follow that the ability to record and play sound comes first? The ability is just there, hanging out, waiting for something physical to wrap around it and make it a reality in the physical universe.

So, when we talk about imagining and inventing things into existence, what we mean is that we weave physicality around actions that inherently exist. They are invisible to us until they come through us as ideas. We like to think we're the ones coming up with ideas, but there they already are. Waiting. Lurking.

Talking to us? Influencing us to conjure an existence for them in the physical?

Perhaps.

At the risk of making a record-scratch moment, allow me to redirect your attention to the subtext of our inventions: we of the Westernized mind invent utilitarian symbols of our disconnection with all beings through heart to remind ourselves that we are disconnected. Unfortunately, in so doing, the reminder gets completely lost because we've invented artificial interconnection.

So, like, if in our disconnected lives we're no longer psychically communicating with one another the way people in nature cultures do, well, here comes the telephone! The phone should be a reminder of that which we're missing, but instead it becomes a substitute that we double down on by scoffing at the "unproven" notion of psychic communication while lauding the proven technology we hold in our hands. Technology that only makes sense if you don't think too hard about how the fuck this is happening. And why would you? It works!

While we're blocking out our wakeup call with our wakeup call, we're also pretending that we are discovering our own interconnecting nature in other ways. We're doing this in physics; we're doing this in ecology; we're doing this in psychology; we're doing this in religion and so-called spirituality. We're doing what nature cultures, First Peoples, heart cultures, and by whatever name—we're doing what indigenous people do indigenously and wholly, and we're doing it piecemeal as discoveries that are only new to us. We're imitating our true nature and calling that facsimile *new*. We, the brain people. The logical people. The rationalizing people. The ones cut off from heart who have traded wisdom for knowledge, Truth for *my* truth, Being *being* for self *doing*.

What are we doing?

Thought's bidding.

Whose thought?

Everyone's. Anyone's. No one's. Thought for thought's sake. A god's. An archetype's. A fairy's. An alien's. The form does not matter. The form is what we focus on. In focusing on it we blur out all else and believe that's all there is to see. We believe that is what's real until we change our minds.

What's real isn't the human, the alien, the higher power, the lower. What's real is what's behind them, what's driving them: ideas. Thought.

The physical universe is thought. We are all thought forms creating constructs for expressing thought in other forms. Doesn't that seem a little tiny wee bit more important than whether or not aliens are here? More important than whether we enter ufology and become babbling idiots because of some Trickster sphere of influence predicting and awaiting our arrival? Or whether, even, we are pulling daemonic beings here from an adjacent dimension through will power?

The aliens think so. So do I. We are both crystalized thought encasing formless thought. Facts espousing ideas. Nouns giving life to verbs. At least that's what we want you to think.

Admires The Trees

Speaking of babbling idiots and recordings, let's rewind to, oh, about a decade and a half ago, when I was a bright, young insight columnist for *UFO Magazine*. Remember *UFO Magazine*? Remember magazines?

Let's see if this essay I wrote for the mag has held up through the years. If it has, let's consider it a barometer for how far we have come in our thinking about high strangeness phenomena. Are we ready for anything deeper?

Sweating Through The Human Costume

Halloween is here and that can mean only one thing: I get to scare children. Seriously, is there any better holiday? Isn't it strange how we have this one annual celebration where if you don't scare kids and then give them candy, the pederast's modus operandi in reverse, the little shits do something awful to you, like egg your house? Adults are cruel and then kind to children lest the children act outright devilish—and this is acceptable for exactly one night per year. Strange.

I don't like being cruel. I'm good at it, but I don't like it. I admit to enjoying the brief high that comes with dominating someone else, from being "better than" the next person, if only in my head—but man alive do I ever hate myself afterwards. I can only imagine how people like Eminem, Joe

Queenan, and Oscar The Grouch feel. What do they do, sleep it off?

When I decided to go public with my alien abductions, I prepared for the worst. It rarely occurred, but I assumed I'd be attacked during interviews by radio and TV personalities with gargantuan craniums housing small minds. Honestly, what's with these television guys' heads? You've got a ticker running at the bottom of the screen, video clips playing on a loop in the top right, the station logo at the bottom right and this giant head clogging up the whole left side. Watching any given cable news show is like watching Godzilla bite the face off a skyscraper: there's this giant creature and commotion and bad effects masking a vapid plot. Can't we just have news?

Okay, not the point. I strayed. Apologies.

The point is, I expected a crappy reception on most programs and figured I'd be the perfect abductee to take on the challenge because not only do I give as good as I get, but I also get the joke. Yeah, *that* joke. You know the one, the dreaded anal probe joke. Not too many abductees will embrace the anal probe joke. I don't understand why. Why is that not okay, but kids dressed in typical Gray alien costumes trick or treating at the door is? Adults wear rubber alien heads to costume parties, right? Abductees generally find these costumes acceptable. How about Grays waving to the crowd from parades? No complaints there, either. Why the costumes but not the jokes?

Alien abduction, however the abductee ultimately ends up

viewing it, is traumatic. Being raped by anyone, let alone a group of nonhumans who have just ripped you from reality and will send you back to it otherwise unscathed when they're finished, is horrifying to the nth degree. If the vast majority of people believed that alien abductions were real would they wear those costumes and make those jokes? Would they own alien snow globes like the one on my desk a friend bought me at the Roswell museum?

I think some would continue to wear the costumes and buy the collectibles the way they do Osama bin Laden masks and serial killer trading cards, but the jokes would stop and the inclusion of aliens in pop culture would take on a vastly new meaning.

What does that make me? Am I a sellout? Or am I playing the game so that I can defuse the jokes and make abductees seem "normal" or "acceptable" to the purveyors of blab asking me how I know it wasn't a bad dream?

Yes and yes. But the deeper questions here are: Where is the line between what's acceptable and what isn't? And who draws it?

Anal probe jokes and celebrating abductions may be unacceptable to abductees personally, but socially they are not.

Facts are important to specialists; however, it is the presentation of facts that is important to the masses. It's the presentation that shapes the passive onlooker's belief about those facts. So, for me, it's not about walking the line and finding balance between what's personally appropriate and socially acceptable. For me, it's about living in that line and on either side of it. In theory, in the eyes of others, I see the line. In practice, in my eyes, it doesn't exist.

If our savoir-faire is so ambiguous and our outlook (and *inlook*) based on belief and whim, then what's real in any of this? Are aliens raping us or are they a Kodak commercial? Are aliens scarring our bodies or are they a punchline to an opening monologue on late night TV? Does the U.S. Air Force hold debris from a crashed spaceship and alien corpses or is it all a wholesome family day at the Roswell museum?

Don't you just love a parade? Aren't the kids cute in those costumes with their big black eyes and their nonexistent noses?

"Trick or treat!"

Up next, a guest who says he's been—get this!—[chuckles] abducted by aliens!

"Trick or treat!"

Whitley Strieber is sick of being the butt of alien probe jokes. Get it, America? See what I've done there?

"Trick or treat!"

Are you dizzy yet? Can aliens and abductions exist for us apart from the context we create for them? Do they embrace us as we embrace their stuffed-animal likeness?

Wait! Hold the phone! Oprah Winfrey just endorsed a book about the reality of alien abductions! And now it's on the news—this thing is real!

Shouldn't we take this subject seriously? For the love of god, kid, why are you wearing that costume? Who are your parents?

Hey, *South Park*: No, it is not time to laugh again. What kind of sick perverts are you to make that joke? I know it's been around since '86 but it isn't funny anymore. Oprah told me so. The news said it, too. It must be true. It must be real. All of this stuff. Overnight. From unreal to real **snap!** just like that.

What happened? Did the facts change? Did reality change? What changed?

I didn't change. I never change. I don't think things through and that's why my thoughts are brought to me by Coca-Cola.

Coca-Cola: the refreshing taste of bubbling cold tar. Grab a Coke today!

Coke. It's capitalized. Like our names. It's one of us. It *is* us. What are we again? Capitalized? Oh, never mind.

Welcome to the Information Age. I'd like fries with that. Up next on the hypno-box, fifteen seconds of other stuff you can attach an emotion to and repeat tomorrow.

Oh my god, what is that on my porch?—FIRE! There's fire on my porch! Stamp it out! Stamp it out!

Awe, crap. Literally. Thanks, kid! I see you giggling in the bushes with your friends! You'll pay for this! "Trick or treat," my ass!

Yet there is no repercussion because the kid dressed as a super hero left that lit paper bag full of feces on the old man's stoop as a joke. Any other night it would have gotten him grounded. Police may have been involved. Not tonight.

Tonight, it's acceptable. No one questions it. No one fears it. If it had happened the night before or the night after it would land him in juvie. But this night yields him a special pass.

Is there objective morality? Is there immutable Truth? Is there reality beyond our perception? Tune in later to find out!

What is the relationship between human perceiver and alien perceived when most of the human perceivers perceive an object while a handful of human perceivers perceive alien perceivers perceiving them? This, mind you, is a far more vital question than, "How much wood would a woodchuck chuck?" They only look similar. Separate but not equal. It's vital because when one human perceives another as an object, we deem that person psychopathic. What would a visiting race deem us?

Don't you find it kind of odd that aliens who speak all of our languages don't openly communicate with us?

Don't you find it kind of odd that Nature is shirking us off the planet six ways from Sunday and the First World is in the midst of Third World War, yet these aliens who speak our languages and know some of us more intimately than we know ourselves aren't saving us?

Do we really know anything with certainty or is everything ambiguous? Hypocritical? What does our celebration of All Hallows' tell us?

Do aliens wear human masks at Halloween?

There are degrees in consciousness like depths in an ocean because One's choice is all choice; One's direction is every direction. One alone knows true creativity, which is total freedom.

Sentience is the gift a person is born with. It is the key to choosing away from the cravings of the old animal brain.

Sentience is also the key to No-Thing and Oneness. It is the means of tasting the ocean in one gulp, not by degrees.

Using the key for free will requires turning the key. Using it for Oneness requires not turning it at all.

Do not use your gift. Do not turn the key and step through the cage. Die into it.

Whoa, what the fuck? Who is this?

Hello? ... Hello?

Ponders The Leaves

Our friend, Tree, has two personalities. First, the breezy, noisy, forward-looking Treetop, who engages with other beings in the air and all around. Second, Deep Roots, who is ensconced in and engaging the underworld from which Tree springs, but never abandons.

Treetop can only imagine what Deep Roots is doing because the roots are buried. However, they may be seen surfacing along the ground, now and again, which assures Treetop of Deep Roots's existence.

Roots are roots. They don't need to imagine. They know what the entirety of Tree is up to. Roots nourish all of Tree whether Treetop knows it or not.

Actually, I got the order of personalities backwards. First comes Deep Roots, then comes Treetop. And much like how the seedling sprouts into Tree, none of this much matters when Tree understands Tree.

If Tree ever does.

This Place Feels Familiar

Much has been said by me and by others about aliens not being aliens because... well... they are not. I still call myself an alien abductee out of convenience, although usually I say, *so-called "alien abductee"* and make those silly air quotes with my fingers. Sometimes I'll call the mysterious intelligence *Visitors* out of deference to Whitley Strieber, who coined the term, but really, how long does a being need to live here to not be visiting anymore? If they're from somewhere else, at the least they are squatters.

The general public knows what an alien abductee is, which is unfortunate since that is pretending to know an unknown. However, it's easier to say *alien abductee* than explain around it and have the other person say, "Oh. You mean an alien abductee?" Perhaps I should stop and just stick with *experiencer*, but then I'll have to explain what I'm an experiencer of. Usually, I'll say, *high strangeness*—and we're back to, "Oh. You mean an alien abductee?"

Because some of the phenomena of what researchers have told us is alien abduction do align with the actual experiencing of this expansive unknown, we prematurely diagnose experiencers with an acute case of aliens. In so doing we lose the richness of experiencing an emotional-intelligence-stimulating mystery that is legitimately beyond us and yet interwoven with our lives. The contact phenomenon doesn't fit in with scientific demands of repeatability and proof, it fits in with who we are. However we see ourselves dictates how we relate to it. We know this because we can, for instance, find glaring similarities between *ye olde fairies* and *modern aliens, yo.* Even so, most of us don't see ourselves as people naive enough to believe in fairies. We tend to assume that ye olde people reporting ye olde fairy encounters would have reported modern aliens, yo, had they been as sophisticated as we are about space travel and physics and been as obsessed as we are with being the smartest organism to crawl out of Earth's oceanic quim.

Yes, we moderns see aliens from another planet where there are none. Or we see the 2.0 version: interdimensional people on the other side of an invisible wall. We see what makes us feel smart and relevant and forward-thinking.

What about time travelers, you ask? Even though we're eradicating the environment that would yield us a future to travel back from, why not?

In all three cases, we see the future before us right now. Why we do this arrogantly and blindly follows the same rationale as how we treat spiritual transcendence: we'd rather collapse the unknown into the known to avoid all that nasty mystery, and we do so by forming a picture that looks suspiciously like us. By "us" I mean Westernized people. There go those air quotes again.

We of the Westernized mind imagine beings no greater, broader, deeper, richer than ourselves. We imagine us from space. And when we imagine us from space, we do so consciously and unconsciously.

Consciously, we theorize from our forward-thinking, future-guessing point of view. Because we have the technological capacity to leave Earth, we surmise that other people on other planets must have done so already. We assume we'd be militarized doctors and scientists in space, so that's what we imagine aliens would be. We think we are the pinnacle of consciousness as we are right now, and so when we imagine what alien advancement looks like, we rarely conjure images beyond creatures who effortlessly build better technology. When we assume that aliens must be lightyears ahead of us, we mean their science must be, not their interior experiencing of life. We don't imagine their interior experiencing at all. We take for granted that they're just like us inside, existing on a sliding scale between animalistic colonizers and Zen. Naturally, they must want something from us.

In science fiction, our shared traits lead to conflict. Beings who are portrayed as peace-loving Zen-like masters of harmony decide whether or not to wipe us out because our crappy human nature produces a cosmic imbalance. We inevitably overcome them with the aid of Hot Pockets, a machine gun, the latest iPhone technology, and the triumphant innocence of the human spirit because they don't have the right, damn it, they don't have the right. This makes a far better story than transcendent beings who are not masters of any "spiritual" aspect, but are instead choicelessly love and therefore choicelessly peace. Not beings who are merely *choosing* to live in harmony, mind you—which carries its shadow side, its opposite, the ability to choose discord—but beings who *are* harmony. Beings who understand us better than we understand ourselves.

Peace without struggle? Unearned love? Understanding the truth of our hearts? Yuck. No one wants that. Not even Christians.

Yes, it is sad but true: when we Westernized brainiacs imagine transcendent beings, our fantasies about them revolve around us. Since we are at war within ourselves, which naturally spills out to the world, we imagine alien allies and alien adversaries—a universe of allies and adversaries. A universe swinging on a pendulum, our human pendulum, energized by fear and anxiety.

Friends and foes are interchangeable because they carry their opposite motives, like two-sided coins.[5] One day your ally may become your adversary and vice-versa. We behave this way because we're stuck inside. We don't acknowledge that we're stuck inside, lazily resigning our predicament to human nature. If it's our nature then we can't be stuck, right?

The question of what an intelligence from another planet, dimension, or living invisibly in the room with you right now would be like doesn't stand a chance of rising above the shallow surface imaginings we create based on our broken lives.

---

[5] As opposed to the alien three-sided coin. True story. Probably. ... Yes, I just wasted your time with this footnote.

***

One of the most depressing lessons I've learned during my stay in ufology is just how many characters who claim to be searching for truth, who distrust the government and the military establishment, who believe they are more aware of what's really going on than the average sheeple, endorse clearcut pathological liars like Donald Trump. Trump is a conman, a racist, sexist, homophobic narcissist who, as of this writing, is dismantling the government, destroying Earth, threatening nuclear war, and who will commit treason if it means "winning." Shouldn't the heroic truth-seekers of ufology be able to see through an obviously sick man who puts children in concentration camps the same way they claim to see through systemic governmental lying and obfuscation over UFOs?

I mean, if you support him in any way then you support a lying fraud with all of the nasty attributes we've been trying to eradicate from our psyches by reciting all the Vulcan dialogue from the many incarnations of *Star Trek*. You are—no matter how you claim to feel insulted by this and protest—you are a selfish racist, sexist, homophobic destroyer of asylum-seeking families, American society, and Mamma Earth. Therefore, not only is your "alien" definition of high strangeness mystery completely made up, so is your call for truth, your self-proclaimed better than average ability to tell truth from lie, and your desire to do so in the first place. You, like your idol, Trump, are a con artist, and you are asleep.

But, hey! At least you're an artist, yeah? A real creative. Like Hitler was that one time.

Talk about sleeping sheeple. The purveyors of nonfiction alien lore are but symptoms of a comatose mind. Oh, how the dozing Western collective dreams of a world revolving around itself. All the characters in the dream and all the settings are projections of the sleeping mind. When a voice from outside such a one's snoozing headspace beckons, rather than waking that mind up, the call gets incorporated into the dream. Because our dream has us on a pedestal, other people have to be less than us. If we had equality, there would be no pedestal.

As you likely know from experience, the easiest way to create inequality is to judge another by surface features, namely skin and gender. Ours is a patriarchal society. Woman, in our dream, is going to be sexualized or mothering or both. Man is going to be a stern leader or a worker drone. Whether or not we go to war with another people is not going to be decided on gender because we've all got the same two. It's going to be decided on skin color and belief systems. Thus far, our dream of us perfectly mirrors our dream of aliens.

Don't see it yet?

Consider our first round of believing that we made unofficial alien contact. This began in earnest in the 1940s. It was nice, wasn't it? The humans involved called themselves contactees, and they claimed that attractive blond-haired, blue-eyed space brothers and sisters landed, freely exchanged ideas, brought them on tours of other planets, and things of this nature. Some contactees even made love to the alien Nordic supermodels, right? Like Captain Kirk and a buxom green lady, except the American South's version where you're fucking your space sister.

Our second round of believing we made unofficial alien contact came in two flavors, both baked in hypnosis. In the first bite of deliciousness, we traded in consciously woven yarns about Venusian runway models for unconsciously woven fairytales of gray-colored insectoids from we don't know where. Probably Sirius, or the Pleiades, or Planet X. These creatures were often cagey and frightening. They treated us like lab rats, forcibly taking our sperm and ova to manifest alien-human hybrids—GMO people who would carry on the lineage of their desperate, failing advanced race through our human mask. We would teach the hybrids how to behave like fat people and shop at Walmart, and they would rape us and tell us not to talk about it. Fair.

The second tasty flavor in our second round of believing in alien contact was a false memory story in which we were assured that the intergalactic praying mantises were space relatives after all. In this version, we were said to have chosen to incarnate here on Earth as humans to learn something. We were they and we chose this, it's just that we had complete amnesia about it until a kindly hypnotist with a soft temperament relaxed us and told us it was so.

Our third round of half-baked contact storytelling, the one we're in now, has us coming to terms with an experience that doesn't actually fit either of the above definitions we grew up being told were the really real case. Neither the conscious tale nor the unconscious tale fit and so now we are more likely to suppose that these beings are us in some elusive way that is unrelated to reincarnation or choice. We're likely, that is, to believe in alien-adjacent origin stories.

Whether through hypnotic recall or conscious pondering, we now, in this third round of myth-making, mistake telling parallel stories for having deeper understanding. For example, instead of aliens riding in from the Pleiades, we might suppose they live in a neighboring universe and can only ride in to our reality on the strength of our ability to perceive them. Or we might believe they are us traveling back in time to fix something in the timeline. Rarer, but yes, still a thing, we might believe they were conjured in the 1940s through magical occult experiments gone wrong.

Reimagining an origin story for aliens is not deep, it's lipstick on a pig. But viewing our reimagining as the last act in a trilogy (gentle contact; savage abduction; coming to terms with our false narratives in a way that is itself a repackaging of those narratives) exposes a real parallel not to another universe, but with our racist colonial conquests. They are, in sum total, expressions of our cultural shadow and the White man's fear of retribution.

Say what?

Uh-oh, here we go....

Picture it: European sailors, who are completely disconnected from heart, land on the shores of Turtle Island.

They encounter interconnecting "alien" people who come from heart. The aliens are accepting and inviting, but the Europeans want to kill and conquer and take, so they spin the narrative and call these people savages. They force them into war to prove their point.

The Europeans stick around long enough to hybridize and become Americans. As Americans, they look back at their history with an understanding that all of their racist killing was wrong. They acknowledge that they are broken inside.

The Americans apologize and want to learn from the aliens, now called "First Nations." They say they respect their equality and want to understand their medicine, but what that means on a societal level is, *We want to steal your medicine, mass-produce it through corporations, sell it, and wipe you out if you get in our way.* What it means on a personal level is, *I want to be you. I want what I think is your spiritual power. I would never call you a slave, but I will suck your culture dry to call myself a spiritual master, a shaman, a kahuna, a medicine man or woman.*

Speaking of slaves, the Europeans, on their way to becoming Americans, stop off at Africa, where they are greeted with open arms, as equals, by other aliens. But the transitioning hybrids don't want friendship and camaraderie, they want slaves. You can't make slaves of equals, so they turn their open-heartedness into weakness. They call Africans savages, less than people, and they steal them away to try to make them that.

But of course they are not that and so the lie cannot hold.

Eventually, on paper, at least, the slaves are freed, and African-Americans are born. The conquering White class apologize and do their best to look upon their Black brothers and sisters as equals.

But doing so is always a choice for the Whites (membership has its privilege), and that choice carries and expresses its opposite. In granting Blacks acceptance, the Whites continue to culturally appropriate from them. Continue to benefit from systemic inequality. Continue to prop up accomplished Black celebrities only to knock them down and replace them with "I can do it, too!" Whites.

See, our vision of equality isn't that we are all born equal, it's that we *choose to say* we're all born equal—a choice we can take away as it serves us. And we model our space alien fantasy on this unspoken ethic.

We used to give inspired names to fantasy beings, like faery, gnome, leprechaun, kobold. Now we've got the Grays. Even when the aliens being encountered aren't gray—are tan or white or blue or glowing—we call them Grays. It's a racist placeholder for "alien." It is no wonder that for decades the Gray has been peculiar to America. I don't know if that's still true, but it was throughout the 1980s and 90s. This may have changed thanks to our friend the internet, with its uncanny ability to cross-pollinate cultural myths, but at least prior to the internet, Americans were the only people being abducted by Grays.

Coming out of World War II, the Nordic Blond was Hitler's wet dream of statuesque, highly intelligent, friendly if calculating, sexy, White people. But... you know... not from here. And the Grays, as we just discussed—try to keep up—went through a metamorphosis that followed the evolving mentality of Euro-American conquest. In the end, Grays were here to emasculate White men, impregnate White women, and steal from us. We abductees were like slaves taken by foreign colonizers. This is what "higher beings" look like when filtered through the inherently racist, colonialist lens of Western mind. They look like how we victimize. They look like enemies.

Put it this way: If we are what it looks like when human nations follow the tenets of a bible that say we own the planet, everything is here to serve us, and everyone else is a soulless, lesser being, then aliens are what it looks like when highly advanced people come here and say, "Oh, you follow that book, too?"

I mean, what are the odds?

As Does The Approaching Monster

Back in the early aughts, I decided to read a book in a park in Queens that I'd never visited before. This, then, is a story about not getting to read a book in a park in Queens that I'd never visited before. It compliments the last chapter well. I'm telling you this directly because I have zero faith in your ability to put it together in your head. I have zero faith in that because I keep meeting people like this....

The Thin Blurred Line

I was situated on a green park bench, burning under the exploding sun, surrounded by whispering trees, whistling birds, WASP children, and now an intoxicated hetero couple. His better half plopped down next to me. Her shirtless male counterpart wobbled at my knees, his bloated outie button nearly grazing my lap. "Is that an alien book? Are you into aliens?" the woman asked, ignoring the fact that I was ignoring her.

I greeted her with an affable smile and said, "Um, yeah. It's an alien book."

I had been reading, *Sight Unseen*, by Budd Hopkins and Carol Rainey, off and on for a few weeks now. I was in the middle of chapter eleven, the one about how aliens may have bred themselves in with the human population to see what living as a human was like. The authors assure us readers that they know it sounds inane, but the probability can no longer be denied: aliens are stealing the human form and coexisting with us. We cannot ignore the facts just because the facts are uncomfortable. And yet the best analogy they give as to why aliens would join human society is that of a tourist trying to get a feel for other cultures by living abroad. I find it hard to believe Budd Hopkins and Carol Rainey feel this way. They must be sugarcoating it the way they say we must stop doing. Ironic, that.[6] An analogy that makes more sense is getting a sex change to experience the opposite sex. A more plausible explanation—the bitter one—is that if aliens are breeding in, we're being bred out. Frankly, I have no problem with this.

The page opposite the one I was tearing through showed three large illustrations of alleged alien babies. Poised uncomfortably close to me, this is what the alky picked up on. There was nary a need for us to bump shoulders since the long bench held no one else, yet there she was, breath reeking of whatever liquor swished within her brown-bagged bottle. I suspected reading time was over.

The woman was plump, in her early forties, had a beautiful golden brown complexion complimented by her tan flower print sundress. By contrast, her companion, the man

---

[6] I have since befriended Carol Rainey. She thinks Budd's work, in large part, is bullshit, but they were married at the time. The things we do for love.

who stood before me, was a sweaty white mess of hair. Most of that grew through his stomach. The *drunkess* tried to convince him to sit with her but he didn't want to. I assumed they'd both leave, so I stuck my ample schnoz back in my book. Of course this wouldn't be a story unless the man left and she stayed, so that's what happened and possibly why.

"You know anything about Nevada?" the woman, now a solo act, inquired. I saved my page with the inner sleeve of the dust jacket and shut the book with a dull *thup*. She now held the full girth of my attention because I knew she'd never let me block her out. Of Nevada, I told her I only knew what I'd read in books or seen in documentaries.

Ah, Nevada: home of the gambler, the brothel, the mad scientist, and the officially nonexistent military base, Area 51. Area 51 is an installation which lies in a desert bed called Groom Lake. This is the UFO hotspot to end all UFO hotspots. Over the decades, stories have emerged from there claiming everything from, *This is the place where the Air Force stores and reverse-engineers crashed alien ships*, to, *Evil aliens secretly run the joint.* The only thing we know for sure is that it exists even though, officially, it does not. We know this because in 1998, several living workers and two widows of dead workers at the airbase sued the U.S. Government for radiation poisoning, suffered not at the claws of aliens, but from having to burn hazardous waste in open air pits, without the aide of protective gear.

Evil aliens? No. Put a check in the evil humans column. Their activity broke numerous laws, including environmental, and was as immoral a directive as one could receive. The Supreme Court chucked the case, essentially agreeing with the U.S. Air Force that because Area 51 did not officially exist, it was not subject to the rule of law. Their judgment contradicted earlier Supreme Court rulings and in hindsight was the dead miner's canary that should have warned us what the Supreme Court was willing to do to abet the military industrial complex years before they handed us George W. Bush, a self-proclaimed war president.

"A lot of crazy shit goes on there, believe me. That's where they store the bodies," my new bestie said, referring to alien cadavers retrieved from downed UFOs, and totally butting in on my political grandstanding.

"Are you from Nevada?" I asked.

"Yes. Vegas. Las Vegas. You ever look at the things in the ocean?"

"What do you mean?" I asked.

"Most of those things are aliens," she said with certainty.

"Most of what things?"

"You probably think I'm crazy but if you look at some of those animals—like the jellyfish. Does that look normal to you? Or the octopus. I mean what the fuck is that? It looks [extra]terrestrial. Look at those old science fiction movies where there's aliens that look like that [octopi]. Where do you think they [the shitty writers of shitty movies] got that from? Think about it [the dumb stuff I just said]."

I was not so much speechless as unresponsive. She didn't let that stop her.

"Scary, the ocean. Lot of strange shit in there. I think aliens came here thousands of years ago and colonized it. Look at sharks. Those are obviously products of evolution—but an octopus? A jellyfish? What the fuck is that? Where does it come from? There's lot's of creatures in the ocean like that. Think about it."

I tried to think about it, but she wouldn't let me. "You ever wondered what your neighbor is?" she whispered starkly.

"What do you mean?" I asked.

"You ever wonder about your neighbors? I mean think about it: You don't know where they're from; you don't know what they're doing. You probably think I'm crazy, right?"

"No," I assured the fat loon, "I'm just thinking about it. I don't think I've ever had a neighbor like that. I know what you're getting at, but I've never wondered if a neighbor was human or not."

"Well it's possible they're not," she assured.

"Sure. Anything is possible," I clichéd. "And it makes sense that aliens might breed their way into the population. In fact I just read a thing about alien abductions that—I don't know how you feel about abductions—"

"—You don't think they're fiddling with us? We've got their hands, you know? We've got their hands in a freezer, you know? We're poking their bodies, seeing what makes them tick—but they're not doing that to us? Of course they are!"

"Of course they are. Exactly," I said, not at all sure what I was being exact about. "So anyway, someone did the math and figured out that given the average number of abductions that take place and the fact that abductions are passed on from parent to child, within seven generations everyone on Earth will be an abductee."

"You're probably a Trekkie, right?" She asked this and for some unknown reason I felt offended.

Oh, wait, I do know why. It's because I'm a *Star Wars* fan, which is kind of like calling a Blood a Crip or a Muppet a puppet.

"I've watched the show," I said, basically shrugging off the implication that I'm *probably* a nerd.

"Well, there was an episode where an entire planet was killed by a disease. Now look at AIDS. We never had anything like that when I was growing up. I'm in my early forties now and I've never seen anything like this. A lot of people blame the faggots, but I don't."

She then launched into an impression of Joe Prejudice wrongly blaming *the faggots* for AIDS. It's no wonder state after state voted to ban gay marriage, when the average person living in New York City, of all places, still felt comfortable saying, *the faggots,* in public. If LGBTQ's can't make headway here, they can't make it anywhere.[7]

She pointed out various passersby, saying, "He could have it; she could have it; that girl could have it, and you wouldn't know. Your girlfriend could cheat on you and bring AIDS home to you. Where did this disease come from? Shit!—Where do you think those writers [of *Star Trek*] came up with the idea?"

---

[7] But then they did. Years later. Thanks to aliens. Wait, what?

"You think aliens?" I scoffed. I tried not to scoff, but scoff I did.

"Of course!"

Eureka!

"But," I tried poorly to interject, "why would it come from aliens? I'm not so sure it wasn't created by us!" I was referring here to the credible evidence that the origin of AIDS may be a military lab, where it was created as a biowarfare super germ used for population control. That this disease favors gay, Black, and Hispanic populations—the most unfavorable populations among the White hetero elite—may not be coincidence. Much like the octopus. Dear God, what was happening to me?

"Did you ever see *Predator*? The movie *Predator*?"

"Yes," I said.

"Well?"

I don't know why everything was self-evident to this woman; however, once I got the pattern down, I could predict her like Sylvia Browne.

"It's just a movie!" I exclaimed.

"Is it? Shit! There could be a Predator in those trees staring at you, how do you know? Do you really think we're the only ones here?"

I'll translate: *Predator* is a movie about an alien that can turn invisible. Humans are its prey. How, therefore, can I be certain we are not human prey to these real aliens hiding in the shadows?

I told her that I agree we're not alone, but if they were

human-killing aliens they might at least once, just once, ah, say, for instance, kill a human being. Anal probe? Sure, anal probe. But I defy anyone to produce a case where the abductee has been killed.

"You know the *Planet of The Apes*?" she rattled.

"The movie or the planet?" Okay, I didn't say this. But I would have if I'd thought of it. First. Okay, so I stole it from an episode of *The Simpsons*. Hot damn, I *am* a nerd. What else was she right about?

Auntie Drunkelton plodded along tediously like Kevin Smith dialogue. "You know the part where they peel off their faces to reveal they're alien? I mean, shit! That's it right there!—How do ya think they came up with that?"

I didn't remember that happening in *Planet of The Apes.* I remember something like that occurring in the 80s TV series *V,* but *Planet of The Apes*? Anyone? There are approximately eight million sequels and one reimagining to that movie; I'm not about to Google search it anytime soon.[8]

I let her have that one, nodding politely, growing woozy off of her 40-proof exhales. She prattled vociferously about these presumably evil aliens who mean us harm and are taking over the planet, presumably by injecting clumsy sci-fi scripts into presumably coked-up Hollywood screenwriters' heads, letter by manic letter, word by jittery word, in what is, presumably, a psychological cry for help. Why else would they give away their plans like that? Of course they are screaming for attention! We aren't being invaded by space

[8] Make that 4 reimaginings, as of 2020.

aliens, we're being invaded by tweens! Oh, this all makes so much sense now!

Presumably.

Just when I thought this barrage of pop culture references disguised as original thought had wound to a Dennis Millerian conclusion, she asked me, "Have you ever seen *Tommy Knockers*? Seen it or read it? It's from Ste*ph*en King." She pronounced his first name like *Stefen*, not *Steven.*

"I think I saw that. Is that the one at the airport?"

"No," she said. "It's the one where this UFO lands in the earth and everyone who comes into contact with it gains power, but they start losing their teeth. They fall apart because the aliens are secretly draining their life force. But they think they're gaining all this power, see?"

"So is that what you think is going on?" I blurted, wanting to end this conversation without delving into a conspiracy theory on, say, *Xena: Warrior Princess*, or gummy worms.

"Yeah!" she yelled instead of, *Duh.* "I should go before I become that crazy lady who wouldn't leave you alone."

Ahem.

"But let me just say this because we may not ever see each other again."

Oh?

"You ever seen, *The Lion King*?"

"Yes."

"Cute movie, right?"

"Sure."

"You remember that scene where the animals are talking

about why the lion is so calm?"

"Yes," I lied. My memory is shit.

"And it turns out, what? He's at the top of the food chain. He has no reason to worry."

"Right."

"Well, that's like us, isn't it? We're at the top of the food chain here, no worries. Now along comes something higher than us. You don't think they're gonna take us over?"

Her eyes measured mine with the searching alert gaze of a person who does not trust that I am not humoring her. I kept my face pure and honest. I humored her with my accepting, warm smile-squint. "No," I responded. "*We're* not."

Okay I didn't say the 'We're not' part—Fuck! Why hadn't I thought to say that?

"No," I stated flatly. And before I could expound, she launched into a diatribe insinuating my anthro-pomposity.

No? No?! How can you believe humans are the only intelligent life in the universe?

How can you believe we're the top of the food chain with aliens here?

How can you believe they're not hostile toward us?

"I didn't say any of that. It doesn't make any sense that aliens are here to kill us. They would have done that by now. They would not be part of our food chain and, in fact, they wouldn't be able to have anything to do with us directly. We see logic as the end-all/be-all of what the brain is for. These beings are translogical. Their minds are broader in every sense, which means we cannot meet them as equals if we cling to logic. We can only drag them to our level and assume they behave according to our limited expectations." Now *I* was sounding like shitty Kevin Smith dialogue.

"What if they destroyed their own planet and now they want ours, you know, for our resources?" she asked.

"Why wouldn't they travel to a planet like ours that isn't inhabited?" I shot back. "They've got the means to travel the universe, there must be another planet like this one out there.

"Hey, you know what? Even if they are breeding in with the population and breeding us out, so what? Is what we're doing here worth preserving? Why should I fear an alien invasion when we're destroying ourselves anyway?"

The drunk and I were at an impasse. Movies made more sense to her than reality. Getting sauced on a Sunday afternoon was precious human activity and worth protecting. All of this misery we call a miracle and take on faith is what life is must not be destroyed, at least not by *them*.

If there are any aliens reading this—or osmosing it—kill us. Kill us now. I spent way too long arguing about your motives with a paranoid, inebriated stranger. And the mental line differentiating us was thin. And I'm not so sure I won.

Please, on behalf of my people, please wipe us the fuck out.

Our Hero Hides In The Brush

I know this book isn't strictly a sequel, but checking in on people is fun. Hmm... I wonder how that investment firm fulla racists I worked at is doing?

Securities and Exchange Commission
Litigation Release No. 17969 / February 5, 2003
SEC Charges Broker Todd Eberhard, and His Firms, With Securities Fraud and Looting of Customer Brokerage Accounts
SEC v. Eberhard, et al. (S.D.N.Y. Civ. 03 CV 813 (RJB))

The Commission announced today that it filed an emergency action this morning charging securities fraud, including looting of customer brokerage accounts, against broker and television investment personality Todd M. Eberhard and his brokerage and investment advisory firms, Park South Securities, LLC ("Park South"), a registered broker-dealer and registered investment adviser, and Eberhard Investment Associates, Inc. ("EIA"), an investment adviser that was not registered with the Commission. The complaint also names Stone House Capital Partners LP ("Stone House"), a Park South affiliated hedge fund, as a relief defendant that received transfers of Park South customer funds at Eberhard's direction.

The complaint alleges that Eberhard and his companies systematically concealed substantial losses in customer accounts by, among other things, issuing phony customer account statements and making other material misrepresentations about the value of the accounts. The defendants also misappropriated customer funds by moving assets back and forth between the accounts of unrelated customers without knowledge or authority of the customers, and by making unauthorized wire transfers out of customer accounts - essentially looting the accounts. The fraud was ongoing: defendants continued to misrepresent the value of customer account balances as recently as last week.

Upon the Commission's application, the United States District Court for the Southern District of New York today entered a temporary restraining order and an order freezing the assets of Eberhard and his entities as well as assets of Stone House that are traceable to Eberhard's customers. The Court also appointed a receiver for Park South and EIA and ordered an immediate verified accounting from all defendants and expedited discovery. The litigation is pending.

The Commission would like to thank the United States Attorney's Office for the Southern District of New York for its assistance and cooperation in this matter.

For More Information, Click HERE.

Gets Lost In The Clouds

Speaking of aliens and doomsday, you know how aliens were once notorious for showing abductees doomsday scenarios? What do you think that was about? Were they psychological tests or trustworthy predictions?

If tests, was the common denominator that whether they showed us a nuclear holocaust, a quick freeze ice age, or some other calamity, they were showing us an event we were helpless to stop? And so perhaps they were testing our reactions to dire situations that are out of our control.

Seems to me the doomsday presentation was really about seeing if we would respond by doing the right thing for the sake of doing the right thing with that information.

How many people do you know who shrug off important issues they feel are out of their control, instead of taking right action? Even politically, millions of people refuse to vote because, "It's all rigged anyway"; "Nothing ever changes"; "It doesn't affect me"—You know all the excuses. So, while the doomsday scenario may be prediction or may be propaganda, since we cannot know either way, it's a useless question to ponder. The only ponderable factor is who we truly are when stripped of comfort, predictability, and control in a gloom and doom scenario. If we see the ending of us, if we fear its inevitability, what do we do with that emotionally-charged knowledge? Do we scream it from the rooftops? Do we hesitate and think about the repercussions for our reputations? Does it transform us or petrify us?

What kind of person are you when you know too much? When you have *seen*? Are you one who speaks up? One who changes lifestyle to suit the needs of life? Or one who shrugs off the burden because there is no use in doing the right thing for the sake of doing the right thing if no societal change will result?

You are not just you, you are part of society, a voice in and an example of the collective. Changing yourself is changing society. Doing the right thing means one more person in society is living rightly. And if you do not do right because it's right—simply for that reason alone—then who are you? And what is the nature of the society that produced you?

Why would aliens want you to take them to your leader?

***

Thus far in my life of high strangeness, I have received three environmental warnings from the enigmatic other: two in dreams that were more than my personal unconscious mind and one in a wake-state vision. The first was a dream I had in high school, which I wrote about in, *I Know Why The Aliens Don't Land!*. This was the event in which my favorite discarnate female voice, who apparently broke out the popcorn and watched me lose my virginity in 2001, warned me about how our polluting the environment and abusing oil were collapsing the ecosystem and murdering all life. The second was that Atari-like green grid Earth vision I wrote about earlier, where a white mass from the North quickly slid over the eastern portion of the United States. The third one was a real charm, and it went something like this....

Dolphin Rescue

The year was 2011. Having spent my post-college life thriving in New York City, it was time to go. Nearly a decade earlier, I had transformed from brain-self to heart-self and lost all ambition. I was a blissed out, smiling kinda guy. I was Being being human, and everything was new and joyful at all moments. I didn't need the arts or a job to fulfill me. I was no longer defined by my wants, my dysfunctions, my work, my creativity. I could no longer feel boredom or anxiety.

Do you know how hard it is to relate to the people you love when you *are* Love and they least expect it? They think you're having a midlife crisis because in a world of partial people, the sudden onset of wholeness looks as deranged as mental illness.

Over the ensuing years, complete bliss wore off, yet many of the effects stayed. I never regained my ability to be bored and I never caught the bug to do what I used to say I loved: work in television and film. I could (and hopefully can) still write, yet there was no longer an intense compulsion to do so. These drives and these ways we define ourselves are a result of not being whole inside.

I was, if you will, “complete.” I am no longer, if you will continue, “complete,” no longer basking in the wholeness of human existence. Yet and still, I am at all times aware that wholeness is me whether I am self-identifying as wholeness or not. I cannot forget who I am—who we all are beneath the masks—although I don’t merely know it. The knowledge comes from formerly having been that and so it is encoded in the fiber of my being. There is no turning away even though I’ve consciously turned away. This conundrum is me.

I’m like a fallen angel without the vengeance streak: at all moments aware of the Heaven that I am and from which I am disconnected. This is my actual experience, not a theory. To you, that may sound melodramatic and depressing. To me, this is my current state of being. I can’t *not* know and understand all of our true nature whether I am self-expressing from “its” point of view or back to being Jeremy.

Put another way, if you are cut off from Source in the way I used to be when I was like you, then what I am now is cut off from Source and cut off from you. But I am also you, for I am also Source, whether I live it or live cut off, because I am unblinded to the transcending realness of nonduality. Unblinded and yet not seeing through that nondual eye at the moment. Or your eyes. I’ve got four eyes, silly, I wear glasses.

So, whoever *that* guy is? He woke up one day in 2011 and realized he had lost his New York ambitions, was working a grueling shit job, and the economy, which had tanked in 2008, was on a false rebound. It was rebounding into one not made of careers but of permanent shit jobs we were all told to be thankful for.

So, whoever *that* guy is? He figured there was no reason to struggle in New York City if he didn't have a goal he was working toward or deluding himself with.

No big plans? Don't bother with the Big Apple, it's far too expensive and unforgiving.

If I'm going to do shit jobs for the rest of my life, that guy said to himself, *why not do them in paradise?*

His lease was up in a month. Time to move to Hawaii. Why Hawaii? Because he had visited a few years prior and fell in love with the Big Island. Visited, because Ted Roe offered to take anyone who was willing to come to Hawaii swimming with dolphins. He knew Ted as a researcher from NARCAP, a UFO organization that preferred the term UAP (unidentified areal phenomena) to UFO (unidentified flying octopus—object. Flying object) because it made them feel like they were above ufology in the way that Wendy's feels like it's above Burger King because they—I dunno what—use meat.

Ted was also a free dive instructor who took a real disliking to Michael Salla, a Ufological Hack of the Disclosure Movement Kind, who also lived on the island. Salla and his wife charged big money to New Age tourists to psychically "call in" dolphins the way other Disclosure Movement frauds charge big money to psychically "call in" UFOs on the mainland.

Excuse me, *UAPs*. Disclosure advocates preferred that term, too, because it sounded more official in a government secrets sort of way. Such twists in terminology made them feel like they were in the know. In the know about the thing they wanted disclosed because they didn't know.

I mean, right? Which is it folks, do you know too much or know too little?

Clearly, they know enough to take your money.

Anyway, Ted called bullshit on the Salla scam and made the offer to take eager snorkelers to meet dolphins for free in Kealakekua Bay, where they enjoyed eating and sleeping and generally dicking around. *That* guy took him up on it and, lo and behold, on his first time snorkeling, he swam with dolphins, as promised.

He was out there floating in the middle of the ocean. Alone. One fat buoy. Ted was off flipping around like a trick seal. Suddenly, as if Michael Salla and his wife had psychically called them in, a pod of spinner dolphins rose up around him. They circled. There was a mom and her baby. It would have been magical if he wasn't acutely aware that these were animals in their element sizing him up. He didn't want to present a danger to the baby, so he floated like a water log. Scared. Like a water log. Probably not a thing, but there he was, eyeing the shoreline, realizing he would have no chance of making a break for it should these smiling dolphins turn into hungry sharks.

They didn't. He lived. It was magical. He knew he had to move here. He didn't know when until *when* hit him in 2011. It was as if an internal light went on and everything in him felt like he needed to abandon New York City for Hawaii

Island that moment. Problem was, his sister was getting married in a few months.

His mom suggested he let his apartment go and come live with her in Massachusetts until after his sister's wedding, then make a break for the tropics, never to be seen again. This was a big move for an East Coast boy. He didn't know when he'd see his family again, so he accepted Mom's offer, and it was off to Ma's to live the Gen-X dream of moving back into his parent's basement. Except it wasn't the basement, it was a real bedroom. And that wasn't the most important dream he lived out at that time.

Or should I say, *I* lived out? You do realize when I was talking in third person I was talking about me, right?

Fucking keep up.

***

So, okay. All of that too-cute-by-half preamble out of the way, here comes the other end-of-the-world-as-we-know-it dream I had shortly after transitioning to Mom's place. In the dream, I am floating in Kealakekua Bay, just like I had done in real life, except I'm totally alone. No Ted Roe 20 feet below the surface. No splish-splashing tourists fighting the current and scaring the fish. It's darker than real life, too, both the water and the lighting.

I gaze at the shoreline, taking in my surroundings, and then twirl around to face the wide open ocean. Suddenly, I am no longer alone. One dolphin, male, pops up right in front of me. I know he is male because he starts talking to me in a calm, almost hypnotic, male voice. I don't remember how he kicked off the conversation, I just remember feeling embarrassed that this was happening and thinking how, on the one hand, it was perfect material for Paratopia, but on the other, I could never speak about it or I'd lose all street cred with our audience. Me, with my too cool for school anti-New Age posturing; dolphin, with his speaking English. Only all of the wrong people would ever believe this.

I didn't tell the dolphin any of this, of course. Wouldn't want to ruin his day with my embarrassment for his existence. What I said in my out loud snarky voice was, "A talking dolphin? No one's ever going to believe this. If you're real, are mermaids real, too?"

Mr. Dolphin asked, "What is a mermaid?"

I thought it was an odd question. I perked up a bit and replied, "It's like a half human half fish."

Mr. Dolphin said, "I have never encountered one in all of my travels."

And with that, the dream became lucid. Something about the honesty of his answer, the innocence with which he delivered it, and the perfect enunciation woke me up within the dream to the fact that I was dreaming and that this intelligence presenting himself as a dolphin was not me. I was not speaking to my unconscious mind, I was speaking to another conscious mind through the avatar of a dolphin.

I changed my tone immediately. No more snark for this guy, no sir. I met Mr. Dolphin's black eyes levelly and said,

"Okay. What do you have to tell me?"

At that, he showed me a vision of a topographical map of the United States. It was an animated map with, like, video game hordes all migrating from the East Coast to the middle of the country and then to California. All the while, Mr. Dolphin was explaining what I was seeing.

A cataclysm is coming to the East Coast very soon, he told me. This will make the country unlivable for people. They will migrate west and won't be able to settle in the middle of the country. Everyone will have to hightail it to the West Coast. By then, the Coast will be choked with people and they will want to fly to the last state they can—Hawaii—but by that point the grid will be down and airplanes will no longer be flying. Therefore, my don't-call-me-a-fish friend told me, "You need to get to Hawaii right now and plant your roots."

When he said that I knew he meant planting roots as a metaphor for becoming a part of the community and also meant that I literally needed to learn how to farm. I had the feeling I'd be helping to form a community there for refugees, or whomever was left after the mysterious event to come. I also understood that for some reason, heading to Alaska, Canada, or even down to Mexico, would not be an option for those left on the mainland. I didn't get a sense of why, nor did I get a sense of what the cataclysm would be, just that it would wipe out the eastern half of the country—if not in population, then in habitability.

As I was processing this, something didn't add up. I mean that all sounded awful—and it fit in perfectly with my vision from 1999 of, essentially, a quick freeze happening when something white slides down across the eastern half of the U.S.—buuuuuut, I was already coming to Hawaii in a couple of months. It was a done deal. And I told him as much.

"No, you don't understand," he said. "You have got to get here now."

"I am," I protested.

"No, right now."

"But I am, I'm coming!"

"No, now. You have to get here now."

"Okay."

I dropped it and so did he. The dream dissolved to black and I woke up. I giggled nervously to myself. I knew this was real contact with someone through a dream. I knew this warning was authentic. I knew I didn't want to deal with the authenticity of this because that meant telling people and there's a real responsibility there, what with not wanting to start a panic and all. Plus, ethereal beings, aliens, talking dolphins and the such? Not a very good track record of giving us reliable information about the future.

And then there was the matter of me being the wrong guy for this message because, stupid dolphin, I *was* coming to Hawaii now, now, right now. But after my sister's wedding. I didn't get the sense that this unnamed calamity was hitting tomorrow or even in the next year. The rush was all about me stabilizing myself in Hawaii so that I would be prepared for... for....

Eh, who knows? If it was important, he'd have told me.

It's not. Just know that most of you in America reading this are going to die soon.

Helpful, right?

The other option, besides shouting, "The sky is falling!" to a world that would only shout back, "What else is new?" is that it's not for them (you) to know and do anything about. It's for me. Selfishly, it's all about me. Except, even in this framing, it's only selfish in that I'm the one to act on it in some small way on behalf of whomever is left on The Big Island of Hawaii. We must create a self-sustaining society. How I, a completely out of shape white boy from the city, would be the right person for that job was anyone's guess.

If I say that I have subsequently found out not *why* me but *how* me, how I will be what I came here to be when the big change hits, would that scare you?[9] Would it make the dream more real for you? Or are you already resigned to a death by disaster because it doesn't take a dolphin in a dream to tell you what the future holds anymore?

Seems to me we are running headfirst into a psycho-spiritual wall that cannot be climbed. The wall is this: There is no better future that we can project for ourselves anymore. Try to. You can't do it, not realistically.

If you are politically progressive, the best you can envision is more of the same with some slight modifications. If you are not progressive, then you are working to bring us back to "the good old days" that weren't even good then. So stagnation or regression, those are all any of us can envision

---

[9] Actually, my wife Carol and I. Spoiler Alert: I got married.

anymore because we are at a place where we can see that the future was never real. This building up of societies toward global harmony was a total and complete fabrication. Harmony begins and ends with the individual. Running toward the ideal future is running away from this fact.

There is something huge coming down the pike, make no mistake. It ain't COVID, but that's a good warmup exercise. All of the warning signs are here, be they of interior or exterior domains. Mamma Earth is about to wince us off her face because we choose to remain clever, irrelevant animals, and we know this. Do we care?

Will we claim responsibility or continue to smile and call it "God's work?"

Will we claim responsibility or continue to bemoan a "shadow government?"

Will we take responsibility or call it "alien invasion?"

Will we surrender to transcendence or commit the ultimate act of substitute sacrifice?

Another "higher" intelligence is here, that much is a fact. But there is no *versus* between *us* and *them*, for they are not alien, we are not human, and they cannot meet us as equals until we meet ourselves, if there's time.

Is there time?

Futures are time. And time has an end. Linearly, we've got one ending. Cyclically, we've got many. Any way you read it, our story will inevitably come to a close, whether we move to another chapter or finish the book. The one determinative question that remains is, Are you a character in the book, or are you reading the book and imagining the character?

Are you feeling the character, going through the motions like it's real, yet it's really you engaging with story?

Are you a dreamer dreaming or a dream dreaming that you're the dream and a dreamer dreaming?

Do you really want to meet you as you are without confrontation? Without judgement? Without turning away in disgust or denial?

Isn't the first move in authentically seeing another as they are understanding ourselves so thoroughly that we don't project anything of us onto them? Isn't that of the utmost importance when we meet them within ourselves during dreamtime?

All of this urgent word vomit reminds me to ask: Why is it that I, a professional communicator, complicate things way more than Mr. Dolphin, who isn't even real?

We love to say people are complicated. And we love to say all characters in our dreams are us. But if the character in the dream that feels least like you is simple and direct, uncomplicated, not neurotic, making way more sense than the stream of consciousness alphabet soup I just served you, then either that character is not you or our saying we're complicated is a lie. Perhaps our self-proclaimed complications are bullshit that we heap upon ourselves, in which case you are unreal by layers and the dream character is repressed, simplistic realness.

Stripped to their simple realness, a talking dolphin, an alien, and a human are all the same. They are honest. They are joyous. They are calm. They are disciplined. They are playful.

They are one.

And wouldn't that be the perfect place to end this chapter? Except I forgot something. Right. Oh, yeah. Why was Mr. Dolphin telling me to get there now, now, right now?

Whelp, in addition to Paratopia, I was cohosting another podcast called, The Good Parade. This was a comedy show that demonstrated how out of touch with popular culture cohost Tim Binnall and I were. Somehow, I ended up befriending a listener who lived in California and wanted me to visit her before shipping off to Hawaii. She was a self-professed alcoholic, somehow financially stable, somehow living in a place of wealth. She was drunk pretty much every time we talked on the phone. At least I think she was... unless that was her sober voice, in which case... *yeesh.*

Anyway, she wasn't herself a racist, but her bestie was the daughter of an infamous skinhead leader who wasn't too keen on Dad's legacy. She wanted me to stay with her indefinitely. Cozy. She would take care of me, she said, and I could leave anytime I desired. I hadn't thought of it until now but I guess I would have needed permission to leave since I wouldn't have owned a car or known where I was.

The totality of her offer sounded every warning bell in my system. Needless to say, I accepted because who doesn't want to knowingly, consciously, act on the worst decision ever? I had to find out how this doomed-to-fail scenario would play out.

But then I remembered the dream. And the warning. And I realized this was what Mr. Dolphin meant by, “Get here now.” He didn’t mean, “Kiss your mom goodbye and forget your sister’s wedding.” He meant, “Don’t be a fucking asshole who shacks up with a drunk with Nazi ties just to have something to write about, you fucking moron.”

And naturally, because I am nothing else if not a complicated simpleton, I ignored him. No dream dolphin is going to dictate my life to me, thank you very much. This ain’t Sedona, Arizona, this is Taunton, Massachusetts, motherfucker. If I am to survive the apocalypse and help others, then you can stick a pin in that shit. The apocalypse can wait. Daddy’s got a drunk to diddle.

So, I bought my oneway ticket to San Diego and met the drunk of my other dreams. We ditched the Nazis and got married, the end.

Wait! No! That’s not what happened! Not at all!

Well, okay, the ticket-buying part happened. But then she got cold feet at the last minute and bailed, which I kind of suspected would happen. She wasn’t crazy, after all, just inebriated. So, I spent the night sleeping on a bench in the San Diego airport and flew off to Hawaii in the morning. I never even met this woman. Never spoke to her again. I had to lure some other unsuspecting soul to Hawaii and sucker her into marrying me. This one doesn’t even drink or befriend relatives of notorious racist criminals!

Thank you, Carol. Hope this isn’t too embarrassing for you, Honey Bunny. Hop-hop-hop.

Holds His Breath 'Til The Monster Passes

I Know Why The Caged Bird Talks.

And Is Psychic.

"Jane Goodall? She's smart for a person. She knows about 950 words from what I can gather from our conversations," N'Kisi, the famed African gray parrot told a bird friend yesterday.

The gray went on: "She's not as stiff as that Rupert Sheldrake. Man, that guy thinks he's psychic or something. He just sits there staring at me all day. It's creepy."

N'Kisi's friend, a cockatoo of little renown, nodded her ruffled head manically. N'Kisi added, "It's like he expects me to read his mind. I mean I can. But I won't."

For More Information, Click <u>HERE</u>.

Time Out
To Visit
The Poor Man's
Dream Factory!

Our Hero Passes Out And Dreams Of A Better Life

I had this strange dream last night. There is this Turkish psychic, right? From The Learning Channel. No kidding, The Learning Channel. She comes to my house to interview me for some radio show or something. She's really pretty and friendly and has a cool accent like Dracula. We share paranormal stories from our pasts and then she turns on her tape recorder for the interview. We talk into it for an hour.

I am relating this time I became God, when the doorbell rings. It is my mother. She brings flowers. "Mommy, Mommy, I was just telling her about the time I became God!" I joke in the voice of a child. Except I'm not joking because that's what I was telling the pretty psychic.

"Who lives upstairs from you?" the psychic asks.

"I don't know. Other tenants. There are two apartments up there. Why?"

"No reason."

I let it go for a sec, but a lightbulb sizzles in my head and, "Hey! You're a psychic! Psychics don't ask things like, 'Who lives upstairs from you?' for no reason. Come on! What are you seeing?"

She laughs a guilty laugh but doesn't tell me.

"Well, there used to be two guys who lived up there, Scott

and Ray. Ray thought his dead brother was haunting the place, so if you're seeing a dead guy, it's just Ray's brother," I convincingly assure neither her nor me.

Next thing I know, Mom, The Future Mrs. Vaeni, as I now think of her, and I are stuck in traffic on our way to a movie premiere. *My* movie premiere!

Dad was supposed to come too, but he left a message earlier in the day that he'd been battling a bloody nose from six in the morning to eleven-thirty. When he finally got it under control, he drove to the emergency room and had his schnoz cauterized. Damned aliens always ruining things. I wish I'd been around to take the call, but my neighbor's rooster woke me up early, so I went and got a haircut.

I wonder what Carl Jung would've made of this?

***

We get to the theater where I meet and greet people like a politician. Some older, thin, pony-tailed guy walks up to me and hands me his card. He runs a Tai Chi center. He is a Tai Chi master. It says so on his card. "I saw you using a Tai Chi sword in the film. Who do you study under?" he asks. He even compliments me on my Tai Chi work, but I don't remember exactly what he said. Dreams are funny that way.

"I don't study under anybody, I just do it," I reply.

He cocks his head. "So you learned Tai Chi from reading books?"

"No. I've never read a book on it. My body literally just

does it. See, I have this energy thing in me that moves my body and—Well, you'll see it in the movie."

Why did he compliment me on my Tai Chi in the film when all he could have seen was the trailer, which shows next to nothing? Weird.

I try to get away because he's kind of creeping me out, but he keeps grabbing my attention. He tells me that he works with abductees because abductions leave a psychological residue. He uses a term I don't remember, no doubt containing the word *morphic* in it, for this psychological residue. It sounds very official. If I need his services I have his card.

Besides being a Tai Chi master and a makeshift psychoanalyst, he's also a pilot. A pilot who has seen many, many UFOs. By the way, he adds, there's a group that meets by the dam in Upstate New York every weekend if I want to go.

What dam?

Oh, never mind. I excuse myself and float over to the pretty Turkish psychic. She introduces me to this other guy, Harold, who she says is an abductee and one of the founders of... something. I can't recall. Actually, it's hard to pay attention to any one thing. My head is spinning; my focus is being pulled every which way.

Harold asks me how I feel. I feel nuts. He assures me that's normal. If we didn't feel nuts we wouldn't be sane. The psychic seconds the notion. Farah, her name is. Like Farrah Fawcett. I tell her that I'd read an article about her and thought she lived in Turkey. When I found out she lived nearby and wanted to interview me I was sure she would end up my wife, but she's already married, and imagine my disappointment.

Psychic, huh? She didn't see that one coming. But it was kind of true.

The abductee guy, Harold, exudes a quality of openness, of honesty. I don't even have to delve into his past to know he's the real deal. In fact he's the first (of only a few, granted) alleged abductees I've met whom I immediately trust.

The theater programmer spots me, walks over, and vigorously shakes my hand. I know I'm going to introduce the film, so I ask him if there's some private room where I can chill like a diva and snort cocaine. He guides me into the darkened theater where I briefly sit alone. No cocaine. He takes a seat next to me and apologizes for putting my documentary in a schlocky sci-fi program. It didn't occur to him that it might offend me.

It doesn't. I embrace schlock. I am schlock.

***

Okay, so now I'm introducing the film. The house is fairly packed. Not bad considering my advertising budget of zero. Friends and family are there. My masseuse is there.

My masseuse?! Now I *know* I'm dreaming! I wonder if it has a happy ending?[10]

The screening ends happily for me in that the audience

---

[10] Yes.

laughs in the right places and winces in the right places and applauds at the end. I do a brief Q & A, then run out to beat the crowd to set up for a book signing. Almost everyone comes up and congratulates me, even coworkers, some of whom I assumed would hate the flick. And they aren't just paying lip service, either. Two of them hang out at the afterparty.

The afterparty! *Weeeeee!*

We're at CbGb, one of the most famous punk clubs on Earth. Somehow, management lets me do this afterparty for free. There are these amazing bands playing. I picked them. They thank me in between songs. My head is still spinning. I turn around. There, in the corner, where Joey Ramone used to face-fuck disaffected groupies between sets, is my mother.

My mother! At CbGb! I can't wake up!

People in the club keep coming up to me and asking me questions about my ass. Why did I include that nude hot tub scene? It was over the top. It was brilliant. It was superfluous. It was genius. Not since *Psycho* has there been such a terrifying bathtub scene.

Is this what Sharon Stone felt like after screening *Basic Instinct* for the first time? Am I going to show my saggy breasts in a sequel like she? Am I going to give 'em full frontal? Is this really my life?—I was God once, for *Me* sake!

***

The dream cuts to the next morning. I am being awakened

by a rooster. A big city rooster living one block over from my apartment building.

What's that, Rooster? Wake up, stupid, the phone is ringing?

I fumble with my cordless phone. "Hello?" I ask weakly.

Greeting me with kudos is a friend and co-worker who was at the screening. Kudos give way to story. *This* story....

Some guy with long, gray hair and one roving eyeball freaked her out after the show. She says one eye was too small and had a yellow ring around it. I ask her if it was a Marilyn Manson-type contact lens. She swears it was his eye.

The creeper asked her how the movie was and if he should see it. If he hadn't just seen the flick, what was he doing there, she wondered? Wondered but didn't dare ask.

She excused herself and turned to enter the ladies room when he grabbed her hand and said, "You're an experiencer aren't you?"

She wasn't into aliens. She had no idea what that even meant.

"Are you sure you haven't had experiences? Abductees have a certain smell. I can smell abduction on you. You've been abducted before."

She thought this was it. She was going to be killed by some *Silence of The Lambs* motherfucker, and it was my fault. That eye. That roving, yellow, wandering eye would be the last thing she ever saw.

But she's on the phone with me now, so I guess it's all good.

Or is it?

I can't wake up. Every time I think I'm awake I'm in another related dream. In this one, my friend Travis is leaving town. He's moving to D.C. with his fiancé. His interview in my movie is one of my favorite parts. I'm reminiscing about it by my lonesome as I walk to the Times Square subway station. It's a typical pleasant, chilly evening in the city, full of people ignoring each other, each lost in their own dreams.

Suddenly, the date January 22nd, 2005 flashes in my mind. I know this to be the night I shot the scene into which I inserted the interview with Travis. New York evening transitions to Sonora night as I transition into the scene....

I am sitting in a lawn chair on the side of a busy mountain road in Sonora, California, with my two brave companions, Sara and Jeanette. Sara is a friend of the family whom I've known since I was in diapers. We haven't seen each other in about five years. Jeanette is a friend I met on the internets back when such things weren't fashionable. She lives across the country from me. We'd only hung out in person once, when she visited New York with her boyfriend, long ago. The two ladies are standing between a tripod-mounted digital video camera and Jeanette's car. They are facing away from me and are chatting and bored and nervous.

Sitting across from me is the owner of that camera, Mark Olson. My camera is in my hand; if something remarkable goes down, I don't want to miss it. Mark's brother, Jed, is standing tall, facing the general direction that I am facing, monitoring the skies for atypical signs of life. He alerts us to any light appearing, be it plane, satellite, or house. He has better eyes than I do, but everything in the sky looks alien to him until proven otherwise. Thus far everything has been proven otherwise.

Mark is devouring a small bag of Funyuns and has a pocketful of Ritz crackers ready to go when the fun runs out. “Yup. This is what we do,” he confides with a giggle on this nondescript roadside. Nondescript because it’s nighttime and black out. Thank the gods his camera has night vision. My camera has everything else I could hope for, just not the one thing I need right now.

What are we doing here? Well, as you know, I’m an alien abductee. Mark may be an alien abductee, and his brother may also be. All the signs are there: mysterious scars on the body, odd marks that fade with time, alien dreams that feel more real than real, half memories of some vague childhood incident, and my personal favorite symptom, nosebleeds. UFOs have been flying near their house and over it for months now. Mark films them. He invited me to see for myself, telling me to bring a camera because, “These things aren’t going away.” I happened to be staying a few towns over, in Sacramento. I had flown in to teach a class at The Learning Exchange, so I decided to take Mark up on his offer. Then, like any narcissist worth his weight in hubris, I decided I needed to make a long documentary on me for which this excursion would be the climax. I figured, if we really were abductees, the aliens—whoever they were—would know we were coming. And they owed us. Big time.

I thought this would be a great experiment to see what happens when we three abductees gather at a UFO hotspot and I let kundalini will power take over. Would the aliens sense it? If they were tracking us, they'd know we were there. If they were telepathic, they'd know I was not quite myself.

Was there an interest level here for them? I was betting on yes.

I wonder if I told Jeanette and Sara any of this before they agreed to come with?

Huh. Anyway. Yeah, like Moses, I'm on the mountaintop. Unlike Moses, I'm not talking to a burning bush, I'm talking to a snacking Olson. Talking over the intermittent roar of the apathetic traffic. Talking over my embarrassed thumping heart—we've been here for hours and nothing. Talking over Mark's munching and Jeanette and Sara's private conversation and Jed's... well... Jed's Jed-eye gaze staring stoically off into space. Literally staring off into space—there's not a star in the piece of sky he's examining, except that one there. The bright white one peeking at us through telephone wires. That's weird. Was that there before? Of course it was, it's just a star. Or maybe—What's that association between UFOs and high voltage wires?

Anyway, as I was telling Mark, "Back in high school I remember this one time my friend Travis and I were driving our other friend, Adam, home from a party. It was like, I don't know, one in the morning or something. Anyway, we're driving by this cemetery—of course we are, right?—and off in the distance, in the woods, there are these blue glowing objects just sort of hovering in the trees. I'm like, 'Travis, you have to see this!' But he's a staunch conservative at the time, right? Set in his ways. And he knows I have a fascination or whatever with UFOs, so he doesn't pay any attention; it's just me being weird. Then Adam, from the back seat, says, 'No, really, Trav. What is that?'

"Trav's like, *Yeah, right. Whatever.* But he glances over casually, sees the lights, and *rrrrrrt!* Slams on the breaks, puts it in reverse and stops in front of these lights. He's like, *Holy shit—what is that?* And then I see this, what I think is a plane, moving over the car, except it stops. Adam and I see this and yell 'Go! Go! Get out of here!' Travis couldn't see it from the driver's side, but he just peeled out of there anyway.

"When we got to Adam's house, his parents were waiting up for us. We told them and they laughed at us, of course.

"So now after this we made a short film based on... loosely based on this experience called *The Visitation.* It was just a five-minute thing, no big deal. Well, okay, so cut to a year later..."

Actually, cut to that star up there. That sure is bright. Bright enough to catch my attention. Was that there all this time? It's white. Is it a planet?

"...My mom had this friend in town from Virginia. She brought her daughter who was this New Kids On The Block freak, you know? Like, I mean how do you even deal with that? So, I call Travis to rescue me, and we decide to bring her to our friend Bill's place. As we're pulling into the driveway—"

What is that friggen light? Is that something or is it nothing? Maybe I should ready the camera—"Holy shit!" I gasp.

"Did you see that?" Jed drawls.

"I certainly did! It just winked out! Oh my god! Did you all see that?"

Nope. No, they didn't. Or don't. What tense am I in?

They haven't been looking and neither Jed nor I draw their attention to the intense white light before it mysteriously vanishes. Mark's camera isn't pointed to that part of the sky. My camera isn't pointed at all. I am so into my story, so into myself, that I completely miss the opportunity to capture the light on film. Or bring forth that kundalini will power in me to see if an interaction occurs. Or role a six-sided die to see if my karma magic beats the Shire Elf—God! What are we doing here?!

This is it! My chance to prove once and for all, if only to myself, that this phenomenon is physically real—and I blow it! Of course I do!

***

I can't tell if these beings have a sense of humor or if humor is just inherent to the situation, but as I type these words I am reminded that this winking and nudging on their behalf, this giving me just enough to say, *Yup, we're here,* and nothing more, in this very grating fashion has happened to me before. In fact, it happened during the rest of my story with Travis and Adam, which I did not get to finish telling on the mountaintop, but will now so do....

As we're pulling into Bill's driveway I see this *loooooong,* like, football-field long, black oval glide behind his neighbor's house. I think my eyes are playing tricks on me; it's a cloud or something.

Maybe it was. Maybe it was a coincidence.

But anyway, we pull into the driveway and Bill has woods behind his house. There again, dancing in the trees, are these two blue lights—the same lights from a year ago way across town!

I'm like, "Travis! Look at that! Look!"

He looks to where I'm pointing and there's nothing there. It's like a cosmic joke. The lights just winked out. He asks, "What was it?"

And I tell him, "You remember *The Visitation*?"

And he's like, "Yeah, right, bullshit."

I never say what I saw, I just say, "Remember *The Visitation*?" which is important because our teeny bopper friend in the back doesn't know about that at all. I mean we never told her a thing about it, ever. But as Travis is scoffing at me, she chimes in with, "What? You mean the blue lights that have been following us since the stop sign?"

I just—my jaw drops. And Travis just keeps refusing to hear it all the way to the door. *Oh, yeah, right, bullshit.* Waving me off with his flailing monkey paw.

To this day, Trav doesn't remember this at all. I mean the first time by the cemetery, yes. But he doesn't remember the sequel. It's probably too synchronistic and therefore personal, so he blocked it out.

***

Yeah, that's what I would have told Mark that disappointing night on the mountain. And Jed and Jeanette and Sara, if they had been fucking listening to me, for Christ's sake.

Like Travis back in high school, these friends had just missed what could have been a life-altering visual for them.

Was that by design? Are those alien NASA engineers hard at work building ships, buying fuel, traveling to a foreign planet to shine a light at a couple of dudes hanging out on some cliff?

Really?

And then do they turn off the light the moment I take too much interest and think about turning on my camera?

Really?

All of these big, silly questions flash through my dreaming mind.[11] I wonder what the truth is here: that aliens come to Earth and revolve around me, or that I'm so self-centered and so out of touch, I'm spinning myself a neat little fantasy world like a caped role-playing nerd?

I learn through this brief experience that I am more into hearing myself talk than interested in capturing a UFO on

---

[11] Remember that? Yeah, I'm still committed to the *All Of This Is Taking Place In A Dream* framing. Don't doze off.

film. *Me first!* No matter what I do to deny it, this is still the fact.

I read the wink-nudge humor of the light in the sky literally winking out as, *Yeah, we're here, kid. But we're not gonna star in your pooptastic shlockumentary.*

But am I drawing from this experience what I want to draw, or am I dissecting an event that was preplanned and, to an extent, personalized for me?

It is illogical and the height of vanity to suppose that aliens would dedicate their time, energy, resources, and inventiveness—would risk crashing a shuttle on a hostile planet and mass exposure to its hostile people—just to flash a light at lil' ol' me to teach me a lesson about the height of vanity.

In fact, if I were a lesser person, which I clearly am not, I wouldn't be able to tell that the so very human lesson aliens were teaching me by making it seem as though the universe revolved around me was, *The universe doesn't revolve around you.*[12]

Conversely, it is also irrational to believe that the synchronicities in abduction accounts, of which this tale is but a drop in the cosmic bucket, are always an amalgamation of coincidences the experiencer wrongly strings together to make dubious sense of circumstances that, with proper investigation, will always turn out to have mundane origins.

No rational conclusion suffices. No logical explanation sums it all up. Yet alien abductions are real. Go figure.

---

[12] Oh, wait, Jed saw the light first? Maybe this isn't about me at all.... Just kidding.

***

Some UFOs are flying craft humans did not build and yet the builders and we are connected. What's going on here?

What's going on?

If logic only brings us to a certain point before it breaks down and becomes irrelevant then isn't it time to try something new?

Researchers have been studying these phenomena for decades now, keenly awaiting the tipping point event or insight that makes sense of it all. The problem is, we are not dealing with phenomena that cater to reductionism. We're talking about an intelligence greater than ours. As far as we can tell, this is a first for humanity, so why isn't it treated as such?

If the intelligence is greater than ours—not just in intellect, but in the full implication of the word *intelligence*—then what do we need to do to meet as equals?

We upgrade outmoded computers, why can't we upgrade us?

We've got all this brain we don't use. What's it for?

These are a child's questions, and they are applicable. They are applicable because we are, in our old age, still children. As with real children, the bratty little kind, there's no growth without questioning.

As *dream me* replays his mountain expedition in the *royal our* head, it's no wonder why it happens the way it does. It's no wonder why these nonhumans come to Mark and Jed, two of the most unassuming men I've ever met. It's no wonder why there is a light playfulness through the dark fear of contact. It's no wonder why this is so personal to so many abductees even if it's illogical. It's no wonder this UFO literally winks at me, telling me I'm not ready for what they are, even though I think I am. It's no wonder we cannot figure them out.

No, *wonder* is what comes when we give up trying to submerge higher unknowns into our knowledge base. Bringing the object of study to our level is predicated upon the assumption that we're separate from and greater than or equal to the object. This is essential when studying things like energy, matter, the animal kingdom, world cultures, and Western psychology. But how do we meet the higher? Mustn't we *become* the higher?

And yet here I am, I realize, all kinds of lower. All kinds of arrogant, bawdy, filthy lower.

God, how do I get away with this stuff? Years and years spent railing against ego and squawking about transcending the self, yet I write books about me, a play about me based on those books, give public talks about me, podcast about me, and make a film about me, starring me, directed and produced by me.

Dude, that's a lot of *me*. But then every character in the dream is me, so I guess it's par for the course. There must be a *me-ness* that isn't narcissism. Perhaps I am teaching me this through the dream?

***

Anyway, getting back to me, the dream cuts back to me at a crosswalk in Times Square. I'm waiting for the walk signal. The gayest gay man I have ever seen brushes shoulders with me. He's wearing headphones thumping with techno music. He looks me over like a pageant judge and lisps, "This is New York, girl. It's walk or die in the city. It's walk or *die*." With that, he struts into traffic. He does a pirouette. He strikes a vogue pose. He primps the hair of a woman strolling by with her boyfriend. The couple stop in their tracks and explode with laughter.

"You better work it, girl!" he hisses. He continues skipping and dancing down the street as I make my exit to the subway. It's a funny spectacle and yet I can't help but wonder what will happen when he invades the space of a homophobe.

***

Home. Finally, I can rest in the sanity of home. It's 1:30 in the morning. I'm watching a flick with a roommate. I see flashing lights outside the living room window. I ignore them for a spell. Finally, my curiosity wins out. I float to the window. A swarm of cops is attempting to hop our locked gate to the backyard. I fly to the front door. There's police everywhere.

"Hi," I say.

"Do you have an alternate way to your backyard?" an officer asks.

"Yes. Follow me."

Six cops jog with me through my apartment to the back door. "Did you notice anyone in your backyard?" one of them asks while I fumble with the skeleton key.

"No. What's going on?"

"Your neighbor's brother slit his wrists then jumped out the window. He's running around like a maniac."

I can't get the damned key to work! This is embarrassing!

"Good thing you guys aren't in a hurry," I joke. They say it's okay. Better than hopping that gate. Finally, I get the door open and they rush out to the yard. Their flashlights pierce all the dark corners. Nothing. Someone spots the crazy guy on a rooftop two buildings away.

"Freeze! This is the police!"

Wow, I actually hear a cop yell that!

The guy is, like, dancing or something on the rooftop, sort of taunting them.

"Don't do anything stupid! This is the police!"

Then, from sight unseen, booms the loudest, shrillest old lady voice imaginable. She's so New York, she's almost Old York, almost cockney-accented. "Who's on my property?!" The severity of her caw reminds me of the possessed grandmother corpse in *Evil Dead II* barking, "Who's in my fruit cellar?"

"It's okay, ma'am, it's the police!"

"Who's out there?!"

"Police! Go back inside!"

"I will not go back inside! What's going on? Who's on my property?"

"Ma'am! Go back to sleep! You're waking the whole—"

"I'm calling the police!"

"We *are* the police!"

"Then I'm calling your precinct! You have no right to—"

"Lady, shut the fuck up, you're waking the neighborhood!"

"What did you just say?"

A male officer turns to me and asks how I put up with her. I tell him I've never heard her before in my life, but when they're done here there's this annoying rooster, and if they have a moment.... Yeah, they don't care.

The old woman carries on with lungs of steel. Who is on her property? Who is that man? Finally, a male officer yells from the dark, "He's got a bomb!"

"He's got a WHAAAAAAT?!"

"He's got a bomb, lady!"

A female officer scolds him, but they're both giggling.

"Never mind! Go back to sleep!" he yells. They hear over the radio that the crazy man has been apprehended. They thank me, then take off. I go back to my movie. The old woman continues shouting for the next twenty minutes or so. Nothing has changed. I'll hear that rooster in the morning.

***

In another non sequitur, the dream cuts to two days later. There is an encore screening of my movie about me to which I show up late because I want to see if the audience reacts differently if they don't know I'm there. Nope. Same reaction. On the whole they love it. Well, except for this one couple.

I do a protracted Q & A after the lights come up. Some guy with lengthy gray hair and elongated glasses asks me why I didn't include more about my own abductions in the film. He and the perfectly round-headed woman he is with share a tight-lipped, repressed hostility. I half expect them to yell at me, such is the ferocity of their disappointment.

I explain that the movie wants to be what it wants to be and that we've all heard the same stories a million times—short, bald, gray aliens, right? Abducting me? Do we need to hear more about that? So I went a different way.

He follows up with a question basically asking if I feel like I'm falsely advertising, and what do I do if people come expecting to hear my abduction stories?

I remind him that I do share a couple of memories in the movie, but it's not about rehashing the same old stuff. Then, because I feel bad, and because his lady friend is burning a hole through me with her eyes, I recount a story or two.

After the show I go to dinner with a pal who tells me that this guy approached her in the lobby. He had long gray hair and crazy eyes. She can't articulate what's crazy about them, just that she couldn't look into them. She thinks he must have been the same man who had asked me those questions, but she wasn't sure because he was sitting down front, and she was in the back.

Anyway, this guy walked over to her and asked her if she

was an experiencer. She said no. He asked her how long she had been interested in abductions. She said she wasn't. She asked him the same. He said since he was seven years old. He asked her what she thought of the movie, what it was about, what her favorite parts were, and so on. She said she liked it, thought it was hysterical. But wasn't she disappointed in the lack of abduction stories, he asked?

"No," she told him, "I didn't come in with any expectations."

His roaming eyeball was too much for her to ignore, so she excused herself from the conversation. The man stood there staring at her for an uncomfortably long time, as if waiting for the opportunity to strike up a conversation again. He must have gotten fed up and beamed to the mothership.

Was he the same man as the guy with the girlfriend? Was he the Tai Chi master? I didn't notice a roving crazy eyeball on that guy, but he did have long, grayish hair. Either way, it had to be the same guy who smelled abduction on my coworker from the first screening. Had he seen the movie once, twice, or not at all?

How many abductees with long, gray hair and a creepy eyeball are there in New York?

Probably all of 'em. And I'm next. I had a cornea transplant in college. I've got a dead guy's eye watching everything in my left socket. I ain't gettin' any younger. Is this my future? Do we all become this?

***

My phone ringing for real at 1:50am finally wakes me. What an absurdly long and lucid string of dreams. I hate being startled awake like this, but at least I know that I am, in fact, awake and back to normalcy.

"Hello?" I slur.

"Wow, this must piss you off being woken up like this," she giggles.

Ah. It's my friend, April. She works the nightshift at a gas station somewhere in Trumpfuckery, Alabama.

"Uh, yeah. What's up?" I say.

"Nothing. Just the only time I can call is when I'm at work. I knew you'd be asleep, though."

I'm trying not to be mad, but I'm getting there. "Come on, I have to work tomorrow. What's up?"

"Nothing. Some guy just stuck a gun in my face and robbed the place."

"What? Are you okay?" Now I'm up.

"Yeah. It was a small gun. I actually laughed at him and said, 'Are you serious?' He said he was serious. The cops are here dusting for fingerprints and stuff. I'm bored so I thought I'd call."

"Jesus, you poor thing. You sure you're okay?"

"Yeah. You know me. I can live through anything. Wait. Hold on.... Hey, they think they caught him passed out drunk in his car down the block."

"Well, that's good!" I begin to nod off again.

"Yeah. I should probably let you go. I was just sitting here bored so I thought I'd call."

"Okay, good night."

"Night."

"Be safe." But she'd already hung up.

I turn off the ringer and drift back to sleep. I dream that I am getting the rubdown at my masseuse's parlor. I ask her how she liked the flick. She's from China, so I think, 'Mmm… maybe saying I have a Chinaman living inside me,' as I sensitively refer to the possession-like kundalini energy in the film, 'is offensive to, for instance, the Chinese.'

"Your movie is called, *No One's Watching*, right?" she asks.

"Yes."

"Then what that part after?"

"What do you mean?"

"The part that come after that."

"Oh. *An Alien Abductee's Story. No One's Watching: An Alien Abductee's Story,* it's called."

"I don't know that word… *abductee*?"

"Yes. As in, *abduction.* Alien abduction?"

"Abduction? What's that? I say to myself, 'What is this word?'"

"It means kidnapping. You know *kidnap*?"

"Ooooh, kidnap. Steal."

"Yes. Aliens steal me. I mean they don't steal me. They bring me back. It's confusing."

"I thought it say *adoption* and then when you were talking about Chinese, I thought, 'Ooooh this a film about Americans adopting Chinese children. This going to be good movie!'"

“Wow, so you must have been disappointed.”

“No, I like movie anyway.”

“Did you get it?”

“Yes. I need to see it again, though. Some parts I don’t know.” She smiles at me and adds, “You know you could make movie about Chinese adoption. Yeah. A lot of people adopt Chinese baby. I think that would make good movie.”

I have the feeling she means *better* movie.

Cue rooster.

I’m awake.

Wakes Up In A Cave

"Hi. It's me, Katherine. I know we've only IMed and text messaged each other, but I thought it would be good to finally hear your voice. I guess you're not around. You must be out at a party or something, huh? Well, anyway, when you get this message, give me a call sometime. It would be great to finally hear what you sound like. Bye."

It's one in the morning on a Saturday night. Is that an oxymoron or is it just what it is? I don't know. I don't know anything. I'm in a frazzled state of mind.

I'm waiting for a train out of Brooklyn. Earlier, I screened my movie about me at a political dissident coffee house called Vox Pop. We were a half-hour late getting started because we couldn't figure out how to get the sound to work. We couldn't figure it out because the one person who was supposed to know the system was too busy schmoozing the new customers to actually help fix the problem. When he finally did get his ass in gear, the gear broke. He knew nothing about the system. My sister's boyfriend and an old heckler fixed it.

A heckler. Who heckles anymore? I found out later in talking to the man that he's not really a heckler, he's just socially retarded. "Sorry I've got to leave in the middle of this thing. I thought it would be shorter. It is kind of entertaining, though. I didn't expect that. That's good, though. It's funny," he told me. Earlier, when we were struggling to fix the sound, he blurted out, "Why don't you get on the mic, Jeremy? Take this opportunity to tell us a little bit about the movie. Come on! Work the crowd!"

The crowd. Hey, wasn't Harold part of the crowd? I know he came in because I shook his hand and said hello. He sat alone at a table in the back. A tall drink, still full, stood on the table in front of where his body should be. Where did he go?

Harold is the immediately likable abductee I met at the premiere screening back in that dream. Or not dream. Whatever happened last chapter. We reconnected a couple of weeks ago at the—where else—Galaxy Diner. He shared extraordinary tales from his curious life, one of which involved being abducted from a coffee shop in broad daylight. Could this be what happened to him ton—*NAAAAAAH!*

Once we got the sound working we were good to go. Well, except for the fact that even with the lights out it was too bright in there, what with the neon signs glowing through the large window panes. Also, the screen? Not a screen. A white sheet I'd tacked onto a wall made lumpy by the immovable framed portrait of John F. Kennedy underneath. My sister assured me later, "It's a political café run by hippies. We would have been disappointed if things *didn't* go wrong. It's all part of the atmosphere."

After the movie, my go-to band, The Violets, rocked the joint, then a handful of us retired to the keyboardist's new apartment for a lil' housewarming party. I left the party early with Katherine, a friend of the lead singer. We had no clue where we were in Brooklyn, so we decided to buddy up and wait for the train together. I'd seen her around at The Violets shows, but I'd never really chatted her up. We got to talking and she told me that she barely leaves her house because her cat can't stand it when she's gone. Then she told me all about the cat. Then she told me more about the cat. Then she showed me pictures of the cat stored on her cellphone and made cooing noises at the pictures. Then I hoped the train would come so I could jump in front of it and die.

Katherine lives alone. Alone with that cat. She is dumpy and middle-aged in that *I can't tell if you're thirty or forty-five years old* sort of way. When she speaks she speaks at you, not with you, and one immediately gains the impression that this is her holdover defense mechanism from when she was part of the nerdling underclass in high school who were esteem-raped by bullies.

I have no idea why she decides to call her cyber friend at one in the morning to speak to his (I assume it's a he) answering machine in a way that sounds strikingly like exposition—and with another person there, no less. Perhaps she has lost her facility for embarrassment.

"So what do you do for a living?" I ask when she hangs up.

"I'm a child psychologist."

"Really?"

"I work with suicidal teens at [insert fake hospital name

so that I don't get sued here]."

"Really? Like you have to spend all day talking them down, or—"

"No-no," she says. "We have a program where we diagnose which kids are happy and which are depressed and need medication."

"Uh, but aren't all teens depressed? Do you just give them all pills or—"

"No-no!" She scolds. "We determine, you know, normal depression from suicidal depression."

"Okay," I reply. "Do you like what you do?"

"Yeah, I do, for the most part. But it's frustrating because there's no way to determine if what we're doing is helping. There's no follow-up. We're working on solving that problem now."

"What do you mean?"

"Well, for example, say you have 10 students. Seven of them are going to be fine and three will need counseling and medication. Now, all we can do is recommend to the school that they get it and the school tells the parents and that's where our jurisdiction ends. You can't force a kid to get help; it's solely their decision in the end, so of those three, we don't know who goes to counseling, who goes but drops out, who gets medication. There's no way to prove that we're even helping."

"Huh. That seems like a pretty big flaw to overlook."

"I know. We're trying to fix that now."

"How would you fix it? Pass a law so you can just drug up

the kids at will, or—?"

I don't remember her answer. At this point I'm just being a wiseass.

"So if a kid came to you and said, 'I was abducted by aliens,' what would you do?" I ask.

"Well, first of all, I'd tell him that he's depressed, obviously. He must be depressed and probably lonely, so he's making up this fantasy about aliens."

"Really? So there's no way that what he's saying could possibly be real?"

"I believe aliens exist somewhere out there, but I can't believe they'd be taking individuals in the middle of the night. I mean, why? For what reason? It's silly."

I ask her what she thinks of my movie and if she thinks I'm delusional. In answer she asks if I really think I'm an abductee. After all that she'd seen and heard about me she has the gall to ask that.

I tell her I am an abductee, whatever that word ultimately means. If it means I've got an undiagnosed form of schizophrenia then that's what I've got. If it means aliens take me in the night then that's what I've got. Whatever the ultimate origin, I have the symptoms.

She looks me over with incredulity. She isn't buying that I believe my own words. "How much money have you made off of your book?" she asks.

"Nothing, really. I self-published it and haven't even paid off that cost. I've got a few thousand copies sitting in my bedroom if you want one."

"What about the movie?"

"I haven't made anything. I mean I plan to, don't get me wrong. I'd love to be making money off of all this stuff, but that's neither here nor there."

She eyeballs me, warily. For the first time I can remember I am face to face with someone who thinks me a snake oil salesman. I'd say *takes one to know one*, but I'm not one for her to know.

One of her suspicions is correct: I don't really believe my abductions constitute an undiagnosed form of schizophrenia. I try to keep an open mind about what's happening with me, but this mind of mine is slowly closing. I may not know what legitimate abductions are, but I'm certain that they are neither the holographic projections of an ill brain nor the invisible friends tea party of a social misfit. We say things that make hypothetical sense and then call them facts. We hide in that mistake and the world conforms to our comfort level.

This isn't to say that fantasy-prone depressed people don't claim to be abductees—*of course* the ufological field attracts crazies and displaced wannabes. So does the psychological field. So does rock-and-roll. Like moths, the needy are everywhere a spotlight is.

Who is living in fantasyland: the abductee who spends a lifetime trying to figure out what's happening to him, and whose experiences force him to live in a state of uncertainty regarding the boundaries of reality, or the psychologist who lives in certainty, whose sex is a computer, and whose human child is a cat? I'm betting that in my obvious depression and probable loneliness I cry myself to sleep at night less than Katherine.

When the train finally screeches to a halt and the doors part invitingly, I know it is going to be a long, uncomfortable ride home. I wonder what it must be like to be her sitting next to me telling me I'm either a fraud or fucked up. Is there satisfaction in that or despair? Or is it neither?

When you're a person who talks at, not with, people, does it even matter what words belch out of you? Is it all about keeping that wall up, keeping that distance? Is the topic irrelevant because the substance of all monologues is, *I am speaking*?

More importantly, what the hell happened to Harold? Seriously, he came to the thing and then disappeared before it even started. Is that rude or what? I hope he's okay. Maybe he got sick and bolted. Maybe he locked himself in the bathroom and is trapped overnight. Maybe he saw a white rat hopping over a cracked pocket watch in the distance, thought it was a rabbit, and chased it down an open manhole.

I don't have long to wonder. As AOL used to say, *You've got mail.* Except not you, me. I've got mail. Email. Although you're about to read it now, so technically it's all of ours.

What?

Never mind. Here's Harold.

Hi Jeremy,

Thanks - I'm AOK.

In a way I did 'disappear.'

Your event, and the loud breaking of a glass mug inside Vox Pop's front door, was the unexpected start of a long 'journey' into another world/place/time that took place Saturday night and Sunday morning, experienced through a thoroughly vivid and lucid 'dream' - on a crescendo of an increased experience of this 'other place' over the past few weeks - and over a lifetime. I will soon 'explain' this - as best as I can of something that transcends language - in a piece on one of our S.P.A.C.E. websites.

The mystery deepens. More questions. Never clear absolute answers.

Incomprehensible 'Communication' - but a hard-earned attempt at communication on both ends - is an open-ended and never-ending adventure.

As the owner of a popular Village gallery told me last evening, 'It's Out There. It fits nothing that humans, hard-wired by thousands of years of cultural-conditioning and blinded by the barriers of unyielding egos, can define. But the interface will change, yes, really transform the human species into something very different. Something like what's Out There, only our own new human version of it.'

I'm sorry that this nighttime 'event' took me away from what I hope was a successful evening for your movie showing....

Harold

Hmmm. On second thought, maybe we abductees do need Katherine's pills. Or some quality cat time.

Brain cells accumulate information, store it as memory, and from that memory you function as a sentient, self-involved defense mechanism. Defending is the same as attacking: to defend you must attack. To defend yourself you attack another. Knowing this fact does nothing to stop the accumulation, as it is just another memory to be stored.
Real revolution can only take place when the brain cells stop running in their self-enclosed patterns. Nothing within logical boundaries will ever, EVER, make them stop.
One must halt thought altogether, which is not to say replace logic with illogic, or some form of mental deficiency. That's not it at all.
Listening happens when one stops trying. Only then will what is heard not be self-projected.

I can't stop it. I'm sorry, Reader. I don't get why this is happening.

Time Back In.

Gray As Ash,
The Monster Looms Over Him

Hey, Reader. How's it going? Sequel okay? Not so much for me. Can't stand who I'm becoming. I feel like all this cruel humor that used to flow so freely from me is corroding my soul. But that's my problem.

Got a voice trapped in my head. Something. I keep trying to ignore him but he comes back with that fancy-shmancy font, all mysterious and crazy-talking. Come to think of it, I dunno if it's crazy talk or not, I just know that one's not my problem, it's yours. You're the one reading this.

No, my problem—my other problem, likely the really real one—is you. Not all of you, but, like, too many of you. The vocal ones. The uptight whiners.

See, here's the thing: I get a lot of complaints about my potty mouth from readers who can't see past the naughty words I enjoy using. I can hear them future-bitching about this book right now. They get put off by the delivery and excuse themselves from the deep stuff being communicated.

So, why don't I just clean up my act and give 'em what they want?

I did! I wrote a wonderful, sanitized book of spiritual deep stuff called, *Urgency*. Maybe you've heard of it?

I knew I needed to write a PG book in order to attract

more people to my super-duper spiritual message, which they would not have read had I peppered it with F bombs that were not *fun*, *fantastic*, *forward-thinking*, and *fifth density*.

Or should I say, would not have read *again*. The fun, fantastic fact is that we've been reading and hearing the same spiritual message for thousands of years and still we don't get what's being communicated. That being the case, 'Why not hear it again from me?' I thought. I thought, 'I can put that slick post-modern humor spin on it and make the medicine taste like dessert.'

But.

It turns out.

As with the previous thousands of years.

They would not hear it from me, either.

What's the excuse this time?

I'm damaged goods. Unmarketable, really. Blacklisted.

While it is true that I've been nothing but honest[13] and, if I may humblebrag a moment, just a wee bit deeper than anyone in the history of ever in talking about my experiences over the years, I also like joking around. I like having a laugh. And a lot of you reading this right now are, if I may put it gently, complete fucking morons who equate having a laugh with lack of seriousness. You condemn me and then have the audacity to take seriously the dumbest, most bullshittiest bullshit I've ever seen.

My love-hate relationship with my audience, as I hope I've

[13] Except for the spots in this book where I lied for no reason. And right now, obviously.

made obvious by now, began with ufology. That crowd loves a good bullshit artist disguised as a researcher. You can dress up bullshit all ya want, but bullshit in a suit and tie, farting out a logical-sounding monotone speech about what the aliens are *really* up to, still stinks, ya know?

You don't know. Too many of you in or into ufology don't know. You don't want to know. You want your belief system fortified by collegial sex addicts, pedophile puppeteers, and postmen with mail-order PhDs. You want hypnotically-retrieved narratives, cozy little horror stories, and space brothers. A galactic federation of light feeding your darkness.

Some of you ask why there haven't been a lot of new alien abduction books lately. Did the Grays pack up and head home or lose a fight to the Reptilians or something?

No. What happened was, fellow experiencer and reformed ufologist, Jeff Ritzmann, and I did a wildly popular takedown of hypnosis as a memory retrieval tool by exposing hypnosis prophet David Jacobs as a fucking loon. Really, Emma Woods, his star subject, did that when she woke up one day and realized she wasn't being raped by alien-human hybrids, as Jacobs would have her believe. She saw that she had been seeded with that plot line by the good doctor through conversations and hypnosis. Together, after hours upon hours of hypnosis sessions performed over the phone and Skype, they grew the germ into a story that felt real but wasn't. It was his gross fantasy, which he was acting out through a small group of people who had sought his help.

Thankfully, she became lucid of the fact before he had a

chance to publish his inevitable book about his/her bullshit alien hybrid revelations. Also, thankfully, she recorded her hypnosis sessions and some of their conversations, including their final "breakup" arguments, and so we all got to hear just what went into the "work" of one of the top two voices in alien abduction research. The other voice was that of Jacobs's bestie, the late Budd Hopkins, who spent part of his final years lying and covering up for his friend.[14] Fucking disgusting.

And so, through our influential podcast, Paratopia, Jeff Ritzmann and I shone a spotlight on Emma Woods and the tragic fact that, yes, we have to start from scratch with alien abduction research. It's not just David Jacobs, we pointed out, hypnosis is the larger problem. It's the wrong tool for the job.

That is why the alien abduction well has dried up in recent years. You're fucking welcome.

Despite all of the blowback we received from Jacobs sycophants; despite the deafening public silence from cowards who privately lauded our work, and that of Carol Rainey, who subsequently exposed Budd Hopkins' biggest case as a hoax, which he promoted to his grave anyway; despite Jacobs going on to win a MUFON Lifetime Achievement Award and publish yet another book of alien hybrid fantasies billed as research; despite hypnosis still

---

[14] For example, in a *UFO Magazine* editorial he wrote in defense of David, Budd claimed not to know who I was. By that point I had interviewed him, had email exchanges, he'd snail mailed me an article he wrote on Roswell, spoke at my Culture of Contact festival, where I introduced him, and went on Coast To Coast AM to promote it after I set that up for us. He knew me.

being used by people who smile from the podiums of conferences, telling you they have your best interest at heart, and they really want to solve this alien riddle the way disgraced televangelists wait out the public bellowing over their fraud, only to resurface and steal poor, sick people's money again in the name of Jesus; despite all of that plus most of you reading this incredibly long sentence right now either not knowing any of it happened or ignoring it because you don't want to start over—yes, against those odds, alien abduction research has died. All that's growing now are the nails and hair on the alien corpse in its sad little coffin.

Why else do you think hallucinogens have made such a huge resurgence in ufology? There ain't nothin' interesting left to talk about!

We're truffle hogs sniffing out the latest, greatest answer we can babble confidently about, and now those truffles are magic mushrooms. Mark my words: DMT is the new alien god. It's the new template. And the aliens are being reimagined, redefined, and soon, very soon, rewritten with drugs so that the suggestible may take DMT and step inside a virtual alien reality that will feel real. Realer, even, than hypnosis. You will swear it is more real than consensus reality. You will swear it's an alien world. And what it is is a thought construct applied to the collective unconscious by people who don't understand that they are building what they are exploring, just like a dream. Just like hypnosis.

But you won't compare it to a dream, will you? Or hypnosis, no. Because that's too mundane. And you're already mundane. No, this must be exotic. You will compare this to video games with randomized level designs and then you will suppose we are all inside an alien computer simulation. We are fake lifeforms who believe we're real. You will be partly right and partly wrong and both parts are your fault.

Is this going too fast? Should I slow it down? Are you like, "Wait, what about hypnosis? Prove it's bad!" like I'm the one who needs to do the reading for you? Like you don't know how to use a search engine or go to the fucking library? I need to educate you even though you won't accept my professorial oratory as education, but view it as an argument you must defend against through ignorance?

No. Fuck you. Do your work. I had to. You think I liked finding this shit out? I didn't. I was friendly with Budd Hopkins; I'd read all of his books and most of Jacobs's. But sometimes in life ya gotta face facts. Bill Cosby played a cute baby-talking every-father, while secretly feeding women the *drinky-drink* so he could put his *diddle-diddle* in their *daddle-waaaaah.* David Jacobs commanded Emma Woods to send him her dirty panties for alien DNA analysis and not remember doing so, while she was hypnotized. David Jacobs offered to mail her an undergarment with nails at the vaginal opening, which he admitted he found at a bondage shop, to thwart the alien hybrids who barged into her life seemingly just to rape her. I don't have to like what these legends in their fields truly are, but I have to accept it. And so all of Jacobs's inauthentic work goes in the trash.

Sure, we could talk over the historical origin and trajectory of hypnosis used foolishly by fools in ufology, but then I'd have to lay out all the reasons hypnosis is wrong for memory retrieval and defend that position of fact from rabid idiots who refuse to "throw the baby out with the bathwater," even though the baby is demonstrably stillborn. It's all very rote by now and it rarely gets us anywhere because I can't argue facts in a world that increasingly agrees that whatever you believe is true for you is accurate enough, because your personal perspective is everything.

However, the unspoken origin? The energy behind the abuse of hypnosis in alien abduction research? *That* we *can* discuss because that is something you may legitimately disagree with until such time as you see it. Or not. Because that origin is not one based on rational facts but on transrational operations, which, by definition, neither the so-called rational person nor the irrational person will ever know for certain is the case. The case I'm talking about is our need to fit transrational experiences within a rational framework.

Oppressed, marginalized people in our culture fit in by appearing as invisibly as possible to the oppressor. If you act like a stuffy white heterosexual, for example, you'll likely have better opportunities for what the culture deems success. You'll be harassed less. Life won't be good, but it will be livable.

For alien abductees, being invisible doesn't mean being totally silent about our experiences, it means making them seem plausible. Rational, even. We fit in by reducing our experiences to the easily understandable and then we provoke or engage in conversation and debate about that. To pull off this stunt, we, along with an interested hypnotist, co-create scientifically plausible and culturally acceptable narratives about what is happening to us. When we report our high strangeness incidents, be they hypnotically retrieved or not, we often leave out certain details that we think might be too strange even for the interested researcher to handle. In many cases, researchers further edit out details they consider too strange for public consumption when they write their books.

Outliers of society burying the full scope of our high strangeness experiences as outlier data so that we may fit in, just a little, on the periphery. This is how we hide.

In fact, as we previously discussed, the term "alien abduction" does not even apply to the phenomenon it labels, which is why some of us prefer the term "experiencer" or "experiencer of high strangeness." Perhaps we should change it to "experiencer of repressed normalcy."

No, I'm Not Done Yet.

As with bullshittiness in ufology, so it goes with New Age spirituality. New Age spirituality is a subject that most people compartmentalize far and away, higher and hierarchically higher, than the UFO subject and its kissing cousin, the paranormal. You don't want the uncomfortable stuff, the real stuff, all you New Age assholes, you want you in a mirror. You've gone from using the mirror for self examination to using the mirror to embrace vanity.

God, you're in love with you.

Because you hate you.

You feel so powerful!

Because you're powerless.

So guess who doesn't matter to you, *any* of you?

Me.

And you know what's funny about that? Most of you who I am insulting right now, who knew of me prior to reading this, believe me. You actually believe that I have an energy alive in me, which moves the body around when I shut up my yapping self. You believe that I became the self-identity of No-Thing, the great *I Am* awakening, God, or whatever. You believe I was abducted by aliens or interdimensional beings or got sucked into a trickster archetype's Bugs Bunny script. You. Actually. Really. Truly. Believe me.

And?

And.

And?

And.

And?

And.

You. Don't. Care.

You don't care in the way that one must care to be moved by such relating. You don't care to listen for the sake of listening; you listen for the sake of adding to your blabbing self and moving on. Adding to yourself where death of self is needed. Moving on where being stillness is the only being that counts. You don't give one shit about the reality of anything real hiding in your lack of shit-giving. You just want a laugh or you want the gossip or you want to feel the sense of mystery that pulses in the gut and chest and maybe, if you're lucky, puts on a magic show in the room by making your electronics go haywire. You want confirmation of your want and nothing more.

No, not *nothing* more, *everything* more. You want to be the one in the know. Powerful. Wise. Austere. Telling everyone what a great sense of humor you have, yet unable to say anything witty to save your life. And it *does* save your life. It saved mine. Care about that?

No.

You don't want to know what it takes to be wholeness, you want wholeness to happen to you. And with "aliens" some of you still argue with me to this day about what they are. You, who have never experienced them, want to tell me what I barely understand and what you cannot know.

No.

Fuck you.

And also fuck you, those who have never achieved No-Thing realization—which is all of you because it isn't an achievement—but want to tell me that I'm wrong about the necessity for the death of self because there are numerous ways to get there, even though there is no *there* and therefore no way *there*. You are fucking stupid and weak and cowardly and I know this because I was you once and that's the part that really bothers you. You know it's true. You know I am correct not because I am anything, but because the information is correct because it's about all of us. You can't *not* know, on whatever suppressed level, the truth of you. I speak it, but I don't wear a man bun or robes or sit in long periods of silence with my eyes closed before deigning to speak and so I am not listened to. You are all trained dogs without the discipline to play.

So fuck you for listening and fuck you for not listening. Fuck you for telling me to stop saying fuck you and fuck you for embracing the curse words.

Curse words.

I curse you.

You who were born cursed.

Fuck you for making prophets out of bubblegum machine truism spewers—and fuck you for handing the alien abduction narrative to liars, cons, and a cottage industry that cares less about any of this than you do. Fuck you.

But also, as I say this, realize that you are not alone. You're the same asshole who's been here for thousands of years. Thousands of years fucking it all up for yourself and taking the rest of us with you while you "learn." Eternally "learn."

Oh, fuck you, *learning.* You don't learn shit. But you learn nonetheless. No matter what I, the one you believe, say, you go on carelessly, recklessly learning and calling it *maturing.* Why? Because it's something to do and you refuse to hear me when I say stop doing things.

I don't put myself on a pedestal above you and dictate,

therefore you judge me as an equal. And if I'm equal to you, which I am, then I can't know or understand anything that you don't. And that part is wrong. I don't know or understand anything that you cannot, provided you don't exist anymore, but I understand plenty you do not because here you are, same as ever. Cursed.

Yeah, you're all the same to me. And you play this crass denial game the same way. Yet and still, one thing I know with solid certainty that you never will so long as you remain you, which will sound pleasant to your ears when you hear it, is, to quote a man many of you find brilliant, "God fails. Perfectly, every time."

You are God's perfect failing. Failing is built in and so it isn't failing at all, it's simply an aspect of what is. Isn't that deep and dark and beautiful? Eloquent, even. It gives one a sense of hope, like the cup's half full. Especially when you can't know what it means. Speaking of which, know who wrote that? Me, bitches, me. The very one insulting you. Cursing you.

Nice work, me.

Thanks, also me.

Oh, now that brilliant quote looks like shit, right? Because it's from me? Because I'm not Deepak? Because I'm hurting your feelings?

Fuck you. Spare nothing. Especially not your feelings.

And when you're done processing all of that verbal abuse —if you haven't thrown this book in the trash—take my hand! My sweaty, sticky hand! My moist for no reason, death-smelling hand! Really, what is in this hand?

Take it anon! Blindly. Faithfully. Pretend you never read this because who in their right mind would write it?

Let's jump into the next chapter together. Just don't be surprised if on the way down I vanish and your twisting, contorting, scared little body looks up and back and finds me standing at cliff's edge, smiling and waving.

And scraping this crap off my hand.

Conduit closing.

Trickster out, y'all.

It Is Him In Dust

I know this book isn't strictly a sequel but checking in on people is fun. Hmm... I wonder whatever happened to Fat Ass, the farty, racist bastard who helped sneak me into that Park Avenue office to make my short film *STUCK*? Oh, and that anonymous investor who backed out of producing my feature film, *No One's Watching: An Alien Abductee's Story*?

United States Attorney
Southern District of New York

FOR IMMEDIATE RELEASE
CONTACT: U.S. ATTORNEY'S OFFICE
OCTOBER 30, 2003
MARVIN SMILON, HERBERT HADAD,
MICHAEL KULSTAD
PUBLIC INFORMATION OFFICE

FORMER MANHATTAN INVESTMENT ADVISORY FIRM EXECUTIVE SENTENCED TO 41 MONTHS ON FEDERAL EXTORTION CHARGES

JAMES B. COMEY, the United States Attorney for the Southern District of New York, announced that JEFFREY N. ZISSELMAN, the former Chief Operating Officer of Manhattan-based investment advisory firm Eberhard Investment Associates ("EIA"), and a former lawyer, was sentenced by United States District Court Judge HAROLD BAER, Jr. today in Manhattan federal court to 41 months in prison, and ordered to pay $750,000 in restitution, for participating in a $1.5 million extortion scheme.

According to the two-count criminal Information and statements made by ZISSELMAN during his guilty plea on May 27, 2003,ZISSELMAN participated in a scheme to extort Todd M. Eberhard, the Chief Executive Officer of EIA, by threatening to (a) report to law enforcement that Eberhard was engaged in fraudulent and illegal conduct with respect to EIA's clients; and (b) report to Eberhard's wife that Eberhard was having intimate relationships with women other than his wife.

The Information alleged, among other things, that co-Conspirator Brian Mercier reviewed Eberhard's e-mails and then delivered to him a bound copy of some of these e-mails entitled "My True Life" divided into sections, including one labeled with the name of the woman with whom Eberhard was having the intimate relationship. In addition, Eberhard was handed a list of the names of many of Eberhard's clients who had been defrauded, it was charged. According to the Information and statements made by ZISSELMAN during his guilty plea, Eberhard paid ZISSELMAN approximately $1.5 million. ZISSELMAN split the payments with Mercier. The scheme began in December 2001 and terminated when Eberhard was arrested on federal criminal charges arising from his fraud on EIA's clients on February 5, 2003. On April 24, 2003, Mercier pled guilty to participating in the same scheme for which ZISSELMAN was sentenced today. Mercier is scheduled to be sentenced on December 12, 2003 by United States District Court Judge RICHARD C. CASEY. On May 6, 2003, an Information was filed against Eberhard charging him with engaging in a scheme to defraud EIA's clients. According to the Information, Eberhard misappropriated funds entrusted to him by his clients through a variety of means, including by "churning" their accounts to generate millions of dollars in commissions and compensation for himself and his firms, and by making millions of dollars' worth of unauthorized and improper withdrawals and transfers from client accounts. Eberhard is scheduled to go to trial, before United States District Court Judge ROBERT W. SWEET, on March 22, 2003.

In connection with ZISSELMAN's sentencing, he made a restitution payment of $750,000 to a Receiver permanently appointed to oversee and control Eberhard's assets for the benefit of and for distribution to victims of Eberhard's alleged criminal activity.

In imposing sentence, Judge BAER described ZISSELMAN's conduct as "reprehensible" given ZISSELMAN**'s** background and experience, including that ZISSELMAN held a law degree.

ZISSELMAN, 37, resides in Manhattan, New York. Mr. COMEY praised the investigative efforts of the United States Postal Inspection Service. Mr. COMEY also thanked the United States Securities and Exchange Commission for their assistance in the case.

Assistant United States Attorneys STEVEN R. GLASER and JULIAN D. SCHREIBMAN, are in charge of the prosecution.
03-252

For More Information, Click HERE.

The Dust Blows Through Him

Wow. Oh. Okay. This whole sequel retrospective thing isn't looking so good. Come to think of it, most of the people I'd do updates on didn't fare so well in life. But, you know, you get what you pay for. Or something. Whatever truism goes here.

I should probably just write it all out anyway because most sequels are lazy callbacks to the prequel. At least that's how it is in movies. I dunno about books. Who fucking reads anymore? Do you? Is anyone even reading this right now?

If so, *mazel tov* to you, I'd have given up by now. Truth be told, I would never buy a book like this. Not anymore. I am waaaay beyond caring about any of this. This is what happens when you outgrow people who believe in evolution, you know?

It's not you, it's me. Me recognizing how much I cannot stand you. You, the complacent one who wants me to spoon feed you wisdom so you can add it to your databanks and move on. You know how sick and tired I am of fanboys telling me how smart I am or how I inspired them to do such and such a thing—and what they're doing is mediocre at best, stealing from me at worst?

And—Oh, and because *Trickster*—these leeches grow more popular than I will ever be.

Actually, fuck Trickster. The real crime here isn't crime

from my former bosses and colleagues. The real crime here is how you treat anyone you suspect is wise. You just nail us to the fucking cross or ignore us by saying everything is relative so that we can't offer you anything wiser than the frauds you pay good money to see. That should be my money, by the way, but I'm lucky if you buy this on Kindle for a cup of coffee. The cheap cup. Not even a venti, you assholes.

You know what, Reader? I'm over it. I'm over you. This sequel is finished.

You don't need a sequel, you need an intervention.

You don't need a sequel, you need an intervention.

Sorry, who—wha?

Repetition and redundancy, the orderliness of a chaotic mind. We project that which we despise in ourselves onto another so that we are never our worst enemy. Everything you hate is you because hate is you. You are hate. There is no division between you and hate. Unravel the weaving of hate and what is left? Space. Something totally new and uncalculating fills it, if time does not get there first. Love acts when you are not there to stop it.

Who is this?

166.

Who dominates the world? The people who live most in it. The people whose lives are immersed in apparent separation. One cannot kill another unless one has invented and attached false meaning to such an act.

Whoah, whoah, whoah! Slow your roll, other voice! Who the fuck do you think you—What's going on here? What is this, some kind of kundalini bullshit?

You know I don't believe in channeling. I'm not a medium. More of a husky, to tell you the truth.

Is someone in this book? That sounds cheesy but I'm askin', 'cause I ain't writin'.

Uuuuuummmm... hello?

What, am I supposed to just go on like normal, like schizophrenia isn't happening?—Speak up, voice!

No?

Nothing?

Fine. We'll move on.

Guess what's getting edited out. Spoiler alert: mystery voice.

You think I won't do it?

He Becomes The Monster

Okay, I feel better now. Not great, but good. Good enough. I think I can handle another chapter if you can. Thanks for bearing with me. The reality is, I just needed a good primal scream to get through this.

The reality. We always say that, right? As a throwaway line. But what is *the* reality?

You know me. I say there's nothingness from which springs *thingness* from which spring human wormholes who bridge the two.

Oh, you didn't know I say that? Yeah. I say that. I'm all about blurring the line between fact and fiction because I enjoy lying. Okay, that's a lie—I'm all about it because I'm an alien abductee in love with my own riddle. It's no overstatement to say that I *am* science fiction: one part tentacle monster, three parts futurist, all too human. Now that I think of it, sci-fi is really about time: speculating on what may have existed long ago, could exist now, and might exist in the future. Abductees live in that speculation; there are no answers for us.

Too many skeptics cling to this notion that we're all fantasy prone, as if that explains abductions. I'll take the bait: okay, I'm prone to fantasy. What is fantasy? Fantasy is whatever one can imagine and I can imagine a lot. Unlike science fiction, fantasy isn't limited to realms of probability. There is no Middle Earth where hobbits and elves battle wizards and legions of ogres. It's nonsensical to even contemplate whether that realm exists because America would have jacked it for oil by now.

Atlantis, on the other hand, is alleged to have been a real place. There is evidence, weak though it may be, that Atlantis once existed. From that evidence we speculate tenuously. Atlantis is science fiction. Science fiction may or may not turn out to be science fact. Fantasy never will. No precious for you, Gollum.

Well, then, I'm pretending you're asking me, what are abductions? Are they the "never will" of fantasy or the "possibly" of science fiction? They certainly have parameters and are not laden with unlimited mystical worlds where magical creatures dwell, such as those imagined by Greek mythology, starry-eyed drooling children, or David Icke. Strip away the fear and the wonderment of the narrator and abductions read like rather bland accounts of space doctors and/or space spiritualists coming to Earth, taking people, and doing some fairly basic, unimaginative things with us. I think a stronger argument is that abductions are science fact and the whole scope of events contained therein is so foreign to our sensibilities that the fantasies we create are those of bland doctor-like, guru-like, or human-hating ETs. If true, then the only fact we may discern about abductions is that something is happening that we cannot experience directly because we filter it through our own fiction, composed of stories, assumptions, and visualizations conjured in fear.

Shouldn't Fantasies Be More Fun Than This?

The fantasy of the debunker is that there's nothing to abductions except a holographic dream that comes alive in the minds of certain delusional people who are sane in all categories but one: for some inexplicable reason we always mistake noises of a settling house for aliens. Not even ghosts! *Aliens*! So weird.

Debunkers are wrong to debunk that which is not bunk, but they are right to be skeptical enough to tell the difference. Most of what passes for alien abduction research is garbage. As I hope I made brutally clear, anything having to do with hypnosis is garbage. It's fiction. It's co-creating a story between subject and hypnotist that, at this point in history, we are front-loaded with before we ever dial up a hypnotist. Abduction lore is so set in the public mind that it serves as a rough draft awaiting our rewrite, our personal flourish.

Once again for the cheap seats, the fantasy of the abductee is that aliens from another planet or another dimension are interacting with us personally, for better or for worse. We may not have all the answers yet, but they are just around the corner, and what we know of the situation thus far looks strikingly like human behavior. These aliens are just little warped people with secrets. We can get to the bottom of the alien agenda, we tell ourselves, and it will all make sense in the end.

The fact that abductions are still completely unknown and ongoing means that neither debunker nor abductee fantasy hold the answer. How about this for a New Year's resolution: I won't tell you there are aliens abducting me if you won't tell me that the three-dimensional beings I've seen, communicated with, and been taken by are an illusion projected by my fantasy-prone brain. Deal?

High-Mind Logicians And Lowbrow Magicians Walk Common Ground In Poetic Science Fictions.

Yup. Here we are again. Back at science fiction where we belong. Where I belong, at least. I did not arrive here because I made up abductions; abductions happen and that's how I arrived here. I am weary of fantasy and unsure of fact. The framing of my 2003 autobiography is fictional in that there's this running Socratic dialogue interspersed throughout. The chat is fake but the information is real. So is it an autobiography or a work of fiction?

I included news articles in the book for humorous effect. I made up two of them. I think it's obvious which two I made up. I lied, but it was all in good fun. Is the book fact or fabrication?

In 2006, I released a documentary on the abduction aspect of my life. Some of it is fraudulent, again, to humorous effect. Does that call the whole film into question? I do own up to the fraud in the movie, so it's not like I'm really tricking the audience, just playing a prank with a point. Is it still a documentary?

What if I can't help myself? What if abductions have caused a rift in my psyche and I cannot write about them without creating self-sabotage? By that I mean it's easy to see an answer in my head and say, "I'm going to write it." Then, when I write it, I don't consciously do this, but what I do is I understand that answering Mystery is the illusion we're addicted to and the real answer is to keep everything in question. So, my writing becomes this snaking journey of words that often tricks the reader into feeling the relief of having received answers, when ultimately I haven't given any.

My inability to answer *is* the answer. This is obvious to me, personally, but I don't know to whom else. One who walks away from my blathering unsatisfied likely doesn't examine why too deeply. One may read my book or watch my documentary and bellow, "You haven't answered anything! I still don't believe you were abducted by aliens! I don't see any solid evidence!" Then figuratively slam the door in my nonliteral face before hearing the answer.

And the answer is, "I was abducted by aliens and so can no longer create something about them that gives an answer because that's not where they live. That's where you live. As a result of my interactions with them, I live somewhere in between, hence I am incapable of giving an answer. All I can do is unconsciously imitate their effect on my life, which usually means I write a normal, steady narrative that gets punctured throughout in such a way as to throw the whole story into question over and over again. Were that not my real life experience I would write something more solid for you.

That is the evidence you're looking for."

I'm not saying I'm incompetent or can't logically assess verity. I'm admitting that when I'm in creative process mode I cannot create art that tells the difference because art doesn't imitate life objectively, it imitates how the artist lives life. Art imitates artist's way of experiencing. I may be a logically sound person for the most part, but the totality of my way of experiencing is not logic. None of us are purely logical beings, that's balderdash. There's a fact for you. Here's another one: we know nothing.

I feel like the most redundant writer on God's green taint, but how can I avoid it when I build this tower of babble, this empire of words, on a groundless foundation? Eventually I'm going to come full circle always, always, always to the fact that we know nothing. The attempt to know something, anything, is a fun and frustrating process that leads me right back to nowhere. That is the truth behind all facts.

There's all of this experiencing, see? And all of this postulating on meaning, right? It's fluid, reality is. The facts of this age are not the facts of the previous. I recognize that we live by facts. At the same time, I know they don't exist. I know that tomorrow will look nothing like today.

What if we're a broken species deluding ourselves into believing that we're not broken, but changing, growing, evolving? What if we're like Super Sea Monkeys: a smiling package with promises of higher consciousness, but at heart we're all just brine?

What if all we are is life expectancy and fear?

A Taboo Narrative Is Born

The abduction experience says one of two things:

1.) There's a new mental disorder that should be called "functional schizophrenia" because most unfortunate saps afflicted with it are deemed sane, except every now and then they hallucinate detailed interactions with sentient nonhumans.

2.) Said interactions are real. They may or may not be perceived correctly by the experiencer. The very fact that they are real throws all of our assumptions about ourselves and the universe into question.

If number 2 is the case then science *is* fiction. Our entire view of the world is categorically false, for we are undoubtedly missing something fundamental if we cannot, in full consciousness, perceive these beings at will. Much like subatomic particles, they are indicated by their effects but are not visible to the naked eye.

Which of the two makes the most sense? Am I suffering a pathological ill or am I struggling with a higher understanding? Has someone or something with a complete mastery of our physical universe entered my field of senses? Is this presence sewing itself into our fabric stitch by careful stitch? Does it puncture our collective senses with occasional UFO waves, or by other means, to preserve itself in social dialogue, while introducing itself to one person at a time? In this scenario, the individual meets the presence and makes the connection back to the UFO wave, which further solidifies it in our world. The abductee's experience is validated by society, which is primed to speak of such things, and the society believes it is learning more about the presence through the abductee.

If that's the situation, it is a mistake on our part to keep the subject taboo. We cannot draw this presence into our partial worldview where we haven't even decided on the realness of it. We may speak of it, but we speak in hushed tones and hold no collective agreement on what it is. We use the word "alien" as a placeholder and define that however we feel comfortable. As previously discussed, the undertones, the subtext, of our taboo alien narratives reflect the taboo underbelly of our society—racism, slavery, and colonialism, at least. The presence, in this scenario, will remain vague, ghostlike, and a reflection of us. We will never meet it as it is, simultaneously holding it at bay while believing we're embracing it and discovering more about it. What we learn about is ourselves.

Our collective suppression is where the speculation of science fiction quickly becomes the horror of fantasy. This is where monsters and angels enter the scene. This is where reptilian aliens and shady government deals take over. You want a link between the fantasy-prone personality and alien abductions? Start here: the suppression of the reality of their presence.

In our worldview there is fact and there is fantasy. This presence tells us, "No! It's all fantasy! Your worldview is wrong!" But that's not our experience so it isn't a message that speaks to us. We have fact and we have fantasy. When it comes to abductions there's no consensus on which case is the fact, pathology or presence, but man do we ever churn out fantasies.

That's as a collective. As individual experiencers who have no choice but to acknowledge the presence, some of us are lost in our fears, our fantasies, our answers, and some of us are caught in eternal speculation.

Humans ask questions to find answers because we live in answers. From those answers, with eyes of the past, we experience the world. One day, someone living in the question comes along and taps us on the shoulder. A voice from the question whispers softly, "Answers are the past. The past is dead. Questions are living. Live with us and be free of time." We turn around to see who is speaking and no one's there. It gives us a chill and so we make up an answer as to what it was because that's what we do.

Science fact is science fiction. This is where I live. My neighbors don't see it. My family doesn't see it. I am invisible to them. That's okay. You only know what you know. And all we can know is that we can't.

In a world run by answers, that's the one answer that will never do.

Possibility is infinite and is Intelligence. It manifests as probability and actuality in any given universe. Thus, your universe has apparent boundaries, physical laws, mathematical constants: the rules of space-time. Humanity—sentient beings, period—are the realization of probabilities and actualities within possibility. You are God self-reflecting. You may discover the beginning of the universe as a fact. In Truth, however, there is no beginning and no ending. This "glitch" in God's imaginative process creates for God a question. That very question is enlightenment.

God awakens. God gains. There is no end to process. This is bliss. In humanity, it manifests in an instant. In this instant, the rules are broken and you become co-creators of reality. More accurately, you become the awakened physical aspect of God—the true creator/creation.

Jesus fucking Christ on a crutch!—ENOUGH ALREADY!!! I'm the only one allowed to talk like that! Me! This is my book about me, get it? My realizations! My truths! Now just... KINDLY FUCK OFF!

He Leaps To His Feet, Coughing Out Madness

Screw that bullshit Trickster voice! I'm done with Trickster even if Trickster isn't done with me! Archetypes are beneath me! I'm just—I'm over it!

Having to pussyfoot around certain subjects, like UFOs and alien abductions, for fear that I am crossing a threshold into the sphere of influence of a dickish formless awareness is fatiguing! And you know what? I know this voice that keeps interrupting my book is Trickster!

Here's the confounding thing about the Trickster prison: people living within the field of Trickster behave like it's a mock-or-be-mocked world. Probably, that's why they're there, sentenced to Trickster, to learn that it's a be-mocked-for-mocking world.

To live in the Trickster prison is to live in a conscious field of mockery with the express purpose of tearing you down for the crime of having built yourself up. To think the world is mock-or-be-mocked is to be mocked once you're confident in your role as the mocker because you're never in control, you're just kept on an invisible electric leash. On the other end is a hand that dares you to believe you're free and act on that belief.

Tug.

Zap.

Put in your place again.

Why?

Because the thought construct that is *you* is never free. Trickster is a lesson in that. And I fucking get the lesson, all right?!

Trickster permeates ufology, is everywhere in ufology, in every move you make. When Trickster events amplify, you should take it as a sign that you're "getting warmer" in the game of hot/cold where the truth about the nature of UFOs and abductions is concerned. But also note, as so few do, that the "warmer" being indicated through your now prat-falling through life, where once you were blissfully strolling along, isn't that you are closer to understanding reality at large—no, no. You are concentrating on a subject that, if you were to understand it entirely, would, yes, bring you one slippery step closer to understanding reality at large. But the Trickster amplifications, the synchronicities that kick in—those are about whichever detail you're looking into and at what angle. If, for example, you're looking at abductions and you believe they are alien in nature, you will likely be led via synchronicities to more and more material that will confirm your theory. You will meet new people at perfectly timed moments in your life who will do the same, and because the timing feels mechanical, you will be tempted to believe that this is all being orchestrated by a higher power and you're being led to the truth.

Driving that false point home, if you stray from your alien

path, bad luck might befall you as negative Trickster effects begin dominating your life. This act of keeping you on a narrow path to the conclusion you began with through bumper guards of consequences will feel like it has to be the unfoldment of truth. All indicators point to it. And so down the rabbit hole you go, further and further into wrong answers that, if you grow too attached, will drive you to delusion with further and further confirmations that you are, in actuality, getting close to the truth about alien abductions.

Buuuuut are you? In any way? Like, at all?

You are not.

You are being kept in thought. And there is no more comfortable a thought than your own belief. Kept there because the truth cannot be gotten to through the thinker but by the cessation of the thinker. The fact that you are the thinker and the thinker is thought means you cannot understand.

You are thought. So, you find more thought, more of you. You're being led down a dark tunnel that appears as though it's being lit with every step you take. Actually, it's being constructed with every step you take. A tunnel that is perceptible to you because it's coming from you.

Archetypes are to people as the building blocks of the universe are to matter: both their own thing and deeply infused with us. We are extensions of one another, aspects of one another, two smokes wafting through one another.

We are one another on a level that, once we hit it, we become gods.

Another delusion.

Cue Trickster.

Oh, goody.

Mock U

Now that we've solved who, what, and why Trickster is in ufology, and made it more confusing for you, lets get back to mockery. Ya ever notice how society at large mocks people who report UFOs and paranormal phenomena? Which is already weird because most of us pay good money to immerse ourselves in fictionalized movies about these subjects, and the five of us left who read pay to read such books. Or pirate them. Assholes.

Point is, it's not the subject matter society mocks but the people who claim it's real. We treat people who report experiences that fall outside the average range of awareness as if what they're saying is so rare that it doesn't fit in with consensus reality.

Buuuuut is it rare? Like, at all?

It is not.

Practically everyone the world over has had some sort of synchronistic, ufological, paranormal, spiritual, or psychic event that we have decided is abnormal. Given that abnormal experiences happen with frequency throughout the world and throughout all time, we may safely say that this parallel track is mocking our standards of normalcy. We cannot abide this because we're so afraid of uncertainty that we need to carve out a piece of reality and call it normal, call it certain. We treat all other occurrences as nonexistent fabrications, call them fringe, even though they aren't. We pretend they are, but they aren't. If they were, they wouldn't happen all over the world, throughout all time and all cultures.

High strangeness experiences may not be consistent in our personal lives, but they are persistent through history. The joke is, these everyday occurrences never gel within Western consensus reality and we never question why that is because to answer that is to unravel the self. The whole thing is one big, knowing smirk. Unfortunately, those self-restrained to normal awareness aren't conscious of the joke. They don't know what they're laughing at, even though they unconsciously know they're being laughed at. They tend to respond to this invisible criticism by mocking or bullying others whom they can see. Their arrogance is from ignorance and fear. Mine is from knowing the truth, which is the same thing. And that swings us to my favorite topic: me.

I am a hoax, not a hoaxer. Am a living, breathing state of charlatanism. Am a trickster. I expose Truth to you through humor, which is often translated as hiding Truth in humor.

Hoaxers knowingly and purposefully present you with a falsehood that they want you to take as true or real. They sell you on something they know is fake by using an upstanding presentation.

Tricksters do the opposite. Tricksters present you with the unreality that there's nothing to see here, no reason to engage them in any meaningful way. They sell you a presentation that is unbelievable enough for you to scoff at and pass them by. This presentation contains a trail of breadcrumbs within it that only a few will bother to notice, let alone follow. Those who do follow are often rewarded with something deep and meaningful and life-altering. Mind-reforming.

Unless, that is, they are following the path of the ultimate Trickster—the archetype itself—in which case the trail leads to more trails, all kinds of confusion, with enough life-altering fulfillments to keep them hooked. This, because such a one is ultimate and what's ultimate must be seen through entirely for ultimate understanding to occur.

Where common tricksters dangle the ol' carrot on a stick to lead you to mind-reformation, ultimate Trickster, the living archetype, dangles an octopus-worth of carrots to make everything so ridiculous that, if you see it for what it is, you stop your self-serious searching and have a laugh. And in that moment, the joke is not on you but *is* you. And in that moment, if you're not the same jackass who started the odyssey, perhaps you will stop with the deep and meaningful life-altering, mind-reforming bullshit and evaporate into nothingness, where the reality of reality will be the case through what was, just a moment ago, your eyes.

A boy can dream, can't he?

Knock Knock

I keep using the word *joke*. If you're still reading this, you may be asking yourself why jokes would be so interconnected with the UFO mystery.

What is humor but a blending of sense and nonsense sprinkled with the unexpected? Isn't that the Trickster? Isn't that also ufology?

How many experiencers of high strangeness build the case that they are normal before delivering the crazy part? And how many experiencers tell their crazy story only to then explicitly state, "The crazy thing is ..." or, "Now here comes the really crazy part ..." followed by something that is on par with what they've already offered?

We've got a term for stories that run along with the calmness of normalcy only to be punctuated at the end by the abnormal and unexpected: *setup/punchline.* Humor is fused into the very architecture of high strangeness experiences and in the way we bashfully relay them. If nothing else, ufology is full of magical satire.

Magical though Trickster may be, the archetype is not a magician. Magicians are entertainers who provoke awe by selling you on misdirection. But what they're selling has no substance. It's all style. It's vapid, really. And this is why so many professional skeptics are also stage magicians: they don't understand substance, but they know all about how to pull the wool over peoples' eyes for thrill and for profit.

If the Trickster archetype isn't a magician, but more like a magical joker, is it a sadist or a satirist?

Ah. Great question asked by no one at all.

Believing Trickster's sense of humor is sadistic because it comes at your expense stems from lack of understanding what you are. The outcome of Trickster's sadistic humor is personal, sure. But the fact of it—the action—is impersonal and indicates that there is some misunderstood transformative doorway here. So, when we focus our interest on high strangeness and kick up a little Trickster dust, we can be assured that the mysteries at our attention exist within and possibly as doorways to transformative understanding.

We're getting warmer.

Truly, we wonder, what could be more transformative than discovering the reality of interdimensional life, an afterlife, or transcendent alien life? And yet, while we tend to approach these wonders as if they exist outside of us, what often kicks in is a set of experiences that lead us away from the shiny objects of external discovery and toward our personal inner lives. Once there, we see that our inner experience creates the outer. So, by the end of it, we understand interior/exterior as one movement, and that movement is us. We see that we were wrong to treat transformative discoveries like scientific discoveries—like things that exist to be found, proven, and the meaning agreed upon. Transformative discoveries transcend and include the rational. This means they will always appear irrational to rational people. On the surface, transcendent irrationality looks like the kissing cousin of insanity and their imminently fuckable cousin, inanity.

In our refusal to transcend and include the rational, we give life to Trickster as an outside force. Sometimes we identify with Trickster and say stupid shit like, "I am a trickster." Trickster replies, "Rimshot, please," because, yes, you are that, just not in the way you believe. In the way you repress. You're more like a spiritually possessed person than a self-aware Yoda.

All of this, see, all of this is one movement of you. One movement in repression looks... mmm... more like schizophrenia. There's you. There's Trickster. There's you not knowing you are this monstrous Trickster and so claiming you are a purposeful trickster to gain some sense of control over what you've become. But you don't know that you've not become anything more than you already were: a false separate-self sense running around saying stupid shit.

Elusive Objects; Elusive Subjects

There are a handful of takes on Trickster Theory in ufology, all of them wildly unpopular. The most useful naturally comes from a researcher who is not a ufologist, George Hansen. Trickster's popularity (and George Hansen's) is growing in some online circles, but it's mainly unheard of on the radio, in documentaries, and at conferences. It's no wonder why. Trickster goes ignored because we want an answer that leaves our false sense of autonomy intact.

On that note, have you noticed how it's not just ufological phenomena that are elusive, but also the nature of the people involved? It's easier to admit that there is an intelligence that morphs with beliefs and blends in with global cultures throughout the ages, from nature spirits to angels and demons to aliens who are human to aliens who are humanoid to whatever the fuck, than admit that the people involved are just as slippery. Researchers pretending to be Indiana Jones-style adventurers; pretending to be scholars; pretending to be doctors and therapists. Experiencers pretending to know what they saw; pretending to know what they experienced; pretending not to want to feel special. The lists go on, and they, too, evolve with the times.

Who wants to look at that when we can all galvanize around a "The Future Is Now" story, which the common man can follow, be a part of, and control?

That's right, *control*. You and I have the power in the alien scenario. True, experiencers may be powerless and fearful in the face of the enigma, but at least we can name it and discuss it and angrily rail against it or embrace it lovingly. We can petition our government for the truth about it. We can vocalize it, communicate it, share it, deepen it, and further it. It's the game of being heard and we're all invited—not just the wealthy elites, the priests, and the physicists.

I'm tempted to say that ufology, not FOX News, heralded the beginning of our age where facts don't matter, just to look cool—but it isn't true.[15] Ufology further illuminates the truth that fact-based living has not mattered to people since the beginning of time. The new priests of scientific materialism and humanism claim that their logical way is the only sane way of being. That's a ridiculous claim. We've made it this far. How did we survive millions of years if we're all delusional and crazy?

---

[15] Sorry, *cooler*. All of this makes me look cool.

As I, a great man, once said, “All things must be expressed.” Insanity is one of these. Delusion is one of these. And it is delusion into which we are born: the delusion of the divided world. We must see through this delusion if we are to live as the full meaning of *human being.*

“All things must be expressed, but you don’t have to be the one expressing them.” That’s how I wrote it in *Urgency.*.[16] And that’s fully correct. Correct in the sense of the choices we make. We don’t have to murder, for example, or take our frustrations out on other people. These are choices.

It is also true in the choiceless sense where what the personal self dying to oneness means is that while the physical body remains alive as ever, our awareness does not have to be of the body, of the universe, of thought. Awareness may transcend and include mind and body, which means transcend and include all apparent divisions. When that happens, the physical is still expressing the illusion of separation, but the illusion of the physical is no longer the delusion of one’s awareness. One is aware of the delusion, but one is not partaking in it. One is speaking through the divided vessel, but one understands that vessel resides within awareness. The body is a megaphone for Truth and the self is the loudspeaker. Or quiet speaker.

Or Trickster.

---

[16] A fine book, by the way.

Regains His Balance

Hey, UFO infatuated. Ya ever ask yourselves why the hell you're talking about this stuff with anyone at all? Like, we know our personal reasons for communicating it, those of us who bother, but what is it we're actually doing by going back over all these cases, all these rehearsed talking points, over and over again to an audience of hungry ghosts, who sit through our blather as if it's news to them?

Why are both ufological speaker and audience stuck on repeat with complete amnesia that everything being communicated has been said before and, in the case of conferences, probably by each previous speaker?

Some of us drone on about tired subjects, like the Roswell crash, using a super serious tone that demands attention. Others pass the story down from generation to generation as a silly joke that only the mad believe in. We speak Roswell from the heart with honesty, from the belly with humor, or from arrogance with a knowing skepti-smirk that says, "Me an' the boys down at the Church of Humanism already made a pact that this is nonsense and you people are idiots for believing it."

Yes, all of us, even debunkers, passionately engage the story of Roswell. And now, after years and years of this behavior, the behavior is as engrained in each of us as the story is in our culture. Roswell is happening whether it happened or not and everyone who comes into contact with it makes sure of that. Why?

The Roswell crash, like any good tale, is a portal to conversations that, when delivered with the right mixture of tone, purpose, openness, and deep believability, may deliver the room to a moment nearly out of time, where our sense of physics expands and we perceive ever-so-dimly the larger, interconnecting ecology of hidden dimensions. We who pay attention to high strangeness as though we are strangely high often trigger paranormal events, synchronicities, and déjà vu by merely participating in deep conversations. When such occur, it's as if for a blip of a moment consensus reality breaks down and the laws of physics break down with it.

But they don't break down. Our ability to perceive them more fully expands and we see what else is happening in our everyday blindspot.

Roswell, New Mexico is a small town whose tourism economy depends on a tall tale. Roswell, the tall tale, is a portal to a bridge between worlds. Through a glass, grayly, we see that the tale is bullshit, but the effects of engaging it seriously, of not knowing it is bullshit and releasing the depths of imagination compressed in the simple story like a zip file, are real.

One is leaves of a tree. The other is roots in the ground.

One is you, the liar. The other is buried honesty.

One is an argument of facts recited time and time again. The other is the moment of Truth.

Unsheathes His Sword And Enters The Darkness

While we're talking about talking, let's talk this over: How is it that we can come to an instant agreement on what's taking place through the act of communicating? Ya ever ask yourself that? Like, what is communicating actually doing?

One thing we're doing when we communicate is describing factual qualities in the world as we pick them up with our senses and know them to be. Another is describing emotional responses that do not require a literal, factual equivalent to be expressed. For example, if you are excited about some good news a friend gave you, you might shout "You rock!" to them. The phrase is a compliment that does not equate to an action of rocking back and forth or their state of being a rock, unless, of course, your friend is a rock—and in Hawaii, incidentally, anything is possible, but let us not belabor the obvious any further than this run-on sentence, which, equally incidentally, by the way, took me less time to write than it is taking you to read. The point is clear enough, yes?

So, how do beings we consider higher communicate with us, be they spirits, aliens, or even so-called enlightened humans? They speak through the heart, which is less verbal and more impressionistic. Less, "This is a rock," and more, "You rock!" We brain people find that type of instant familiarity a tad off-putting. Intimidating, even. Heart people don't and so they have an open relationship with beings who speak heart language.

When we are scared, we brain people call the unknown entities who pop in and out of our lives *aliens*. We call them *visitors* when we're trying not to be scared, trying to relate, if we're at all curious, and if we're stealing from Whitley Strieber. Our reaction to our fear is to close ourselves off with answers. Although our answers lead to further questions, the lines of questioning stem from our answers, and that's comforting. We feel like we may have a handle on who or what these beings are. We follow our own lead, often repressing the truth that the phenomena behind our word choices are still unknown.

But heart cultures don't see contact from the point of fear because they don't call them *them*, they call them *us*. To heart people, we are all family—nations and nations of family throughout the multiverse. Heart people, as one heart person told me, don't get abducted. Alien abductions, one could argue, are for teaching us dominating Westernized brain people, who are used to doing the abducting, what unstoppable trauma and lifelong helplessness feel like.

All of this is to say, brain people are exclusive; heart people are inclusive. When someone speaks through heart to brain people cut off from heart it feels to the brainiacs like an attack—a heart attack, if you will. If we were healthy we'd never be brain people. We'd be expressing *human being* in the following way:

Oneness is aloneness containing and being all.

Heart is the interconnecting fiber of all and beats in full recognition of oneness.

Brain is the aloneness of rationality, a tool whose usefulness lies in its ability to ponder and dissect all that the divided mind can grasp.

According to this model, if you want to talk about *aliens*, use your brain. If you want to talk to *aliens*, keep using your brain.

Tell, in other words. Dictate. Control.

If you want to speak with *family*, live in heart. If you want to learn from *family*, live in heart.

Ask, in other words. Open up. Allow.

If you want to find out if there is anything to you beyond these brain and heart modes, die.

Dissolve, in other words. Nothingness.

One who lives in neither question nor answer—one who is silence—is uncomplicated by all those interference patterns of the self. Perhaps this is the only person qualified to understand the whole of what "higher" beings are communicating. To such a person, they would no longer be aliens, visitors, or family. Nor would they be higher.

True equality and decipherable communication are just a quiet moment away.

Slays Gods

I wrote *I Know Why The Aliens Don't Land!* with an eye toward appealing to rational non-experiencers, while uplifting my fellow experiencers. I'm writing this as a poke in that same eye using your own finger. Except it's not my eye, it's your eye. And your finger. But it's my poke. So it's not the same eye. But you're doing it.

I've made my point.

I need to be clear about something else, which I've already cleared up like a million times throughout my work: when I say *die*, I do not mean physically. I mean die while the body is alive. And when I say that, I don't mean for you to take any action that results in egoic death because you will only end in a false alarm. What I do mean is, understand yourself so thoroughly that the self dissolves through no action of your own and nothingness (or No-Thing) becomes the self awareness of that there body you say is yours.

And no cheating. No hallucinogens. Drugs: the new gods among us.

Actually, they're the old gods.

Actually, they were plant medicines that were innocent before we got our greedy hands on them.

Now what?

Now I launch into a rant because now we've got Youtube

video after Youtube video of the new prophets speaking the word of their god, Drugs. Drugs used to get you high, now they expand your mind. Now they alleviate your psychological problems. Now they eradicate your ego and bring you to the Witness. Now they introduce you to aliens. Now they give you oneness.

Except they don't.

The difference between, for instance, DMT-inspired oneness and actual oneness is the difference between stepping into a onenessy simulation created by someone else and self-identifying as oneness. It's another Halloween mask that you wear and regard how cool you look in the mirror before taking it off and going back to routine.

When you're shown something on a DMT trip that you can neither articulate well nor understand, how useful is it when you come back to normal? Is not the problem that we're taking a version of nondual mind and trying to make it useful back in pure duality? But you cannot articulate an experience that was dictated to you, shown as an extension of you, felt as you, and also contained the element of you having always known it, all at the same time, can you?

Knowledge from such a mind cannot translate well to our mind of isolated explanations. What it does do is give us a sense of oneness through a clever act of twoness. If it were oneness, there would be no entity teaching you anything. Seeing through the eye of oneness means being all of the contents of the universe as well as the Spirit who permeates them, rides along on them, and is them. The contents of the universe are the contents of consciousness and you are all of them, plus the self-awareness of the consciousness in which they arise. You are the twoness in the oneness and the oneness—and as unfathomable as it seems from a rational point of view, you would experience self as all of the above *at once.*

When hallucinogens turn us inside out and bring the fluidity of dreamtime into the awakened room it makes us postmoderns wonder if we're living in a computer simulation, when actually, our having invented computer simulations is a way we remind ourselves what's missing in our lives: the interconnectivity of heart and identity as wholeness. Inventions like these are physicalized metaphors, our unconscious screaming at us to wake up.

But we should not mistake metaphors for a reality that we need to wake into. We should not go into the invention, in other words, any more than we should take our having invented can openers to mean that we need to implant can-opening technology in our mouths. Likewise, if you have a DMT trip that shows you can-opener-mouth people, and you feel at one with them, this is not to say you need to come back and be a convenience store cyborg.

You would know all of this if you were truly self-identifying as oneness. Suspicions about the meaning of extraordinary experiences and your purpose in life would never creep in. They would be self-evident. Others would call your new batch of self-evident understandings *wisdom.* You wouldn't name them. You wouldn't form a narrative around any of this.

Admit it: our addiction to narrative-building is why so many consumerist tribespeople nowadays are crawling up the ass of hallucinogens and calling it their shamanic journey. It's the same old story about an author named *You*. You want to be the one who knows something others don't. You want to be the first to dictate what the unknowable is, the first to espouse facts where none exist. You want to say, "This is what the DMT aliens look like," or, "This is how the ayahuasca goddess behaves," as though your experience is universal. As though others will experience exactly what you did, or variations on your theme, when they take these substances. And they might after you've front-loaded them with suggestion. Just. Like. Hypnosis.

Oh, I can see why hallucinogens have taken off in ufology in recent years. It's not just New Age assholes who go on shamanic retreats so they can qualify themselves as spiritual masters to other New Age assholes. No, now it's also "psychonauts" who think they're reinventing the McKennas. They want to be the deep thinkers, the narrators, the talking heads in documentaries. Meanwhile, what are they talking about? They're talking about something their audience has access to—something verifiable. But they're talking about it like it's unattainable to mere mortals, a mystery, an abduction, enlightenment. But I can pluck a mushroom from cow turds just like these brave frontiersmen and women and tell you what's what. So can you. So where's the mystery?

It's not about mystery. It's about answering. We want

answers. We want power. We want control. We want more *me* in our diets and this is especially true of those who say they have cut *me* out of their diets altogether.

Psychonauts and trust fund shaman are full of *me* full of mushrooms full of shit.

You. There. Yes, You There.

I see you laughing at this. Loving this. Finally, an experiencer eats his own. Finally, in a mental fit, an abductee breaks down his own mental breakdowns.

If you're at all smart you'll assume I'm projecting onto others what's wrong with me. And if you're a debunker of all things paranormal, spiritual, magical, and peak experience food poisoning, you're not laughing with me, you're laughing at me. I know you're here with me right now, so many of you eye-rolling scoffers actually bothering to read this—and you know why? Because you're fucking broken, too. And a liar.

You're broken. Do you know who buys magazines and books and documentaries on subjects that they whine they find repulsive to anyone who is trapped in an elevator or on Twitter with them? Fucking crazy people, that's who. But you don't know you're crazy because this book is crazy to you and you're rational to you. How can you be rational *and* insane?

Oh, I dunno... like this?

I mean think about this. Here you are, a good little atheist or agnostic or humanist, and you're spending your limited time alive attending to the subjects you find repulsive. Why would you do that? Oh, you'll say it's because you want to educate people, but after decades of debunking, who has learned shit from you and your ilk?

As with the overly enthusiastic true believers you despise, what people learn from you is to stay away from you at parties. You're not just a bore, you're a triumphant bore. You're an asshole of assholes about it. As Jeff Ritzmann pointed out time and again on Paratopia, you need to be the smartest person in the room. And so, what do you do? You pick on the stupidity of people who believe in things that may or may not be real, by claiming that you know for a fact they aren't. And the evidence you cite, again to steal from Jeff, is usually the low-hanging fruit, the easiest thing in the world to debunk. In this way do you maintain your sense of architecture over a reality you know nothing about and are afraid to engage with openly and honestly, while taking a piss on honest folks whose only crime was to open up to you about the thing you lied and said you were interested in.

Yeah, debunker, you're a liar and a con just like the liars and cons you go after. You don't call yourself by your name, do you? Rarely does a debunker say, "I'm a debunker." They usually hide behind the more palatable word, *skeptic*.

"Oh, I'm skeptical."

No, you're not. You're a debunker.

De-bunker? More like *add*-bunker. More like an Archie Bunker, all armchair and mouth.

I am what skeptical looks like. You are what a secular humanist looks like. And that's your other lie. You've got a belief system—secular humanism, usually—which states that you're correct about everything and brain people are the greatest organisms alive and fuck you, shove yourself into the computer already, plebeians, it's your destiny.

You say there is no such thing as the transrational. As proof, you debunk some other thing that is so obviously irrational it doesn't require investigating in the first place, let alone proving wrong. Sometimes a cup on a string really is a cup on a string and no believer telling me it's a picture of an alien ship will convince me otherwise because I'm not a fucking moron. But sometimes those pictures look like more than a cup on a string and the account that belies them sounds like more, too. You don't like that challenge, so you stick with debunking cups and string. And you say you do it in the name of objectivity, science, skepticism. No, you don't. You're a rational reductionist, a materialist, a secular humanist. You're Isaac Newton trying to keep the universe mechanical despite its airy-fairy underpinnings.

You're outdated tech, friend. And that's okay with you because your obsessive-compulsive need to be right was never about needing to right the wrongs, it was and always will be about the fear that you don't know. Not even the fear of the unknown, but fear of the unknowable. Fear of that which cannot be learned by you.

Oh, that's a real problem for debunkers. They think everything will be learned in time, we just haven't gotten to it yet or don't have the means right now—but we will. Have faith. In humanity. Not all humanity, just brain people. Not the superstitious medicine men living in nature where life is, the scientific men of medicine working in labs where sterility is. Have faith in them, for they are the new priests. Sterile is the new celibate.

Scientists are perfect, you see. Their minds are totally pure, unblemished. They exist in a vacuum uninfluenced by petty things like culture or greed or fear. Scientists are so perfect they can be completely wrong about everything and then reassure us that while no scientist is perfect, we will get there. Yes, even imperfection is accounted for in the Word of the Science God. As long as we're forward-thinking, whatever we discover right now that throws everything we previously discovered under the bus is a-okay. Nobody loses a PhD after the diploma for the very specific subject they spent their younger years focusing on and learning about becomes as relevant as a McDonald's placemat. Actually, that placemat has more relevance—at least you can color on it and do the dot-to-dot to form real pictures.

Meanwhile, just as the debunker will rarely tell you he's a debunker and will never admit without prodding that he's a secular humanist; just as he will spit away the notion that science is a religion and scientists the new god-priests, he will absolutely barf at what I'm going to show you next.

You ready? Got your barf bag in hand and your laptop booted up to troll this online?

The Origin Of Modern Western Science... Is Christianity.

Oh, shit! Whaaaaat? And here you thought science was a response to Christianity or an altogether separate track. Here you thought it was an evolutionary stride away from Christian beliefs and missionary persecution, by embracing rational observation the way ancient Greeks embraced rational arguments. But just as the Greek emphasis on logic had a hidden origin in the teachings of Persephone, Goddess of the Underworld[17], so too does modern science owe its existence and furtherance to the father figure they thought they were slaying: Baby Jeebus. In fact, if science had a bible it would begin something like this....

In the beginning there was the Word and the Light. The Word was Math, and it was good. The Light was Electromagnetic Radiation, and it was not so bad. Whatever you could see and figure out was real, not that poetic shit.

And it was gooooood.

But not good enough.

No, it was not good enough to transform the radiating, nebulous world of action through equation into solid things that we figure out and tinker with, while sharply proclaiming

---

[17] For more on the hidden-in-plain-sight origins of the rationality-addicted Western world, read anything by Peter Kingsley and prepare to have your mind blown. Except, maybe, *A Story Waiting To Pierce You.* That was half-assed. Not saying the info is wrong, just that the book feels rushed.

You know what it feels like? It feels like the author didn't think we had a lot of time before an extinction event, so he rushed through the writing process because we're all a buncha dopes who won't get it in the way that we need to get it to be pierced by it, so fuck it. Eat a Twinkie, fatties. Kingsley out!

But my book review is neither here nor there. Get back to this chapter, chucklehead! You left off in the middle of a sentence. Look for the word "Underworld."

that the journey of discovery is what life is about. Not at all good enough. The scientist, in all his priestly modesty, had to be a star, not an observer of stars. In fact, he had to be *the* star, the only valid observer. He had to be the observed star's voice telling the rest of us its story, its truth. Anything else was less. And less was magical thinking. And magical thinking provoked a knowing smirk and a rolling of the eyes in the scientist, which was everyone else's cue to fall in line, for a mature adult hath judged.

Scientists do this still with everything. And what would we do without their knowledge from on highest? Without these unimpeachable witnesses to reality as it is, who, no matter their race or gender, are cut from the same patriarchal White truth-teller cloth? And whose body of knowledge gets churned up and spit out every few years or so under the banner, *Latest Modern Discoveries*?

What would we do?—Bathe in our own toilet, I tell you!

Listen, you can only run from your parents' influence for so long. You can only deny your genetic inheritance for that same so long. When science was alchemically transforming out of alchemy into what it is today, scientists had to hide their work from Catholic priests who would have murdered them to keep their Christian vision of the world firmly in place. Because that's where they clawed out from, a shit-ton of scientists today believe they are above religion.

Killing people who negate our worldview is neither specifically Christian nor exclusively religious. Defending our worldview is what we all do; Christians just happened to make an art out of it for a couple thousand years.

Cut to a couple thousand years later and Christ's Word is not the exclusive word. There are lot's of competing world views. Some societies are more *killy* than others in the name of what they believe. For a while there, it looked like science was going to be the new Word going forward, indefinitely—and a decent one on the less-*killy* side. But scientists showed their asses by becoming the very thing they struggled against: people with the final say.

Scientists might not murder you for thinking anything beyond them, but they would ostracize you. They would repress antiestablishment research. They would claim that the world worked exactly as they said it did until they themselves could demonstrate otherwise, blinded to the narrowness of their monological gaze.

Like priests working for the Roman Empire, scientists would sell out their self-professed purity to the capitalist corporatocracy because lack of funding was a fate worse than death—and the people doing the funding were nothing if not murderers. Nowhere to run there except into the same-old/same-old pattern.

Here is where scientists became the *killiest* of all cult figures, having invented weapons of mass-murder, poisons that look like food, poisons that go into the food supply, plastics, electricity, the ability to strip entire jungles of life for wood and paper, animal testing, human testing—the list of what scientists have done in the name of war and all the "modern conveniences" we once thought were evolution, but have recently revealed themselves to be our extinction, would be endless if we weren't on the brink of coming to an end.

Here we arrive at the understanding that our new savior-god, Science, doesn't have the final answer on reality, will never have the final answer on reality, and is funded and promoted by the empire to sell you *everything is under control* comfort. It's no wonder so many people have gone back to their mainstream religions.

Christians. Muslims. Jews. Hindus. Raelians. Scientists. They're all reality TV stars in the end.

Who Are Also Him

Now comes the part where defenders of the faith lay out all the good things science has given us because they have to reassure themselves by bitching at me. They're not necessarily wrong, they're just blind to the things I'm pointing out and wish to remain so.

If you think I need to balance out the last chapter by citing the scientific advances in medicine, inventions, and observations I enjoy so that you may feel better, this is an indication that science is your religion. Imagine demanding that someone who critiques the Inquisition must qualify it by admitting that Jesus had some good stuff to say. We all know Jesus had good stuff to say. We all know Western science has made great contributions. This isn't about that. But, if it segues us into the next paragraph tightly, I'll admit it: science does have a proven track record, which is what gives the priests their power in the first place.

And with a track record like science's, it's no mystery why so many people put their faith in its ability to ferret out the root cause(s) of paranormal and ufological phenomena. Who better to examine experiences with the dead, claims of the afterlife, and technology so amazing that it must not be from here than the people who accidentally invented Silly Putty when they were trying to make silicone rubber for war machines?

Scientific conventional wisdom on all things paranormal states that because some wild claims prove to have normal explanations, the inconclusive claims also must, even if we never discover them. Therefore, we are fine to dismiss the topic as a proverbial dust bunny in the corner of our collective psyche—an amalgamation of hoaxes, misidentifications, delusions, and story-telling—a smear in the tighty-whities of life that no amount of washing gets out.

But what if the priests of science are looking at that eternal inconclusiveness the wrong way? What if the perpetual inconclusiveness of scientific inquiry into such events is itself the important discovery? What if vagueness is the one detectable, repeatable quality inherent to all authentic paranormal phenomena?

What if scientists have discovered paranormal reality and don't know it?

Has any scientist ever set out to prove the hypothesis that no matter what paranormal event they study, their results will be inconclusive? That no matter how advanced technology gets, it will only ever be able to detect something vague enough to indicate paranormal phenomena's existence and nothing more? That the paranormal tantalizes us with the promise of an agreed-upon answer akin to Lucy tantalizing Charlie Brown with a football and the promise to let him kick it this time?

Stupidly, it is taken as a truism in Western society that

technology is far more honest a broker of sensing all that is around us than human organs. Your eyes deceive but the camera never lies. Though that is vastly overstated on the technological side, it is both true and untrue when it comes to the paranormal. It may be the case that our technological implements perfectly record and amplify exactly what is there: vagueness. And no matter what instrument the scientist uses, no matter how flawless the experiment, all one will ever conclusively find is vagueness. This alone is predictable and repeatable.

Can We Glean Anything About Paranormal Vagueness?

What have we learned about this vagueness? Anything concrete?

As a matter of fact, yes. And this, too, we've been learning since forever. The objective reality of the paranormal is not just vagueness but also meaning. Meaning to the person or persons involved in the event(s) and meaning (although perhaps a different one) for the collective, when it gives attention.

Vagueness is a generator of meaning. No amount of denial diminishes that meaning. Experiencers of the paranormal are adamant that they witnessed extraordinary things. Some are adamant that what they witnessed literally unfolded as they perceived it. Others see the literal event as a surface-level smoke and mirrors act covering something they did not, or cannot, ever understand. In either case, they are unshakable in their understanding that something profoundly off-script from the norm happened, and this alone forced them to rethink what they'd been taught about existence.

Rethinking what you have been taught about ordinary subjects necessarily includes rethinking your teachers. But reality is no ordinary subject. Reality is the subject of ordinariness itself. Rethinking what you've been taught about the limits of reality necessarily includes rethinking the ability of teachers to exist for this subject at all.

Can we be taught anything about reality? Who here is an authority? All we can know is that we cannot know.

All of life is vague. The rules that govern us are malleable. They are not rules at all. It is tempting to apply mechanistic thinking to this and conclude that laws of physics are simply limitations that get discovered as such when we advance our knowledge—as if we are evolving to a point where we will discover and comprehend the final, factual laws that govern us. But then what are the governing structures behind those laws?

If it is never-ending then there are no laws. If it ends at a set of laws and those laws exist without reason, then they are arbitrary. They might as well be anything. They are illusions, too.

And, see, that's where our science is heading: nowhere. We're catching up with the one immutable meaning beneath the surface of paranormal vagueness: it's all vague. It's all folly. It's all play. Even the parts that jump out and go, "Boo!" Even that which we deem to be normal.

And now we find ourselves here at the *now* precipice,

teetering on the edge of time and timelessness, space and void, things and nothing, with a final question that has an answer sloppy sages might gussy up in riddle language and call "an answerless answer." That question is this: What are we really, truly left with when we strip it all away?

If there are laws governing reality then there must be a governor, unless those laws exist for no reason. Reason without a reasoner. If they just exist then they are woven into the fabric of the universe so tightly that there can be no universe without them. In effect, the laws of the universe *are* the universe. If one were to dig away at matter/energy until there were nothing left but laws, there would be nothing at all, for laws cannot exist without substance to govern and substance cannot exist without laws.

What are we left with? We're left with nothing. No-Thing. Literally, an answerless answer.

Irrefutably, nothingness is a concept; concepts exist in intelligence; therefore, nothingness is intelligence. And this intelligence, in simply being, is being all things at once. That is our true identity, and it is beyond the capability of our instruments of perception to discover. It is beyond, even, the person wielding those instruments; beyond the brain projecting that person; beyond the cells that comprise the brain projecting that person; beyond the molecules that comprise those cells; beyond the atoms and the quarks, the particles and waves.

Yes, beyond that sea of energetic clay and the intelligence that governs it lies formless awareness. This concrete Truth

—this fact—is only seen through the eyes of one who neither knows this nor denies it, for answers are things and nothing (or No-Thing) demands a mind that is clear of answers, including the correct ones.

One who is No-Thing-aware acts rightly. Such a one's actions come from Source; such a one's words are Truth.

Truth speaking is wisdom. Truth regurgitated is knowledge. Knowledge teaches the what of things; wisdom is how you use knowledge and why.

Science lacks wisdom because it doesn't make moral judgements or approach the why of anything, just the how and the what, which are appearances, illusions. And this is why our understanding of the universe is fluid, not at all the concrete answer we're seeking. It's not our lack of comprehension skills getting in the way, it's that the universe isn't real. It isn't real and what is "real" is only perceived thus through direct experience. Not through knowledge, study, and practice. Not through building upon another's work.

One could say that known reality is obscured by vagueness and this is contained in clarity, like murky water in a clear glass. You see it when you properly interpret the mystery presented by intelligent movements on the liminal stage between the vague and the opaque.

One could say that, but then what in God's name would one be saying?

A riddle for the ages. A riddle for the sages. The same old fucking riddle nobody gives a shit about anyway.

Believer, debunker, DMT psychonauts, I've got your

medicine right here. It's the same for all of you because you're all the same: ***Shut. The. Fuck. Up***.

Kumbaya, bitches. Ready or not, your oneness is happening riiiiiight now!

Vaeni, out!

That was tedious.

Welcome to my world. Who the fuck *are* you?

The ranting grows stale and the ending is meaningless.

Thanks. I haven't ended it yet. Oh, and did I mention?—Who in the high holy hell are you, dude?!

Why are you so hostile to the very people who pay attention to you?

I explained that already.

VOICE: Did you?

JEREMY: Redundantly so, yes. Like everything else in this book. Round and round.

VOICE: Your problems with your audience apply to society at large.

JEREMY: True.

VOICE: Then why are you being myopic and lashing out at the people in front of you?

JEREMY: Because they're in front of me.

VOICE: Because they listen to you and so you feel that you have some semblance of control over the situation.

JEREMY: Whatever.

VOICE: Your audience is dead to you. They are an object in front of you. You don't even write for them, you write for you—and you expect them to react to you positively?

JEREMY: Every decent writer writes for themselves.

VOICE: Yes. And with an eye for writing their material well enough to earn an audience.

JEREMY: Agreed. And your point is?

VOICE: Why was the section on your documentary so long?

JEREMY: That's why you're here, to critique my work, dude? Okay.

Why?—Because it shows how dream-like, how fluid, normal life can be. That's one reason. Another is that it's a callback to both the length of the Nickelodeon chapter in the prequel, which is about normal life, and the "Time Out/Time Back In" segment, too. There's a bunch of other reasons, you want me to list them all?

VOICE: Are they reasons or rationalizations?

JEREMY: I'd argue they're subtext. Unless you know something about me I don't?

VOICE: You wrote a long section on a proud accomplishment that you know few people will see the point in slogging through. They're not here to read the literary equivalent of your slide show presentation of past events, Jeremy. You wrote it because it makes you feel like a somebody to read it back to yourself. For a hair of a second you may feel good about having made a movie that few have seen and for which you ultimately feel like a failure. This is the type of insecurity that, if it goes unchecked, leads to narcissism.

I don't see you disagreeing.

JEREMY: I don't see me disagreeing either.

VOICE: One must now ask: How are you different from those you smack around and defend against?

JEREMY: I'm self-aware.

VOICE: Then you are evil.

(*Jeremy ponders that a moment*)

JEREMY: I think I might be.

VOICE: You are the post-heart/post-enlightenment self whom you must understand for No-Thing-self awareness to be the case. Not the case, *again*, because that would be falsely dying into the memory of your *I Am* experience and getting trapped in a different thought construct. Yet you waffle to remain as you are and you understand all of the implications of doing so. This is why you are evil.

Currently, you are evil. Next moment, you might feel good and enlightened. Evil and good are irrelevant. Feeling enlightened is irrelevant. Constructs, all. Noises, all. Once and always again, silence is key. Not exorcising the growing choir of inner demons. Not indulging the sanctimonious vibes. Silence.

JEREMY: Clearly, I'm the one who doesn't deserve a sequel.

VOICE: No one deserves anything. You know this.

215.

Our Hero Repents

JEREMY: How did I become this? I feel like a raging shell of a man. And there's sorrow beneath it. I don't mean that passively—I am the sorrow. I'm all of that sorrow.

I was God once. I was happy. I was joy. Now I'm a cancer eating myself. How did I land in a junkyard full of old me issues after blasting off of Planet Me, sixteen years ago?

VOICE: You understood you so thoroughly that you dissolved. You resurrected in heart and were subsequently opened to universal oneness. When you chose to come back to your separate-self sense, you chose to live what that meant. Like a magnet, all of your old resolved issues attracted back to you again because the me is the me's history.

But you aren't as solidly dysfunctional as you used to be, are you? Those issues want to be you again, yet you can never go back to being as unconscious of them as required for that to happen, and so they feel as though they are haunting you.

J: Yeah. They're like phantoms. They haunt me, but I can repel them because I know they aren't real, and yet there's a friction to that.

V: Remember that coming back from the universal wakeup provides an opportunity to start anew, which feels like a good idea until the corrosion becomes apparent. The dysfunctional ghosts of you come back home. They are not you anymore but they are familiar and they form a monstrous presence, as if a differentiated being. The friction you feel becomes you if you are careless.

Think of it this way: your personal history is ancient history to you. You can get bogged down by it, grow obsessive with it, and then there you are, the old you again, but worse. More delusional because now you're blocking out the wholeness that you know you are from direct experience.

J: Would this happen if I came from a different culture?

V: It would be far less likely to happen if you lived in a culture that understood all of this and supported you, but that culture would funnel you into a new set of circumstances from which to wake.

J: I'd probably get a cool title, though.

V: The title of another story in which you are the main character.

J: I used to be a true story. Now, I'm based on a true story. But whatever that is—whoever *this* is—is real now.

This is who I am and who I am to see through. I'm getting it. Thank you.

V: Thank *you.*

J: What's your name, anyway?

V: You will recognize me if I tell you. You will take from the known and make me knowable. Is that important?

J: Nnnooo? ... Is this a trick question? You're Trickster, right?

V: If I were, which answer would I give? And would you be foolish enough to believe me? Better not to ask. Tell me what you really want to talk about.

J: I already was talking about what I wanted to talk about before you interrupted. Are you here to tell me something different?

V: We need to talk about what you want to talk about first.

J: I want to talk about whatever you want to talk about.

V: You don't know what I want to talk about.

J: Yeah, who's on first, dude?—Let's hear what you have to say.

V: How can you hear me when what you want to hear is you? You want to get me out of the way to go back to your book, but I'm not here to be in the way of your book. I'm here to help you write it. The real book. The one you need to write. But first you have to finish writing this one.

J: You want to get rid of me before I get rid of you, is that it?

(*no response*)

J: I already told you I don't do channeling. No psychic shit here.

(*no response*)

J: 'kay. That's how you want to play it. Then I shall dub thee *Mystery Voice*, for that is what you are, and it's the least cheesy thing I can come up with on short notice. Actually, it's still pretty cheesy. But, whatever, Mystery Voice.

Mystery Voice? Let me ask you this: What's the difference between a voice in my head that sounds like me, an alien in the room that feels like me, a hallucination that is a projection of me, and a vision that is projected through me?

MYSTERY VOICE: Encounters with beings and archetypes of the inner world seem like they are at once coming from you and separate from you. This is because when you go searching for them, or they for you, the point of contact is one of instantaneous, symbiotic, world-building through known ideas, symbols, and facades. The resulting virtual space is brought to life so that you will find the shared moment comprehensible, just like with, and often in, dreams. And just like with dreams, you can learn to come consciously clear, have a bit of control there, and seek out teachable moments.

Although nonphysical in nature, none of these beings, instances, and ideas reside outside of your universe. We are talking about awarenesses inhabiting the nonphysical interiority of your universe. The physical universe is, roughly speaking, concretized thought. Given that you exist within it, you are also, therefore, thought. In the end, any conversation with beings from the interiority of the universe is you talking to yourself, even though it feels like a conversation with someone else.

But there are also beings outside of this universe of thought and time. When they speak, their voices cut through your dream and you'd better listen. Only such a one may impart wisdom or knowledge that has any bearing on the outside world—the world apart from your self-building, self-fortifying adventures.

Communications with unconscious, impersonal, universal thought forms are for you to understand within yourself or about yourself. However, the other voices from outside your universe use these very same thought forms as the mouthpieces through which they speak. They speak to provoke you to step out of your universe. The way to know the difference between universal thought forms speaking and external beings using those thought forms to speak through is to listen with the intent to understand yourself so thoroughly that you, as controlling thought form, no longer exist to make the distinction.

J: Wait, what? I think that's beyond my pay grade. Or below it, I dunno. This is the problem with these types of dialogues: they become word salad real quick and then I'm supposed to smile and nod along.

MV: There is an important element to what you call the *I Am* awakening that you overlooked when you wrote *Urgency*..

J: I'm sure there were several.

MV: This is the one we're talking about: At the onset, you felt as though there were people in the room. You disregarded that feeling as a psychological byproduct of the experience, not as the cause of the experience. You also disregarded the female voice and the choir of voices at the end as versions of the same psychological theme. Why?

J: Because they have answers in psychology, or at least

likelihoods.

MV: No. You did not want to tarnish how others reading it might perceive your experience.

J: True. Yeah. Debunkers are going to debunk no matter what, but I didn't want skeptics to scoff and believers to believe.

MV: You didn't want people who do what they do to do what they do.

J: (*laughs*) Well, when you put it that way....

MV: You cannot control your audience.

J: Tell me about it!

MV: You rationalized brushing past the otherness in the room by equating the feeling of people behind you with accounts of sleep paralysis, saying the *I Am* experience must have triggered this in the brain. But your rationalization was not your reason. Your reason was fear. Fear of the known seeping into the unknowable. Fear that moments of duality would call your nondual experience into question and it would be ignored as a dream or hallucination by much of the readership. You were not making your experience clearer by dividing its aspects into knowable and unknowable parts, you were obfuscating. You did what you're so very upset with debunkers for doing: you conjured false yet reasonable-sounding answers to a major theme of your experience—namely, the multiplicity in oneness—to gain a sense of control over a situation that, frankly, was all in your head to begin with. Nobody called you on anything you wrote.

J: Nobody could. They aren't qualified.

MV: Fine. Then nobody would have, so who were you controlling this for?

J: For me?

MV: Of course for you. You are fear.

J: But I never once thought, even in the tiniest bit of *ever*, that this experience wasn't real—wasn't reality itself. So, I wasn't afraid that I was deluding myself, in other words.

MV: That's correct.

J: Then what fear could I have been covering up?

MV: What are all selves covering up? What do they exist for and as?

J: The fear of nonexistence.

MV: Yes. And this was your new resurrected-self version of that fear. This is what you are now a reflexive response to.

J: The fear of death. Annihilation.

MV: Yes.

J: I don't get how.

MV: Those other beings you felt in the room were not psychological constructs. They were and are real. They exist beyond the veil of duality. They decide when you are ready for the *I Am* awakening, not you.

And it *is* a decision. It is not a result of being silence. That result had already come to pass as you described.

J: Okay, now I'm confused. How do others exist nondually? Maybe it would help if you walked me through the *I Am* awakening as I experienced it. First, I read Jiddu Krishnamurti and got what he was saying, and in that moment—

MV: No, first you believe you're an alien abductee. And then you aren't sure what you are. You don't know how to define this presence that has partially come to define you and so you cannot define yourself fully. You cannot say, "I am an alien abductee," and mean it. You can, as you've explained, use the term as a placeholder for Mystery. And this Mystery partially defines you, colors your outlook, partially *is* you.

Next, you read books of Jiddu Krishnamurti's dialogues, and what happens? All of this "Truth is a pathless land" talk of his grates against the part of you that you believe you *do* know. You actually think you know something about yourself and here is this man claiming nobody knows anything and furthermore, knowledge itself is the problem. Thousands of years of spiritual search and culture-building have been wrong. What you think are spiritual ladders to Truth are walls blocking it out.

Krishnamurti bothers you. He angers you. You want him to be a rambling lunatic, but you're too vain to block him out and move on because you realize people you consider intelligent find him intelligent. You deduce you must be wrong and you don't like being wrong, so you stick with him, reading his work until you finally understand what he was saying in the way that one must to dissolve brain-self into heart-self.

And for the longest time you believe you've got it. That's enlightenment. You feel joy. You feel unburdened by psychological issues. Truth is flowing through you, replacing your rote databank of knowledge with the living flow of wisdom.

However, bleeding through your feelings of fulfillment is discontentment. You are heart-alive and you realize that you're still a self-sense. As you say, you're now the guy who gets it. That's your illusion, the new you one must wake from.

You're the guy who completely comprehends Truth but has mistaken that comprehension, with its many deep understandings, for full understanding, and the moment you understand this, understand who you are, you cease to be.

Jeremy died the day he realized he was still alive, happy as a clam, completely comprehending "Truth is a pathless land" as a means to not fully die into the whole of Truth. And in that moment of death, what you came to identify as *kundalini energy* blossomed within the body.

Is this making sense?

J: I couldn't have recapped it better myself. Please keep going.

MV: You're now heart-alive and kundalini-alive and you're wondering what this new force of will in the body is, exactly.

Truth is living freedom, right action, complete health. When Truth is spoken into time through heart it becomes wisdom, morals, and ethic. Decisions and knowledge. Playthings of the personal self center. When Truth is performed as the action of the body, its willpower is what you call *kundalini.*

Kundalini may look to you like possession by entities or a distinct intelligence. This is what happens when nonduality expresses within the dualistic framework: the expressing both feels like you and not you. What that's really saying is, it feels like something of time—something you can recognize—and also timeless—that which is untouched by recognition and is deeply you.

When you step aside and allow kundalini to maneuver, it comes on as a bunch of personas and deities manipulating you to your great benefit. You may have heard of them or you may not—it doesn't matter. They are the dead and the otherwise immaterial, but not presenting as ghosts and possessions and the visions one picks apart as an ordinary perceiver of "another realm," including as a psychic. Instead, they are presenting as the personifications that are historically associated with the actions the body is performing to aid in its health, such as yoga postures and mudras.

Is this at all clear?

J: Barely. I think you're saying that if I weren't divided inside I would not be witnessing multiples of beings funneling into my body via a separate energy that connects us. I'd be the whole damn thing. But since I'm fucked up, I feel buddhas doing buddha shit when my body moves around on its own. Something like that?

MV: Close enough.

J: Alright, but when you say the energy is a flux of dead people and entities and stuff, what does that really mean?

MV: Formless awarenesses, archetypes, impersonal beings—the entire ecology of the mind of your world—

comprise kundalini energy. Just as you talk about all life being one in the physical, so, too, you are all one in death. The nonphysical interiority of your universe is death.

J: Right! When we say all is one, we forget that! We talk about all life and objects that we see and feel as being one energy manifesting in different ways, but there's also this inner world of formless beings and immaterial stuff that is also one. The neglected is also one. The misunderstood and forgotten are one.

MV: Let us say this: just as the body feels like it is both you and something you reside in, kundalini feels like it is both you and other beings residing in you. Kundalini presents an immaterial version of that feeling.

An immaterial version. Not the only one.

Truth also feels like you and not you when it informs you as wisdom and insight. You might suppose it's the voice of a guardian angel whispering in your mind. The more complacent you become, the more identified within time, the greater the distance between you and Truth.

Are we with each other so far?

J: Yes. I could talk about me all day.

MV: Clearly. But we only have two more versions of you to go, and they're quick. The first is you while consciously being the *I Am* awakening, which is what you've been asking if people can live as, not just visit. And then you, the aftermath of that. You here right now.

Recall that the *I Am* awakening felt as though it began when a slit opened in the spine. This is something you've only felt a few times, and each time felt like someone was opening you with surgical precision. This is not the same as kundalini, which you can allow to express and turn off at will.

It's like a door in the spine, right? And the question is, who is opening it if not Jeremy and if not kundalini? Who decides when to do that?

J: I... I don't know.

MV: That's right. And you cannot know. To know is to recognize. To know is to kill the moment, to kill the now with knowledge, which is time.

J: Definitions from within time kill the timeless, same as answers kill mysteries.

MV: Yes. This is uncomplicated, but words complicate. You have an experience of oneness, and that oneness is administered by others. Why?

J: You're asking me?

MV: I'm asking.

J: Because duality is how it begins. I'm experiencing duality, which is separation, so I am going to perceive someone or something separate from me bringing me into the nondual moment, birthing me into it, deciding it's my time. However that plays out.

MV: Yes. That is true. You will always experience the machinations of duality right up to the moment you dissolve into timelessness and right after you come back to time. But it is also true that there are others sharing the nondual moment with you. If that is confusing, consider the act of reading this book as an analogy. If the book is nonduality, there are multiple people reading it and yet you are all one consciousness.

J: Okay, but then nonduality... In your analogy, the book is separate from the readers?

MV: Not separate from but vastly different from and yet relatable to its readers.

J: Wait, the book isn't all of nonduality in your analogy. It's got to be a universe. The readers are from different universes reading this one book—this one universe—which is the universe I live in. And when I, as a character in the book, spontaneously self-identify as the book itself, then I become like them, right? A character out of the book reading the book?

The book, then, is still me, but I'm out of time and so not just identifying as a character in it or even as the whole book. I now understand myself as part of a multitude of universes. I'm a library.

Is this... Is that close to what you're saying?

MV: It is, but it's jumping the gun. You woke up to universal oneness. You did not wake up to multidimensional oneness, even though you were surrounded by people from other configurations of dimensions. You experienced the *I Am* awakening of the universe exploding into life within nothingness, which is pure consciousness. You did not experience the aliveness of multiple universes. And because you did not, the part of your oneness experience you deny is that there truly were other beings in the room. They are of oneness consciousness, but not of your experience of it—not yet. Not as you self-identify now, because they transcend and include universal oneness.

J: How's that?

MV: You experienced the *I Am* awakening of seeing and being the universe from and within nothingness, right?

J: Right.

MV: What happened to the multiverse?

J: I don't know. I assumed it was all-inclusive.

MV: It *is* all-inclusive. But you didn't experience that all-inclusiveness, you inferred it intellectually after the fact. What you woke up to in the moment was you-as-universe. Universal oneness.

Always when such occurs, one experiences and understands elements of consciousness and emptiness that transcend and include even you-as-universe, so one assumes that's all there is. You've experienced yourself as all there is. But this only holds if one does as you did and ignores the fact of other people in the room during one's awakening—others opening the door in the spine.

When multidimensional oneness remains hypothetical and unexperienced, it is unreal for you.

J: Whoah, boy. Is there a further awakening, then?

MV: There is.

J: How does that work?

Finds Family In Forgiveness

MYSTERY VOICE: Think about what dimensions are. What does the word describe?

JEREMY: In physics?

MV: In reality.

J: Is there a difference?

MV: We shall see.

Dimensions describe the spacial relationship and perception of the universe and you in it. When you think of dimensions in science fictional terms, you imagine a veil between completely separate worlds that you need to invent a way of opening. But dimensions compose not just the universe, they compose every single thing in it. They compose people.

There are other dimensions to people than the ones you have mapped out. They are also available to you consciously. When you step through—or when something else comes to you—it *is* an other who is also you, thence the feeling of familiarity. You and they are living in and as these same dimensions—only you are blind to most of them.

Now, space and time may take technology to move through so long as they are treated as isolated dimensions. However, when you become conscious of all of your dimensions—and clearer, still, that they *are* you, the fabric of you—what happens? There may still appear to be separation—someone stepping through a portal. But even that is not fully the case. They are not stepping through anything. Rather, they are manifesting their intelligence before your eyes using avatars from the nonphysical interiority of your universe.

Likewise, when they "abduct" you, they do not take you anywhere. They wake you to a shared space, like a dream or a vision, inside your universe. Some call this subspace; others, the underworld.

J: Why is the fear level off the charts during abductions?

MV: Fear plays a role. We will come to it.

J: This is confusing.

MV: Confusion also has its place. Logical breakthroughs can lead to personal transformation. What are you doing when you say you are "making sense" of something?

J: Bringing something that seems senseless into the realm of the senses? Bringing it alive by understanding its workings.

MV: You're confused about something, which nags at you until you understand it. Once you understand, you let it go. You drop it; it's finished. You brought it alive, but in so doing, you let it go, making a little space in yourself, a pinprick of nothingness in the womb of your psyche.

All of your building, all of your creating in life, is not to the end of finding answers or concretizing ideas and expressions and inventions, but to the end of letting the whole rigamarole go and finding sweet release in nothingness no matter how brief. So it goes for orgasm. So it goes for drug highs. The addiction is to nothingness. The gratification is in nothingness. Nothingness is you, authentically you, and when you come back to normal, back to inauthenticity, that's coming back to struggle, back to pain.

It takes more energy to be you than to let go, but it's evenly distributed throughout your life, so you don't feel like a tulpa. You feel like a real boy, Pinocchio.

J: That's adorable. I'm not sure I caught it all, but hopefully someone reading this will get it. But I want to go back to something. You're saying dimensions are not just macro-scale. That dimensions—the way we think about dimensions—is like a bunch of universes bumping up against each other, something you could step through, if you knew how, into another world, but that's not right?

MV: It's right, but it's limited. The reality is that the universe doesn't exist without its content. There is no dimensionality without physicality, no architecture of appearances, no underlying defining characteristic, without things to characterize. So, the universe is composed of dimensions, and if you were to step through them, well, you'd have to step into the body of the person conjoined with you in whichever configuration of dimensions you were stepping into.

Luckily, you, like all else, are composed of all dimensions, even though you consciously inhabit just a few. So that body you'd need to step into already exists. It's already there. It's already you. But it's also already occupied. Occupied with an aspect of you in the largest sense, but one whom you would consider a person.

J: This sounds like schizophrenia in reverse. There are other versions of me wandering around and I *don't* hear them.

MV: Yes, but to say other versions of you... they don't look like you. They don't sound like you or think like you. They are born into a different configuration of dimensions, a different physicality. Their world is not another version of yours that, for instance, had Hitler won World War II, the future would have been different. It's not like that. It's a completely different sense of existence in a truly alien world and yet all of you share the same need, even if you are not conscious of it. Most of you are not. The need is for conscious unification into the one being that you are. Your example of schizophrenia—all of your psychological and spiritual examples are fractal versions of this need.

J: Huh. Wow. Okay.

MV: Shall we continue?

J: I... yeah. There's more? (*chuckles nervously*)

MV: When have you known there not to be?

J: At a dead end.

MV: This book is alive. Everything you've written until now was the dead end. From death comes life.

J: Every shit has a rose. Or a shroom, come to think of it.

MV: Do you know what humor is?

J: Funny? I dunno. Does anybody know what humor is?

MV: You all do. You even say it. It's a sense. A sense of humor is an actual sense. Taste, touch, smell, sight, sound. You have these five basic physical senses and then some of you jump to a sixth sense you call *psychic* or *intuitive.* But humor is a sense. Beauty is a sense.

J: Some people don't have a sense of humor, though. I worked with a guy who had Asperger's Syndrome. I was warned not to be sarcastic with him or playfully antagonizing because he didn't understand humor at all and would either take offense or be confused.

MV: Yes. And there are blind people and deaf people, numb people, and people who cannot smell.

J: Oh. Okay.

MV: Humor is a sense. What people find funny and how they find it funny are personal developments.

J: And now that you say that, I guess he did vaguely comprehend humor. He loved to host a comedy show. It was like a fake game show, or something, at the community theater. He didn't have to be funny but he was involved in that way.

MV: The deaf feel the beat of music. The blind form their inner vision of beauty through the other senses. Senses exist in humans whether the individual is cut off from them or not. This fact is also a metaphor for your multidimensionality. You are cut off from your other senses of self and yet you are all here right now. In fact, those others who opened you to universal self-identity and you are one multidimensional being.

J: Wow! Okay. Yeah. That's kinda the obvious elephant in the room now that you've said it. Right. They're me. Not just random others in a multiverse. We share this space like facets of a diamond. Do we share any traits in common?

MV: Yes. The nonphysical senses. This is why humor is used as a tool of communication. And fear. And yet from these people, if you don't feel frustration and hostility, you feel joy and innocence.

J: So, okay, So you're talking about alien abductions again. You're saying there are at least some versions of me who do know how to pry open more dimensions.

MV: Of course.

J: Of course!

MV: They know how to make themselves perceptible to you and then have you pull them into existence here through greater and greater perception. You already suspected that.

J: Is that what synchronicities are for? I mean does the process start out as small, nearly invisible signs, and then evolve if we latch onto them?

MV: No. Think about how it happened for you. It was big and flashy. A parade that did not exist when you were a toddler, which was clearly there for you to witness. The conductor of the marching band looked at you and smiled. This was for you to remember. It was an imprint on your brain at a stage of development where your ability to discriminate between internal and external phenomena was just beginning to form.

Your parents denied your experience because they didn't see it. How could they? It was for you and you were a child, so they assumed it was just your imagination.

But you knew it did not come from your imagination and could not be persuaded otherwise. This friction is what has kept the vision alive for you all of these years. Other people's denial—especially that of authority figures—benefits those who have a strong sense of themselves.

J: I've always been full of myself. Admitted. But what are they actually doing, these people we call *aliens*?

MV: The universe is thought in different states of itself. If you obsess over an idea, a possibility, with the proper intensity, you may transition it from an idea to the physical—from the possible to the actual—if only for a brief time. In this way may they, through avatars, be physicalized in your world in fits and starts. Long enough to do what they need.

J: Which is what?

MV: You mean you've spent your entire life relating this to people and you don't know?

J: Oh, *aha*. You're not gonna tell me?

MV: We will come to it in due course.

J: Okay. Where do synchronicities come in, then? Or do they? Or did I just make that up?

Can I ask that?

MV: Synchronicity is complicated because it is a universal language spoken by manipulating the fabric of the universe and is spoken by different sources. It is often so difficult for you to tell who is speaking that you mistake the identities.

J: Is déjà vu related to synchronicity?

MV: Déjà vu has multiple sources, too. You could have thought something before and then lived it out later. You could have dreamed something similar to, or the same as, what you subsequently lived.

Sometimes, though, déjà vu is the echo that occurs when you are moving in and/or out of synch with the flow of right decisions.

J: Meaning what?

MV: Meaning that when you are at one with Truth, flowing in Truth and Truth flowing through you, you cannot make wrong decisions. You act out the healthiest choices possible. But when you are not in the flow, when Truth is a flow running parallel to you, not through you and as you, you still may veer in and out of Truth's stream. And when you do, when you pass in and out of the flow of Truth like a drunk driver weaving in and out of his lane, you create what you call an echo. That echo is the sound of two voices speaking the same thing. Those voices are Truth's and your own.

J: That is stunning. That's like how even a broken clock tells the right time twice a day.

I thought déjà vu was what happened when other versions of me in parallel universes made the same decision. Like, maybe when universes line up, there's an echo through the fractal.

MV: No. Although you are prismatic beings, that type of multidimensionality does not exist. There are not infinite timelines carrying infinite versions of Jeremy making every decision you discard. Ideas are alive and they will make their homes in the voices of other people.

However, you are prismatic in that you do live multiple lives at once. From within time, when you believe in this or theorize about it, you call it *reincarnation.* You suppose those other lives happen before and after this one. But within the timeless moment, all lives are living simultaneously.

J: We're talking about reincarnation now?

MV: For the moment.

J: Huh. Okay. So I am expressing as a number of people in this universe and a number of people in other dimensions?

MV: Not just people. You know you are a sun. You experienced that. You experienced being Sun as if you were Sun right now, but also with the sense that you will be Sun in a future lifetime. Humans are not the only sentient life form you put on the blinders to "become," one after the other, when you're stuck in time.

J: Why is there a discrepancy between unfolding as reincarnating selves one at a time and actually being all of them right now? Like, why can't we perceive how we really are if that's how we really are?

MV: Recall your chapter, *Ponders The Leaves*. Stick with that metaphor. People are like trees in that they have surface personae and a persona of the depths. Now, let's make you a specific tree. Have you ever heard of the pando?

J: The bear?

MV: Not the panda bear, the pando—a single tree that appears to be a massive forest. It's not. It is one root system sprouting tens of thousands of trees. One organism with many bodies.

You, as individuals, are like the pando. And the surface world that each of your bodies exists in is time. In time, you have amnesia about the other trees also being you. But the roots know. The roots know all.

When it comes to people, the roots are not timeless, but they are formless and ancient, so they feel timeless. Yet, how can they be? They exist within the interior experience of the universe. The underworld is there. Heaven awaits. All the shapes of death—pitstops on the way to identifying as one of your other lives that exist concurrently.

J: Whoah, slow it down, there, Chester. This is a lot to wrap my beady brain around.

MV: For you, it shouldn't be. You experienced the unfolding of creation out of nothing and saw through the perspective of all that you witnessed and were, at once. You saw the expanding and you were that expanding. You saw rock forms hurling through space and you saw as if through the eyes of those rocks and that space. You knew yourself as no picture, the big picture exploding out of no picture, and all of the details of the picture, as well as the force of explosion. You experienced the unique qualities of all of those separate elements in their separation and also as one movement and also no movement—in a single instance. And you know that this is what you are. This is what you call *Truth* with a capital T.

Now we are saying that there is more to oneness than universal identity. You will wrestle with this intellectually before you understand it in the way one must for transformation.

J: Wait a sec, I just thought of something. If all of my lives are living right now like a pando grove, could there be more than one of me somewhere in the world right now?

MV: Somewhere out there is a star with your name on it.

J: Huh. Yeah, I'm a sun.

MV: There are many death realms, all of them thought. Many births, all of them you. You *are* Sun right now but will experience such as an increment of future time if you physically die without transforming into universal wholeness.

J: What if I believed in Jesus? Would I see him in a death realm?

MV: Very likely. You die into your expectations and you experience yourself recycling back into the physical. Saying that you keep your sense of self is saying that you keep yourself asleep. The universe dreams you anew. You dream you anew. Round and round you go in time.

However, out of time and apart from thought, conjoined to your universe, are other universes with other beings, some of whom are specifically stuck to you. To *all of* you—your whole spectrum of lives. You'd say *lives lived,* but from the timeless perspective it's, *lives living.*

You are a living, breathing string of lifetimes in a living, breathing universe and you've got living, breathing multidimensional people who are stringing along with you as well. Some of them understand all of this; some don't. Those who do are trying to wake you. You translate this as them trying and failing to wake all incarnations of you in the past, present, and possibly—if they fail with you now—future. But to them, all of those individuals who make up your lifetimes are one at the root and living right now.

They do this work because waking you is waking themselves. If that sounds selfish and personal, it isn't. They understand their action to be one waking oneself, not them waking you to benefit them.

Now, the only reason you struggle against this—you, Jeremy, who have awakened to universal oneness self-identity and yet continue to ask the same questions over and over, untouched by the answers you're trying to memorize—is because you fell back asleep. Contrary to how it felt, you did not fall back asleep the moment you came to normal awareness and jumped off the bed after the *I Am* experience wrapped up. You fell back the moment your universal focus centered on a giant red planet and you heard that familiar female voice ask, "Do we humans not understand that other planets cannot help us if we continue to block them out and kill ourselves," while thought on a loop in the background repeated the words, 'Lisette Larkins, *Talking To Extraterrestrials.*' That moment was the beginning of the end for universal self-identity.

Stay with me now. This is going to get very specific and I need you to see this.

The female voice and the red planet were a ruse. A ruse set off by you as you flailed in fear that you were dying. You-as-fear as a background noise is negligible. But when you-as-fear come to the fore, you unconsciously reach out in all directions for safety.

Safety came in the form of something you knew: this voice with her alien message—a cover for the multidimensional truth you're refusing.

You are not blocking out other planets here to help you; you are blocking out other dimensions trying to wake you. Small twists like these give lie to the truth and change the scenario into one you can survive. More than survive, you may come back and train yourself to work with "beings from other planets" through, for instance, channeling.

J: What would I actually be channeling?

MV: Voices of the unconscious mind. In other words, thought constructs. More you.

Now, when you came to and jumped off the bed and knew

you had a decision to make to be Universal Oneness guy, or be *this* guy, Jeremy, you had already made your decision. The decision was an aspect of that universal experience, which now, back in Jeremy mode, got broken up in time as something you could choose into—some future event just waiting for your signal to become you. And you figured you could put this decision off, write a book, be relatable to people, and get back to it whenever you were ready.

The decision wasn't real. In fact, as you know, you cannot chase nothingness in the hopes of becoming Mr. Universe again through an ego death. You didn't choose it in the first place. You were opened up by multidimensionals.

J: Who are also me, though.

MV: It's irrelevant. Right now, for all intents and purposes, they are not you. Not until you all merge as the conscious self-identity of One. Until then, your oneness with them is a fact we may talk about, but you still encounter them as separate entities.

J: So, what was the Lisette Larkins riff for?

MV: It was a psychic failsafe from the multidimensionals to insure that you would not let any of this go. Despite the fact that you cannot choose universal self-identity the way you assumed you'd be able to, there was a very good chance that you'd try. You haven't tried with any real effort to be that again, but if you had, you'd have failed and eventually given up hope. You'd have questioned the validity of the experience.

This is the depth of selfishness of people: you give up on the actual when it does not behave according to your desire. The multidimensionals understand this. They intervened by throwing in that chorus about Lizette Larkins, which turned into prophesy when the Learning Annex representative asked you to teach her class. You cannot deny a callback like that, one which acts as a psychic prediction. If ever you began to doubt the experience, your mind would go right back to that prediction and you'd be stuck with the reality of your ordeal. And then maybe, you being you, you'd question not the realness of the experience but the realness of the feeling that you chose to come back to normal. From there, we would end up here in this discussion.

J: Funny enough, I never questioned the experience, but I did end up questioning the nature of that intuited decision, and here we are!

MV: We are here.

J: Okay. Let's go back to reincarnation, cuz I find this topic fascinating for once. If reincarnation is a misnomer because there is no time, and all incarnations of me are alive right now, are any of my other human lives being lived right now in what I think of as this lifetime?

MV: It is possible. Sometimes you run into them and fall immediately and inexplicably in love. You call them soulmates. More often, you never meet.

J: Wait, what? Soulmates are me? Incestuous me living other lives right now?

MV: Sometimes.

J: Not always?

MV: No.

J: Is it pointless to try to figure out who's who?

MV: Acting on anything in this conversation would be another diversion. This is the problem with getting into detail. Details become Cray-Z Straw holes and before you know it, you've sucked the life out of yourself chasing white rabbits.

J: Rabbits in a Cray-Z Straw? Sounds like a Beck lyric. Wait, one more tiny, little detail. What's a near-death experience? Does that fit in with reincarnation at all, er...?

MV: You're born into a collective identity. Your adult identity is shaped by a series of other people's agreements through your formative years. In the West you'd call this collective identity, "objective reality." And some of that you slough off throughout your life, replacing what doesn't work for you, personally, with what does.

When you die, you die into a personal, subjective vision. However you truly perceive life and death to be at the end of your life is what you die into. Thus, people experience a variety of near-death experiences, and they're all valid. They all reflect the subjective reality of the person.

J: Huh. Okay, kinda suspected something like that.

MV: Yes. In death you are formless, although you may appear to yourself to have form. Whereas in waking life you feel differentiated from the events you experience, in death you *are* the events, there is no separation between experiencer and experience, which is why it feels hyperreal. All is immediately you and you are not dreaming.

J: And then what next? We pick a flowering tree from our root system and sprout up into that life?

MV: If you've mastered the ability to will yourself into an available lifetime, yes. If not, you are born automatically and at random.

J: Why? Are we learning something from this?

MV: No. You are performing the action of life. You are the spark of life within your bodies.

J: Not just *me*, me. All incarnations. We're all zipping and bopping around lifetimes like a pinball machine with a shit-ton of balls.

MV: If you like.

J: To what end?

MV: Forever. Until you aren't.

J: Oh, don't be cryptic now. What's the end to that?

MV: Let's back up. Rewind to a different angle for the lead-in to your *I Am* awakening. First, you unified your psychological interior. When you were working properly, coming from heart to inform the brain, not working from brain in denial of heart, you were interconnecting with life in the way nature cultures never forgot. But then you realized that as joyous and freeing as that natural you was, it was still you. Finding out if there was anything beyond you would take more than reform, it would take death. And the only way for the self to die was to realize that it was still alive. Reformed and healthy, yes, but alive and in charge, nonetheless. The moment you understood this is the moment you died.

In the next moment, you came back. And an energy that may only maneuver when the self is out of the way came alive. You treated this energy as you had your own dissolution of self. You stayed out of the way as much as possible, never trying to insert control and domination over its unfoldment.

The other "alien" aspects of you, who are awake to the fact of their multidimensional nature, knew precisely when it was time to open you up to the big reveal of all that you are. All that you are in-and-as this universe. They did that for you, which is secretly saying you did that for yourself because you are all one being. And now you are approaching the next reveal: the oneness of multidimensional being.

These people you call alien do not want equals. They want what you want: to wake up to wholeness. But they cannot do so until you and the other aspects of you, clinging to other configurations of dimensions, do the same. You *are* one waking oneself up, as you've always known. But you never knew the fullness of the meaning—never knew what it takes—until right now.

The universe wakes. The multiverse wakes. This is simply how things are. It's the beating heart of existence. The heart beats because it must or you'll die. Any other explanation, no matter how factually accurate, how meticulous, how scientific or magical, is a flourish.

J: When I had the *I Am* awakening, did all incarnations of me have it, too?

MV: No. When one of you awakens to universal oneness,

that one alone awakens. The others feel a spiritual stir, like a calling to engage Mystery. However, when one awakens to multidimensional oneness, the other incarnations do then spontaneously awaken to universal oneness.

J: That's crazy! Everyone else is always a step behind!

MV: More like the conscious and unconscious aspects of one's entire existence get recontextualized.

J: As whole other people! Whole other people are my unconscious baggage and I'm theirs, is what you're saying!

MV: They are not baggage when you completely understand all of this. At least you'd better hope not, for you are fractally the same unconscious bag person to awakened multidimensional versions of you right now.

J: This is insanity! So do we all carry around each other's karma, too? Is that real?

MV: What is real about it is that the health of the individual trees affect each other in the pando grove because they are interconnecting at the root. Some struggle in shade; some receive more sun and thrive. All feel aspects of the health and the lives of all.

However, this needn't be one's burden. Those who say they have experienced their karma burn away actually experienced their own compassion for themselves in a moment so powerful that they came clear. Staying with the metaphor, they stopped leeching nutrients from the other trees in the cluster and stopped being drained by them.

J: Now, that one tree is a loner. A loner reaching for the stars. Like Pando Calrissian, am I right?

(*Jeremy throws a hand in the air hoping for an invisible high five from Mystery Voice and is left hanging*)

J: No? ... *Star Wars* reference? ... Nothing?
Fine. I'm ignoring you ignoring me.
Are there people who have woken up completely?

MV: Yes. Many people wake up to individual wholeness. Fewer wake to multidimensional oneness. Both actions create novelty in the universe, adding to the richness of its interiority and therefore your interiority.

J: How so?

MV: The universe takes from the transcending stages and creates false wholeness wake-up scenarios within itself, which you might call *spiritual hierarchies*. Their function is to keep the inquisitive mind occupied and waking up within itself, never truly transcending the universe in a sustained way.

J: Are you saying the universe itself is working to keep us asleep? Be nothingness, but bring that back to thingness as a novel experience?

MV: Yes.

J: Wake up for a few and have a lovely chat with the multidimensionals—but be sure to fall back asleep and keep dreaming?

MV: That's right. What you call "asleep" the universe calls "alive." The universe has no problem waking you up to higher and higher levels within itself. In fact, doing so is it hanging onto itself for dear life, fractally similar to the personal self who does not want to die to "wake up" to wholeness.

The difference is that unlike the personal self, the universe is its own healthy wholeness. The universe is an autonomous being.

So, the universe keeps you on paths of waking up slowly, which means moving around archetypal environments that comprise the interiority of the universe. We'll talk about that soon. The universe does this for the very same reason you're willing to play its game: This is how it remains alive.

J: Okay, so from our little human point of view, when we dissolve into nothingness, which transcends and includes the universe, the universe converts that experience into new information it can use to entertain us, keep us occupied, and keep us here. Not just me when I come back to normal awareness, but all of us. It becomes part of the collective mind.

In other words, something new for the universe's interiority translates into something new for our interiority—new imaginative realms, for instance.

MV: You've got it.

J: That makes sense to me because, obviously, even when I had my awakenings that transcended the physical, the physical body continued to exist.

So like, brain-self shuts up and there is a moment of pure nothingness. But when I come to, the body is going to do something with that information, if I'm not careful. This is the problem gurus and the such have had through the centuries: One moment of pure honesty becomes a shitstorm of teachings. It's insane. We're insane.

MV: No. You are the universe and this is how the universe works. There is no right or wrong in this. The universe isn't asleep and afraid of its own autonomy the way people are. It's impersonal. It deals in reflexive response, not decision-making by a personal self to deny Truth. That's your job. Seeing through the necessary illusion that is the personal self is also your job.

All of this is a description of how the universe works with

authentic transcendental moments—including your personal responses, whether you come from brain or heart or wherever. All of what you may consider obstacles to wholeness are natural, from universe at large to the universe that you are. It's just what is.

J: It's mechanical.

MV: It's organic but it's predictable, if that's what you mean.

J: Sure, I'll take it. I like looking smart.
So, okay. I'm starting to see this massive picture here.

MV: It's a lot.

J: Says the master of understatement. But I still don't see why the moment of complete transcendence, or awakening, into multidimensional oneness wouldn't have a detectable mark in the now that the multidimensional people could locate from their vantage point out of time. Presumably, they'd know which of my incarnations to focus on because, like, they've done it already, but they don't know it yet. Or something. God, I'm starting to talk like people I hate.

MV: If the man-bun fits....

J: Ha!

MV: Imagine that your universe is a pond and you're a fish. The pond is connected to another universe called *land.* Beings on land see all of the pond. They see all of your time right now in the blink of their eye. And when they touch the pond, they see the ripples of their actions. Their goal in touching the pond is to influence you to jump out onto land. However, they cannot see you, dear fish, leaping out onto land until you do so because the ripples didn't exist until they tapped the pond.

J: But if we pull out from there, does this become its own act of time? Is it an act that some third being from a place called *air,* may already be witnessing?

MV: Perhaps. How will you know?

J: That's not an answer.

MV: You're asking to gain something.

J: Yes! A cheat code! People in air can tell people on land which incarnation of me to wake up because the people in air already see it!

MV: Ah. This is where your rational inquiry needs to rest. This is the point where you want to make selfish sense of reality to gain that wholeness. And so you're falling into the trap of believing that if you can imagine something, that's how it is.

The key to seeing what's false is in seeing that the same dilemma would plague the person on land who switches their attention from the factual fish to hypothetical birds in the air watching all of this. The hypothetical birds would also be interconnecting with the land and the pond and so they would want you both to wake up. All of this is one waking oneself. They would know what the land dwellers would not: looking to the hypothetical skies to give them the perfect vision of their awakening is to be trapped in time, dreaming.

So, no. There is no cheat code. This is not a video game. And it does not extend forever and ever in fractal pulled-back visions from entities of greater and greater heights or depths. You may imagine it. You may experience it through the dreaming mind of the universe in a mushroom trip. But the depths of being end in that which transcends and includes them all: *Being.*

Pure Being existing prior to and inclusive of all. Pure Being imagining the multiverse, which is imagining the universe, which is imagining you imagining there's something else.

Imagine that.

J: (*laughs*) Alright, alright, I get it. I'm more clever than Pure Being.

MV: That wasn't what—

J: No, it's cool. I get it. So, okay. We're fish in the pond. People on land throw dynamite in the pond and some of us blow out. But not all of us do. My question now is, what are we to each other if only some of these conjoined me's wake up to multidimensional wholeness while others stay asleep?

MV: Family.

J: So if I wake up and join my woke family, we would what? Work together to wake up other creatures that are me in the multiverse?

MV: Of course.

J: Of course! We'd be fishermen. My grandfather would have loved that.

MV: Just as universally awakened humans spend their lives stirring others to universal oneness, you would help do the same with other beings in other dimensions, some of whom you would know to be you.

J: And would I get to tool around in a cool UFO?

MV: If you were aiding other people, or they you, you could appear to be. Remember: they are thought forms materializing and dissolving, too, not technology. UFO waves help keep the mystery alive in the culture at large and give it a visual, which becomes a recognizable avatar for the individual. Shall we continue?

J: Let's.

MV: You are right now experiencing duality. That means you are experiencing life as though some things are coming from you and some things are not. Let's explore this is/isn't dichotomy.

J: Let's.

MV: From the nondual point of view both is and isn't *is*. Both are always already happening and that happening is you. Maybe a rough analogy is reflexive action, as opposed to consciously thought out action. Both are your action, but one is reflexive, not of your conscious will, and so it feels like it's not exactly coming from you. Both are you even though only one comes through your conscious decision-making process.

If you've got a handle on that, let's move on.

J: Let's.

(*no response*)

J: Sorry. One too many?

(*no response*)

J: Nothing? Okay.

MV: Stick with writing; you're no comedian.

J: Some version of me out there is!

MV: And we will have a different conversation about this very topic.

Collapses To Ash

MYSTERY VOICE: One senses a growing discontent in your humor.

JEREMY: I'm getting antsy. I'm at that place where I think I need proof that you exist or I'll get lambasted by critics, even though I won't because I'm not important enough to comment on. So, yeah. It's another stupid problem in my insecure head, but if you could give me something, some proof that you're real, it would go a long way toward my imagined critics believing this is nonfiction.

MV: Stars are living beings. You experienced that. That's real.

J: But not to anyone who hasn't experienced it!

MV: That is the point. You want me to give you something you cannot know but will discover. Future knowledge, is that it?

J: Yes!

MV: Future knowledge isn't real for you until it is. That cannot validate you until it comes to pass.

J: So then give me something we will discover soon. What do you see right around the corner for us?

MV: Western science tells you that life crawled out of the ocean and kept going. It's the myth of evolution and you live it every day like it's a fact. But the actual fact is that the ocean creates life and then recedes. The ocean leaves its bounty of organisms on dry land and whatever survives thrives. Evolution starts from that point and moves until the next literal sea change. Everything you need to know about spiritual transformation is contained in that simple fact of organic nature.

J: Really?

MV: Yes.

J: Are you sure?

MV: Yes.

J: And science will be discovering this soon?

MV: Not just science, *everyone*. Not just everyone, *all*.

J: Oh, damn it—I knew it! You're just being cute, right?

How about you name the correct number of dimensions to reality? I think people will pay attention to that.

MV: You explained Truth correctly in so far as such may be explained. Do people believe you?

J: Many do, yes.

MV: Do they pay attention in the way they must for that to matter?

J: None that I'm aware of.

MV: And so you're looking for the wrong result. People believing you does not matter. Careful articulation is the result you are looking for. That is the whole of your job. There is no next step of convincing people because to convince is to win them over by persuasive arguments, correct prophesying, and so forth. That does not produce transformation, it produces followers.

J: Great. No payoff for *this* guy. But if you don't give me something and I leave this in the book, I could be accused of lying and being coy or something. Answering without answering—I mean, if anyone with any smarts reads this and gives a shit. So I kinda do need an answer now. Isn't that part of meticulous articulation?

Plus, I want to know! If we can know how many

dimensions there are then we can figure out how many universes exist—how many alien me's are enfolded in the one super being.

MV: How many dimensions are there? None. And also one. And within that one, all. And the number for *all* depends on who is looking and where.

Your universe is and has dimensions and everything in it is and has dimensions. There are more dimensions than there are grains of twoness in oneness. But not all of them are populated.

Now I ask you, is that at all helpful? Are you convinced of anything?

J: But we don't need that many dimensions to exist. We know this!

MV: You're looking for elegance in the architecture of a universe divorced from you. The universe is its content and all of the content are exuding dimensionality, not just the universe at large.

Picture an enormous, thick glacier with infinite crazing cracks throughout. As far as the inhabitants of the glacier know, the glacier is the whole of reality.

Next, understand what the inhabitants do not: the glacier is frozen liquid. The crazing cracks, like the glacier itself, are illusions. Yes, they are there, but they don't have to be because solidity is not water's fundamental state. The glacier melting away immediately deflates any and all experts who made the case that the glacier was the whole of reality.

J: But... so... other versions of me waking all of me up is an impossible task.

MV: Then you'd better get started.

J: I'm being serious!

MV: The inconvenient fact remains: there are not an elegant amount of dimensions. There are far more than just enough for you to exist. Far, far more. There are enough for all things that can exist to exist. But they can't all exist in the dimensions that are the architecture of your physicality, obviously, so when you encounter them, they come to "exist" here in imagination. Through imagination, through psychic means, through dreamtime, through the fundamental "fluid" state of all realities—that which you can articulate you can move into and/or become.

J: Through drugs, too? Am I completely wrong about hallucinogens and plant medicine?

MV: You are right, if shortsighted.

J: Okay.

MV: Hallucinogens blur and often outright destroy the boundary between personal and impersonal thought. So, you are right that the trip one takes is always within the realm of thought, but you misunderstand just how vast and alive thought is. The universe—the inner and the outer—is teaming with alivenesses. Archetypes are alive. Ideas are alive.

The alivenesses of imagination need to be expressed in space-time. They are alive but not life. Not organisms. They are the interiority—*your* interiority—and they are born through you as you are reborn through them.

Alivenesses make you come alive through your process of bringing them to life. All wants to be inspired and transformed and seen. You go in to bring them out or have a spontaneous eureka moment in which they appear to you. This is how the heart of the universe beats.

J: There's a lot going on, but it isn't interdimensional, is what you're saying.

MV: Altered states of mind are immersions in what you may call the underworld or the matrix, whatever word you fancy today. They are like floors and apartments in a high rise building. You occupy one apartment on one floor. There are a number of other floors with apartments. They may be decorated differently; you may be moving up and down to get to them—but it's all one building.

The building is death, the floors are the collective

unconscious, and the apartments are filled with alivenesses.

J: You keep saying alivenesses. Are they intelligences, too?

MV: All is intelligence. But ideas, for example, are one-note, self-contained intelligence. They are not having conversations with you, they become the conversation, if that makes sense.

J: Sorta.

MV: Let's not get bogged down. The question you're really asking is, *Do hallucinogens open windows to other planets or other realities populated with alien entities?* And the answer is, *No.* They bring you to the alivenesses within what you call the collective unconscious. This is why you may learn a lot about yourself but nothing at all about the entities you're talking to, or, say, schematics on how to travel to them in a ship. They don't exist out there in the physical universe or in any adjacent dimension. They are of the interiority of the universe as expressed and experienced through humans. This is why people often walk away from hallucinogenic trips with a feeling of universal oneness. Like cells in a great body, you're all interconnecting within-and-as the interior awareness of the universe.

J: So, if we can't get to other dimensions through DMT

and the such, can we move around them in a normal woken state of awareness?

MV: Yes. But, as you know, *that* normal wake-state is not what most people live and call normal. If wholeness, as you've been calling it, were your normal, you could make appearances in other dimensions in the same way those you call aliens are doing with you.

J: How are they doing it?

MV: From within time it looks as if life is unfolding and expanding. It looks as if the psyche of humankind is unfolding and expanding, too. As you look back you see the building blocks of collective consciousness—primordial patterns and personas. You wonder if these are alive in some way. You have all of these questions because you remain as separate selves parsing out separate aspects of self, examining them, wondering about them, testing hypotheses against them, and utilizing them. None of this is an issue when you are in the flow of oneness. It's an issue when you're married to the idea of a glacial world, if we may go back to the water metaphor.

Actually, let us change the water metaphor to a quilt and see if that doesn't work better.

Oneness is timelessness. All of the events and experiences you think are following each other already exist timelessly, like color patterns on a quilt. Similar to how we talk about the now being a painting, the quilt is you.

The quilt is a tapestry of colors that fade at the edges of their patterns. You, the quilt, have a problem, which is that you don't know you're the quilt. You think you're a single thread weaving along the quilt. That's your sense of oneness —you as a thread. You're not wrong, but there is vastly more to you than that.

From your vantage point as a thread, weaving in and out of color gradients is a process of time. If you believe time is linear, then you see the color of the pattern in front of you growing brighter and brighter as if you're traveling into a color. You look behind you and see where you believe you just were is growing dimmer and dimmer.

Of course if you say time is cyclical, what you're recognizing is that the colors have contours. They actually are patterns and they are similar, with slight alterations. To move forward, backward, up, or down is to enter the space of another color and reset the clock, as it were, on the amount of time you have before the colors change again.

One day, the quilt wakes up and discovers that it is not only a thread, it is all threads. Not just moving through a color but is the color. Not just one color, all of them. The quilt is now wholly quilt-alive.

J: In biological terms, this sounds like each cell, each organ, of the body is at that moment self-aware, not just what we call the self or even the soul, but everything. Or—I shouldn't say *self-aware*—aware as oneness. All organs are oneness awake.

MV: Let's stick with the quilt. Talking about the human body gets tricky. Let's keep it simple. You are a quilt. You spent your whole life believing you were a thread on a quilt. Now you realize you're the totality. Not just intellectually realize it, that perspective is now you. Not just feel it as a joyous reassurance that you're interconnected with all fabric —it's you. And so you see that what you thought was life unfolding through time is a limited perspective within you. You are always happening right now, which means the fades in color gradations are actually fully realized colors, not a progression of color changes through time.

So, we are saying that experiencing life as a thread who is living in the quilt you're weaving through, the gradient nature of the colors come upon you and you pass through them. And that is time. But when you step out and see the whole tapestry from above, you see there is no color manifesting and revealing itself to threads as the threads go along—the whole quilt exists and gradation is a property of the colors. That is timelessness—that is the now.

Again, this is hard to explain to the thread who is unconscious of the larger perspective. Colors look like they are growing brighter and dimmer as you travel a path to and fro, when you believe you are a separate entity who happens to live on the quilt.

J: Okay, got it. The colors already exist in all states of themselves. The thread is going nowhere. The act of weaving, which is like traveling and discovering the new, is an illusion because the quilt is already made.

MV: Now, let's change those colors to archetypes. From your perspective within time, there is an evolution from animal to human. Adjacent to that, humans seem to be creating this collective unconscious mind, and within that, archetypes.

Archetypes are you but not you. They are the personas you drift in and out of and can be read as characters in morality plays, myths, and so forth—but they also seem to have a life of their own. There's something peculiar about, for instance, the Trickster. Trickster is no petty symbol for mischief and mystery that you may experience anywhere in the world merely because it is a universal story about a trait of the human character—no. To enter the field of Trickster is to have your life actually go haywire, right?

J: Yes!

MV: And so here you are trying to figure it out. Is Trickster a life form? Does it live symbiotically with you?

Or are you fantasy prone? Are you going crazy and reading into things that aren't there?

But in oneness, these are not questions. Archetypes are thought forms. They are formless awarenesses, hyper-focused personas, which, in you, would be as keys on the piano of your person.

J: The way you explain archetypes brings to mind a conscious fog bank of ideas that express a single feeling we waft in and out of through mood swings and pressures in life.

MV: I was going for a color on a quilt, but what you suggest is also a valid way to visualize it, if you can picture those ideas as landscapes, feelings, and choices. Ideas become landscapes when you consciously commune with the archetype in a visionary way. They remain feelings and choices when you unconsciously identify as the persona.

J: But Trickster seems different.

MV: Trickster would.

J: Well, true. But why? Trickster phenomena happens at you. If I enter the sphere of the Sage archetype, for example, I behave accordingly, as I try to figure out the world, but the world isn't coming alive around me and attacking me with a smirk. Trickster seems to be an entity who actively throws roadblocks at us, lies, and is ultimately corrosive if we're not paying attention. Am I wrong?

MV: Earlier in this book, you wrote that in one's refusal to transcend and include the rational one gives life to Trickster. This is an aspect of what happens, but the bigger issue is not one of rationality, per se. The bigger issue is one of shallows and depth. To that end, your favorite psychologist, Carl Jung, came to understand through firsthand experience in the underworld that people have two distinct personas: one who is surface and of the modern times and one who is much deeper and connected with death.

J: It's the difference between Justin Bieber and The Doors.

MV: (*a beat*) Thank you for your contribution.

J: (*laughs*) Oh, now he has a sense of humor.

MV: If I may, let's finish this.

J: Please.

MV: You experience yourself as a shallow person and a deep person. When you experience yourself mainly as a shallow person—a category that includes intellectuals, not just yesterday's pop singers—and you come upon the depths, you give great resistance to being the deep person. Why? What does it mean to be shallow and deep?

J: Shallow is surface, like you're saying. Some people equate that with being artificial, but I don't think they are synonymous. I mean, they can be. But shallow—if I have to put a fine point on it—I think to be shallow is to overly identify with the obvious. And then you keep hiding the depths of yourself from yourself. The more you do that, the more fearful you become of your own buried nature.

MV: True. Now let's put a microscope to it. Simply put, depth is the universe's death realm. Repressing what you fear, burying it, forms the ground between you and death. It is the dirt you must dig through to reach the underworld.

The shallow self has to recede to engage with death. This is not the total annihilation of self, yet it is what most mean when they refer to ego death. They mean the shallow self relinquishing control to deep self. This is what happens in a flash with all hallucinogens, which is why anyone who clings to their shallow self when tripping experiences fear. When they give up and go with the flow, they have a much better trip.

J: But then why are deep people also often deeply flawed people if they had to unpack their fears and psycho-baggage to achieve said depth? Shouldn't they be over themselves?

MV: Not necessarily, and for reasons you already understand in different contexts: working out one's fears and personal issues creates a strong self, a deep self, one that may travel into death. This is not the annihilation of self but the reformation of self. The death realm of the universe, the human underworld—these are the interiority of the universal self and therefore the personal self, which exists within the universal self. They are active. They are imaginal. They are not, in other words, nothingness.

J: Is Jung right that our two personas cannot ever merge into one?

MV: No. He was right that *you* cannot merge them. You may only delude yourself into having done so. Jung never experienced total dissolution of self, but he was a master of relaxing the shallow so that the depths may rise. He experienced the ancientness of death, which has a timeless feel but is not timelessness. He carved a path through the realms of archetypes in the underworld on his hero's journey. He remained a hero, a strong self, throughout his life. A strong self in a weak world, which tortured him to his final day.

J: What do you mean by *ancientness of death*? What's ancient and what's timeless?

MV: The universe is intelligence. We've said that and we see it. The contents of the universe are intelligence. We've said *that* and we see it. From within the universe—within time—the experiencing of these contents is the experiencing of intelligences. Some are physical, what you call the living world, the material world, and some are nonphysical, what you call the land of the dead, or the underworld.

From the point of view transcending and including the universe, all is happening right now. There is no time, only aliveness. However, from within the universe, within time, you experience nonphysical intelligences and states as if they are ancient and perhaps eternal. Within time, you see formless forces giving rise to form. You inherently know through feeling that archetypes are ancient—far older than humanity. And yet they are given rise by humanity.

How is it possible that entities and dreamscapes arising from your species and residing in you are far older than your species?

You rarely ask that. It feels like a glitch in the system. It's not. The answer is that time is a perspective held from within the universe. The answer is that all is happening concurrently, right now. *Ancient* and *new* are conceptual fabrics on the tapestry of now.

J: But as we experience them it seems as though we draw from the depths to create the shallows. For instance, we collapse wisdom of the depths into trite yet effective words to live by. The grandness of archetypal personas filter into dull, routine behaviors. What do archetypes get out of engaging with us?

MV: The time-bound answer is that they reap the benefit of your senses and imagination. They create the architecture of your personality and you create the landscape in which they reside. Because you exist in relation to one another, you make them comprehensible as beings in a place, give visionary form to their formlessness.

The timeless answer is that neither of you are selfishly gaining anything. The circuit between people and archetypes is an ever-present flow. You give each other life and you are each other's lives.

J: Yeah, but Trickster seems to selfishly screw with us.

MV: Trickster is the one who screws with you during betwixt and between moments. Trickster resides in you betwixt and between the shallow and deep personae. What, exactly, is the nature of Trickster's activity? It's to call reality as you know it into question for long enough to remind the shallow self that it needs to relinquish control to engage the depths.

J: So, Trickster is like that asshole who claps his hands in your face to startle you out of your daydream.

MV: Trickster alerts you to the necessity of changing the guard internally, so to speak.

J: —Of applying the shallow persona or the deep. Trickster tells us we're applying the wrong frame of mind in a situation by making us look the fool. It's like learning through anxiety and frustration, which is why ufology is so damned frustrating—because we never learn! Or, at least, too many in the field have a difficult time treating the subject with the appropriate depth and as a result get picked apart by Trickster.

MV: Yes. This is also why, for example, when you have conversations about the nature of subjects you believe to be deep, when the tone hits a certain depth, the room comes alive. Electronics go haywire. The lights flicker. Something in the next room slams to the ground. Internally, you may feel like you've triggered an echo chamber of déjà vu, or the hair on your arms might stand up and a chill run down your spine—these types of things. The thickness you feel in the room is the energy building as you resist switching over to the person of the depths. And you must resist to remain in conversation, for the person of the depths is a loner.

J: I gotcha; that makes sense. And actually, that makes sense of the sadistic humor, too. There always seems to be that aspect, like there's someone laughing at your expense. Someone familiar but you can't place who.

MV: Think of it like being a belligerent drunk in front of sober friends. They know you're drunk. You kind of remember that you drank too much. But on you go, arguing with them that you're not drunk. They need you to sober up enough to leave the bar. It's time to go. But you resist. You fight it. Maybe you take stumbling swings at one of them and land on your face. They laugh and try to break your fall.

J: Ho-ly shit, that's *exactly* what this is! I've never heard it put that way before!

MV: It's yours free of charge.

J: Well... not for the reader, but thanks.

One thing I'm stuck on is how the universe incorporates the timeless into time. Like, what's the actual... I dunno... mechanical explanation for that?

MV: Hearken back to your immediate reaction to your *I Am* experience. What did you do? You jumped out of bed and jotted it down. You called your father to retell it. And you have been dissecting it ever since.

You speak it; you speak about it. You solidify the oneness of it and then smash it to pieces. Each piece now has its own meaning, its own set of intricacies to examine. Anyone who listens, anyone who reads, engages those pieces. They do not experience the whole, which is timelessness. They engage and sometimes get caught up in the stories. The stories are time. And sometimes Trickster imbues these stories with life, which is to say makes them a gateway to a larger ecology of formless awarenesses.

J: How does Trickster choose?

MV: The reader chooses by allowing his or her

consciousness to be expanded by the material they are reading. Trickster behaves as an extension of the person. When you authentically ask and are ready for such a change —for growth—which means you're asking both consciously and unconsciously—Trickster surges up from the depths.

And you will grow. Or collapse. Either way, you are still divided inside. You're still conscious and unconscious. You're evolving, or falling only to evolve again in some other way. You're moving, in other words. You are not stillness. You are not No-Thing-self awareness. You're not timeless but a chapter in someone else's story, which is becoming your own book. And because it feels new and leads somewhere, you think you're getting somewhere with this transcendence business.

What you are is an animal free-roaming on the farm. Better than a barn, which is better than a cage. But it isn't total freedom, is it?

J: You know what *trickstery* thing in ufology really gets old fast? The constant drum that something big is around the corner. The feeling that this alien abduction stuff means something when it doesn't. I mean societally. Grand-scale. It obviously means something to experiencers, but is there going to be a mass landing?

No.

Is there even going to be a great cataclysm for which I, myself, have moved to Hawaii to act out a special role?

I doubt it.[18]

It's like there's this clandestine, intelligent presence that acts as a motivational factor for our species under the false pretense that it is going to expose its reality to the public in a big, undeniable, materialistic way. We cannot tell if aliens are a cosmic U.N. or cosmic saviors—but aliens are here. And they'll be making themselves known to all soon. Very soon. When the time is right. When it's important to do so.

And it's bullshit, so what is it they're doing? Guiding our actions with false promises? Motivating us to act like our lives depend on it?

What's the fucking point, dude?

MV: Don't your lives depend on the way you act?

J: Well, yeah! But they do either way! I mean environmentally, there's going to be what for us is a disaster. What for every other species is probably a relief. But that's an inevitable consequence of our actions. I don't need aliens or ayahuasca to tell me that.

MV: You live in duality. You live in the brain, as you say. You live a separate-self sense that runs so deeply, you still think you can take time to plot your course. You've already plotted your course and you're sailing to the edge of the flat

---

[18] I don't think the COVID-19 pandemic counts. I suspect it's a harbinger of something far more drastic to come. In other words, I do now lean toward the dolphin dream having relayed accurate info and I'm playing my part in what's to come. But who wants to write that in an uplifting, feel-good book such as this? Not I, fly. Let's stick with doubt.

Earth. You're thinking about turning the ship around, or not, unsure, maybe will, maybe won't, while at the same time realizing Earth is not flat, but really not understanding those implications. Really not understanding any of it because you refuse to look at yourself as the fundamental element in your life to understand first and foremost. Understand you and everything worth understanding follows.

This life you are living is the consequence of that one denial.

J: It's the butterfly effect.

MV: It's the not chewing out of your cocoon to be the butterfly effect.

J: We're not even flapping our wings. We're wingless!

MV: You're feckless. Now, this is the world you create and inhabit, so you're the one living a lie and therefore living in reaction to that lie. Reaction, because first and foremost you sustain how you are living through conscious and unconscious defensive posturing. Anyone who needs to speak truth to you for you to act, not react, must pierce you—you who are this deeply-engrained defense structure. Piercing you triggers your deep terror of annihilation. If you really think about it, you'll see that gloom and doom prophecies are not what terrify you. Alien boogeymen are not what terrify you. What terrifies you is the existence of this intelligence in your life at all because its mere presence instantly calls out the lie that you are—the defense against fear of annihilation that your entire life has secretly been about. They murder you when they come, tear you down when they come. Remind you that who you are, this center of the world you believe yourself to be, is nothing more than a hardened shell suffocating the truth within. They are that truth and so are you and that is who they need to speak with.

As you know, this terror is not your fault. The body is alive and it wants to remain alive. The body is self-aware and wrongly equates that self with its own aliveness. It wants that self to live, not die to the transformative moment, because it doesn't understand that the moment is transformative.

The body is so cunning it will say, "I understand what you're saying. There's this moment of death, which is a transformative moment, and I am afraid of it, so I avoid it by living a life of avoidance and being in complete denial of that. I get it." It says that, it gets it intellectually, maybe feels a bit of grief—feels sorry for itself—all to avoid dying to the fact. Then it seeks to act on this knowledge by reading books on mysticism, spirituality, religion, occult, maybe doing a shamanic retreat. Anything to avoid its death of self-sense.

It will accumulate knowledge and experiences and immerse itself in false egoic death scenarios where there is still a person witnessing it. And then build itself up, strengthen, embolden the sense of self and in so doing say, "I have died an egoic death and now I am more powerful than ever."

This is what you do. This is who you are.

You are duality. And in your duality, brain people fancy themselves individuals who can act on their own through free will and self-determination. It's all so very silly and yet here you are. And you call that the pinnacle of evolution despite being surrounded by heart people who don't have to pretend they are the discoverers of new frontiers of consciousness, like adolescents, because they never abandoned the adulthood of their interconnecting nature for pretending they were alone in this world. They are not playing at being super heroes and yet you idolize them as if they have super powers. They have all that you disconnected from to be you and now you want to be them, too.

Too.

You want to add them onto you. You want interconnection, heart, to conform to the standards of the disconnected brain. You want to scream like a baby in his terrible twos because the adults in the room aren't taking your identity as seriously as you take your own identity as the center of the world.

And now, here you are. Just like all of that. And an intelligence needs to speak with you. But not *that* version of you. Again, not the unhealthy, dysfunctional fake individual chugging along on will power, thinking therefore he is. No, not *that* person—the one buried underneath. The one not building up a character in time, but timelessly being the case. That person lives in the now.

How does one speak to the aspect of you living in the now

who is being smothered and muffled by the self of time?

By shutting up that self of time. And one only does so by bringing your body's focus into the now.

J: You're saying beings living in the now catalyze us with fear and bring all of our senses sharply awake. That makes sense. They bring us to a hyper alert state of attention.

MV: They make mentally ill people lucid long enough to receive healthy instructions that they may act on, consciously or not, when they fall back into their fog of self absorption. And they don't just use fear, they also use urgency. You won't act quickly in a way that breaks up your routine if you have no sense of urgency about it—which is why you wrote a book called *Urgency.*, yes? The word implies a choiceless need for action right now. So you should be familiar with this.

J: Right, but I didn't lie about anything to instill urgency in readers. I didn't put on an alien mask and go, "Boogety boogety boo!"

MV: You're still focusing on the wrong aspect of the interaction with this intelligence. You're like an unlit match that needs to be fire complaining about the ways in which matches are struck. It doesn't matter how they are struck, what matters is that they become fire. And only fire may understand this. The unlit match cannot.

J: But we're struck again and again. We don't just become fire and stay fire. We become fire over and over.

MV: Because you refuse to be fire forever. You put yourselves out. The match wants to remain unlit. It wants to stay that rigid structure, yet life requires that you be fire. Until you actually be fire on your own, outside forces will keep striking you, creating sparks, flames that blow out quickly. They'll take what they can get if it means you doing what you need to do to survive.

Imagine a global pandemic of cancerous, mentally ill people doing everything in their power to gluttonously and psychopathically destroy everything around them—everything they need to survive. Billions of unapologetically homicidal/ suicidal people. And imagine that there are other healthy people who want to help, even though part of the sickness is that the afflicted want to cannibalize the healthy people.

You do this with heart peoples who extend a familial hand despite your torturing and exterminating them. You do this with so-called aliens. *You* do this. This is who you are.

The healthy people want to help because they know you are one being manifesting as separate people. And a part of you knows this, too, it's just that you're ill and so your expressions of oneness are corrupt.

And so one wakes oneself up whether one lives in a forest on Earth, the cheese of the moon, or in another configuration of dimensions. You don't do it by speaking the sick people's mentally ill language. You do it by snapping them to lucidity. If that means making them feel like prey so their instinct kicks in and their senses rush to the now, so be it.

J: It's true. This is why people living in heart cultures would never be terrorized by aliens.

MV: People in heart cultures would never need to have any tool used on them to force them to act consciously on behalf of life. Their lives *are* conscious actions on behalf of life.

No Fire Burned Him

JEREMY: I've got another question, if we can back up a moment, about archetypes in general, not just Trickster. I get that we're symbiotic with each other, but if we can visit them or commune with them in deep-self mode, are they autonomous? Are they living lives like we are?

MYSTERY VOICE: That which you deny has a life of its own. Just as repressed personal issues dance your conscious self like a marionette, so do repressed transpersonal issues.

Archetypes are transpersonal, symbiotic overminds, which a strong and disciplined self can treat as allies, enemies, or useful programming. You may travel into them, travel with them, see them as separate. You may visit their thought-form realms that are not you, yet both influence and are influenced by you.

J: Is that a yes or a no?

MV: It's a no. What is it a person does as a skilled lucid dreamer, a dream warrior, or a sorcerer who knows how to explore other realms through dreams?

Such people build their character through repetition and then, once stabilized, enter various spheres of influence—

archetypes—filled with spirits, demons, and deities. Isn't that so?

J: I guess. I don't really do that, but—

MV: But many people do. Heart cultures have, in Western terms, made a science of dreamtime and vision quests, both of which entail consciously entering the unconscious. Such provides quite an adventure, but that is not wholeness. One does not adventure in undivided mind, for that would require division.

If you were whole, archetypes would be aspects of you-as-universe whose intentions you would not need to question and whose actions you would not react to. You would not seek them out or flee from them as self-proclaimed heroes on a journey. You would be neither strong and disciplined nor weak and chaotic. All would flow naturally and appropriately. Whatever is real and correct about them would be the case. Unquestioningly the case. Similar to how so many animals don't need to be taught what look like astonishing feats. They live those feats of flight, of strength, of coordination, of instinct. They are living the flow and so there is no question, only right action.

Now, let's further the discussion. Let's ask this: If you were from another configuration of dimensions and you needed to examine this one, how would you go about it?

You could not come here without getting reconfigured within the limitations of these dimensions. As you say about oneness, you cannot take you with you when you go. The self has to die for oneness to be the case in the body. Well, now we're talking about the interdimensional version of that. You cannot take your form with you into another configuration that erases your form, so you must settle for peering into other universes from your own. How do you look?

J: I have a feeling you're going to tell me.

MV: You look by pressing a hand, so to speak, into an archetype and using it like a puppet. This gives you a presence through which you may be a force of influence, even, not just an observer. Once you have peoples' attention, they imagine you. What you look like; what your purpose is. Pardon me for skipping around analogies, but recall the one about being glacial.

J: —No, this is good. I'm beginning to get this.

MV: Okay. So, in the glacier analogy, from your point of view, these other-dimensional beings are fluid and you are solid. You only know a solid world, a world of thought. They are invisible to you as fluid. But they are awake in a way that you're not—which really means they have more freedom—and so they have the ability to use your collective thought forms to their advantage. To put it crudely, they can manually override archetypes.

J: Wait a minute. You said something key there. Our glacial world is thought. You keep saying the physical universe is thought, an idea I've been toying with lately.

MV: Yes, I've been reading along.

J: Ha.

MV: From the physical to the mental, your universe is thought. All gradations of thought. It's beyond an idea, it's what is. The contents of the universe are consciousness existing in various states of itself, and the universe itself is also conscious. You got that right.

J: Maybe let's say that nothingness is pure formless consciousness and that consciousness, in simply being, is being all things. And what you're saying is that all things have their own sense of being, as well.

MV: Yes.

J: So I am me and I am conscious. Then one day I wake up and realize I'm also the universe and I'm, like, hyperconscious. I am all of these individual consciousnesses that comprise the universe, as well as the universe's sense of self.

MV: You are.

J: And you're saying that archetypes run living programs. So the less conscious we are, the more out of control we feel. The more out of control we feel, the more power archetypes hold over us—or the more we play out their programs is probably the better way to put it.

When you're unconscious, the program runs you. When you're conscious, you are in synch with all of the programs like a body being in synch with and as its organs.

MV: That is roughly accurate, yes.

J: So, me waking to universal consciousness and then controlling the archetypes isn't a factor.

MV: No.

J: I don't wake up into universal consciousness and then control the archetypes. I wake up and whatever the right action is in any given situation will happen choicelessly, naturally, and in proper proportion.

MV: That is true when you wake up to Truth. However, if you only wake up to universal consciousness, you may control archetypes.

J: Well, then I'm confused. How many wake ups are there?

MV: How many do you want?

J: How many do I need?

MV: None.

J: Well, I would like there to be only one. I mean, what do I want? That's what I want.

MV: And if there's a you there wanting it, what happens?

J: I wake up into my own desire. It's a self-fulfilling prophesy. Self annihilation plus desire equals self-fulfillment. I get that. But then if there are all these wake ups that happen, how can I ever know if I'm awake?

MV: You'll know when I am dead.

J: Nice.

MV: I know you're frustrated, but let's stay with this. Human beings do not need to wake up. The result of not will eventually be the end of humanity, but that's no reason to try to force yourselves awake because any effort gets in the way.

There is no reaction that takes you to ultimate Being. Ultimate Being is who emerges in the cessation of reaction. Reaction only ceases when one understands this so deeply that its self-evident nature dissolves the reactor. When the reactor is no more, Being is the actor. Not reactor, but the actor.

Now, if you were awake as the universe, ultimately you would still be asleep, still be living in reaction. Reaction to nothingness and to other universes knocking at your door.

You may imagine you'd be something of a superhero, with superpowers and control over all the things that are you. Perhaps you would send Trickster out to do your bidding.

J: *Perhaps*? I totally would!

MV: Not so fast. What is the universe as an entity actually concerned with? Is it that type of control? No. It is concerned with its expansions and contractions. Its breathing. It is being the joy of living. It is delighting in the life found within. The universe is radiant and you are that radiance. All life is. So, your fantasy of becoming a controlling universal self would actually, unbeknownst to you, make you a super villain, not a hero.

J: See, now you're being cute again.

MV: I'm telling you that there is no awake except AWAKE. Nondual consciousness is impersonal. It is untouched by the dichotomy of good and evil. If you come alive as the universe and use it, you are not nondually awake, but are asleep and dreaming of many powers. Awakening to wholeness is very much the all-or-nothing proposition as you've understood it.

J: And backwards, of course. It's actually a nothing-or-all proposition. Because I can be cute, too.

Now, riddle me this, Batman: Are these multi-dimensional versions of me utilizing archetypes appropriately in the way one wholly awake would? Like, do they put them in natural alignment or right order, whatever the term is that applies, and flow with them that way like a universally awakened human would? You get what I'm asking?

MV: No. They are using them to communicate. Remember: you are the universe and so you want to contain the act of awakening within you. Waking up to universal consciousness and then utilizing your own archetypes would be like talking to yourself through a sock puppet. The effect is, you would immediately put yourself back to sleep in duality.

J: Hold the phone! You're saying that the universe at large has the mentality of a New Ager? The universe wants to absorb that which transcends and includes it, not transform into it?

MV: That is not behavior exclusive to people with New Age beliefs.

J: But still, that's what you're saying, right?

MV: Yes. Have you not been listening this entire conversation?

J: Shit! That's a problem!

MV: It's the same problem through and through: you clinging to your own definition so as not to relinquish your sense of identity in death. Your personal psychological tricks of the trade are like tide pools in the shallows of oceans that are the universe's tricks of the trade.

Now, say there were another universe with its own archetypes—its own tricks of the trade. If you were to wake up to universal consciousness and use those to speak to the aspect of you residing in that place, you would remain awake, or nondual, if you like.

J: But ultimately, isn't another me in another dimension a form of duality?

MV: Yes and no. Let's call it transcendental duality. That other person *is* you. If you understand this and they are ignorant of it, you become the waking factor of a sleeping being. Pando tree one is awake. Pando tree two is asleep. Pando tree one cannot move along the ground to wake pando tree two, so she travels into his dream via the root system that is deeply, authentically who they both are. They are this oneness expressing as differences.

J: Okay. We're pando trees and glaciers and quilts and shit. Got it. And now these archetypes... I know you said hallucinogens can't tune us into the multidimensional people, but do they use our archetypes during our drug trips? Do they ever talk to us that way?

MV: No. It would cause too much confusion about who is talking. You would be far less likely to ever understand what was really being communicated and why.

J: Well we're pretty confused as it is!

MV: Right. Why make it worse? Conjoined aspects of you are nudging you to wake into universal wholeness and, after that, initiating you into the multiversal project of waking other conjoined aspects to multidimensional wholeness. They are not interested in talking to you while you believe you are floating through other realities that are actually the interior domains of your universe.

J: No one wants to talk to someone when they're high. Makes sense. It'd be like entering someone's virtual reality game and trying to convince them you're real, not part of the game. We've seen this movie. Its got a cliffhanger ending.

MV: Worse than that because with hallucinogens the game player believes they've already tapped into reality. They believe the trip is everything. The trip is higher consciousness.

It is expanded consciousness, to be sure. And you're there to learn about you, whether you know it or not. You're there to grow, not dissolve. The universe knows what dissolving looks like from people who have done it and may thus replicate it for purposes of growth disguised as ego death.

J: Imitation enlightenment.

MV: It is enlightening. But it isn't transcending and including the universe. Just as nothing in you, the psychological doer, can transcend you, nothing in the universe can transcend the universe. Hence, the need for multidimensional beings who transcend and include your universe to facilitate the big wakeup. The universe has you work on your psychological baggage, engages you on a level of health and healing through natural substances, for example, so that you will be as awake as possible within itself.

Multidimensionals work on the same issues, if need be, but to a greater end. You are not to just wake up within the universe, as the universe, but also wake out of the universe. This difference may be hard to detect but it is the way one may differentiate whether they are dealing with multidimensional intelligence or intelligence within the mind of the universe.

J: Alright. Before I completely lose *my* mind, I'm just gonna steer awkwardly into this.... For something like archetypes, it sounds like there are five ways of experiencing them:

—like gods or entities, which is when they're on autopilot because we're unconscious;

—like a natural extension of ourselves, which is when we're in the flow of Truth—when we're all-caps AWAKE;

—as something we can control when we're kinda/sorta awake, but not fully—like sorcerers would, maybe;

—like deities in realms that we can visit as a shaman or a prophet might;

—and as megaphones, or puppets, of other-dimensional beings who, oh, by the way, are also us.

Is that what we're saying?

MV: That is roughly accurate, although archetypes on their own are more alive than that. To say that they are on autopilot, or a program running when you're unconscious, is to say that they act as guides and guardrails to humans through cultural guises. They are impersonal alivenesses that have very personal meanings in your lives.

J: Then what is the point of archetypes on their own? I mean doesn't the universe want me to wake up to my wholeness?

I am the universe, right? Doesn't big me want little me to become no me and therefore all of me? How can I do that if I believe I am being guided by higher powers? Or fighting them? Doesn't that belief, that reaction to them, keep me asleep to Truth?

MV: The universe as its own entity would love to meld consciousness with you. The universe, per se, isn't the roadblock. The roadblock transcends and includes universe-as-entity. The roadblock is thought.

Thought is what everything is. Thought is in the way. For you, as an observer, you would say that thought is in the way on the macro and micro level—macro being the universe; micro being the individual. But it is thought, through and through.

The problem is that thought does not want to be transcended and included. Thought wants to be informed by Truth, not rendered obsolete as the controlling factor within Truth. The universe wrestles with its fear of annihilation through you. You are an expression of that fear and that wrestling match.

Before, when you asked how many wake ups there are and I asked how many do you want, this is what that was getting to. This is the whole point of you. You, the self, the ego, are thought. You experience yourself as the result of impersonal, formless selves of the collective, archetypes and so forth, informing and giving shape to you, who give life to archetypes. It's that circular. In the now, both are happening simultaneously, but in time you experience the former creating the latter, which energizes and transforms the former. And you will, as you know, do anything to remain as this thought circuit. Again, not only true for the human body, it is also a fact of the universe.

There is a reason you died egoically and came back "the same but different," as you say. Because the body is thought and thought wants to live—wants to be aware as itself. It doesn't care if that self-awareness manifesting as you is falsely autonomous as a brain person or interconnecting and natural in heart, so long as the perceiver is in control. It will keep casting you into the void and reeling you back like a fisherman.

We should add that thought is not an entity who is nefariously manipulating you because it's afraid to die. This is simply what it does. It reacts. Just as you're not consciously calling in troops of antibodies to fight off foreign bodies, bacteria, parasites, and the such invading your organs. Calling them in is simply how the body works.

To thought, health and wholeness mean stability and growth. Go ahead and be bigger and better. Self-improved. A higher self. More powerful. All-natural. Artificial. Good or evil. Ignorant or the greatest intellect. All of that is fine as long as the force of your will remains thought. In fact, feel free to manipulate the universe, to "create your own reality," so to speak. It doesn't matter to thought, for it is all within thought.

As for completely dying to Truth? As long as Truth converts into a body of knowledge, which is thought, go ahead and die to the moment for a moment. What does that awakening become when it's in the past?

J: A story.

MV: For other people who hear it, a story. For the universe, it becomes like the funny pages on Silly Putty—something to work with and warp and absorb. For you, the experiencer, the awakening becomes an explanation. It would never be anything else because the second you come back to normal—back to time—the aliveness of the timeless moment becomes only a feeling stuck on repeat for you to chase, if you decide to long after it. Either way, timeless experience dies within time. It becomes *your* timeless experience, no longer impersonal. The result is that you've helped expand thought by adding to it from outside of itself.

Now, if one may suggest, let us review the *I Am* experience with fresh eyes and all that we've learned here as background.

J: Jesus, schoolmarm much? *I Am*, take three?

MV: If you like.

J: Let's call action!

Heroes Don't Exist

MYSTERY VOICE: Let us start here—

JEREMY: —I'm glad you were able to work Silly Putty into the conversation.

MV: We're not staring there. Let's start here: you are prismatic beings. If we were to break you up in time, we'd say that you live past lives, future lives, and this present life. With some training, or by accident, you may come to know at least some of your other incarnations. Otherwise, you remain unaware of them. Either way, you are not awake as all of them happening right now.

Similarly, you may, through training or by accident, make kundalini energy rise and fall, yet, either way, you are not perpetually kundalini awakened.

Brain-selves utilize ideas in the form of knowledge, things learned, to exert a feeling of control over their fear of the unknown. They also use intuition rooted in past experience.

Heart-selves use intuition rooted in interconnection. They also use knowledge rooted in past experience, though they are far less likely to fumble through the present by clinging to past experience. Their decisions tend to be more fully formed than brain-selves. One could say they feel and think their way through life as one flowing movement, while brain-selves behave in a stilted manner, thinking and then feeling.

JEREMY: Got that.

MV: In kundalini aliveness there is no brain-self thinking or heart-self feeling. Ideas are alive and are now free to express as themselves, not as your interpretation of them. Not as learned acts. Although you may request that kundalini do certain things, like work on your backache, heal your wife's injured thumb, or make rain during a drought, it plays out in whatever ways the body, psyche, and environment require to be healthy, which may or may not include your request. And if you request nothing, kundalini expresses nonetheless.

J: Who determines what's healthy?

MV: Truth determines this. You may think you've diagnosed a problem correctly, but Truth knows the truth, as you may have guessed by Truth's name.

Truth knows all the right moves, when to perform them, and in what order, as one flow. We're breaking it down as if into sequential components, but it's as instantaneous as your personal conscious mind playing out the will of the unconscious. You relinquishing personal conscious mind into Truth is allowing Truth to play all the right notes with the collective unconscious for your body/mind to sing in perfect pitch.

Unawakened people who are educated to much of this are hard to jostle awake because they already believe they're not in the choir, but choir directors.

Unawakened people who don't know about any of this find great astonishment in their waking. Waking to wholeness incrementally feels like becoming someone newer, someone powerful and deeply fulfilled, step by addictive step.

Educated or not—lucid or not—you are still asleep, still dreaming. The lucid dreamer has far greater freedom, has expanded consciousness within the dream, but that is false freedom. It is a trap to keep you sleeping.

J: It's like mastering kindergarten and then being held back for all the rest of your school years. You never leave! You're too good at this!

MV: But you're the one holding you back. No one else. You're doing it. You're doing it because you are this thought bubble called *the universe,* which is full of chatter.

However, you're also part of the multiverse. To self-identify as the multiverse is to burst your bubble, to go silent. As we've talked about, the universe does not want that. The universe wants to exist in solitary confinement. It wants to keep you.

Keep in mind that saying *it* and *you* is saying the same thing. The universe is you, whether you're aware of who you are or not. And what you want is to be the ultimate, to be he who transcends and includes all. You want it all in you. You don't want to be transcended and included in anything. Transcendence is unacceptable to the universe, except as a fleeting bunch of experiences that add to you, add to your body of knowledge.

J: I think we've made that clear.

MV: But the fact is, you already are the one who transcends and includes you. Such a one does not come along and swallow you up. Such a one already is you, for there is no time, no movement towards you, no swallowing. It is already the case out of time, out of the universe. All you can do is break that up into a past or future event and fear it, for you are a projection of the body. You are psychological time. You assume that wholeness is an unknown height you have fallen from or a mountain you dare not climb.

This is all you. Face this. Face yourself as the universe and therefore time. Face the fact that you are thought and thought is limited. The limitless cannot come from you; you must cease for limitlessness to be the case.

J: I dunno. Waking up other me's in other dimensions sounds like a hamster on a wheel scenario, too. How unlimited are we, really?

MV: Wake up and find out. There are other aspects of you to which you must wake to be truly and finally whole. Each of these is their own whole. Each may be explored and questioned. Putting a stop to it with cynicism is your way of keeping this in imagination so that you may judge it invalid and discard it. You've never been multidimensionally awake and you're trying to apply how you feel hearing about it to the unknown experience of being that full awareness.

J: In total ignorance. Just like I chastise others for doing. Okay, great, I'm a hypocrite. At least I'm the ultimate hypocrite.

MV: You name yourself to not abandon yourself, but you must.

J: Why must I? There are a kajillion people who come and go and none of *them* fucking have to! So what if I die unfulfilled? Who gives a shit?

MV: And that again is thought struggling in fear against being transcended and included. Understand this. All of this. Let the weight of the totality sink in. If there is another death, perhaps someone truly universal arises. Someone who sees from all points of view as one vision and sings joyfully, *I Am*, while remaining... curious.

J: Let's leave it at that.

MV: Yes. And now you are ready to write the book you needed to write.

J: What book is that?

MV: The children's book.

J: Are you serious?

MV: Are you angry anymore?

J: No.

MV: You have reconciled the shallows and the depths. That was the source of your anger. You were not mad at the world or the foolishness of ufology. You were sad that you were back in the world at war within itself and that you found yourself again at war within you.

Knowing oneness intellectually isn't enough. Knowing Love from past experience isn't enough. And there is nothing you can do about it. You, who have seen. What hope is there for they who have not and who have no conscious interest? What hope is there for they who have conscious interest but have not seen and so must convince themselves they have, just to carve out some psychological comfort?

J: It's the same old tune: my anger is secretly sadness, a perversion of compassion that I feel but don't live. Life's a pity party and we're all invited.

MV: Miraculously, though, the solution is also the same. When faced with the insurmountable, what action must one take?

J: None. There is no true giving up as a reaction to the insurmountable. All I can do is understand that I haven't got the tools to do anything about it at all.

MV: The challenge is irrelevant if it's insurmountable. It's a false challenge if there's no overcoming it. Seeing this, understanding it beyond the intellect, beyond the shallow self, beyond, even, the depths—because there's no answer to be found there—seeing this so thoroughly that the seeker of answers dissolves is the only understanding that makes room for oneness to be the case.

J: I can't do that by writing a book.

MV: Of course not. At most you can reconcile the shallows and the depths. You cannot dissolve them. You cannot dissolve you. You cannot cause the reader to dissolve. But you can dissolve this book. You can make a symbol of it—an articulation in the form of a visual.

J: Sounds pointless.

MV: If you make it with passion tempered by care, it is something more, something alive for people. Not just alive the way all ideas are, but that which takes root in and blossoms through people.

A symbol is a seed. Yours is one of renewal. Plant it now. The reader now has all the information needed to understand that the ancient is not timelessness and renewal is how time represses timelessness.

Plant it now. Plant it in that soil and see if a mutation occurs on the way from seedling to tree. Not a difference in leaves manifesting, but an entirely different tree coming up.

Plant it now and see who grows.

"Joy In Repetition"

Song created by Prince, a musical icon who had a career-long love/hate rivalry with pop legend Michael Jackson. He died April 21, 2016 of a prescription drug overdose, seven years after Michael Jackson's death by prescription drug overdose.

The Story of Toe

A Love Story for Adult Children

by Jeremy Vaeni

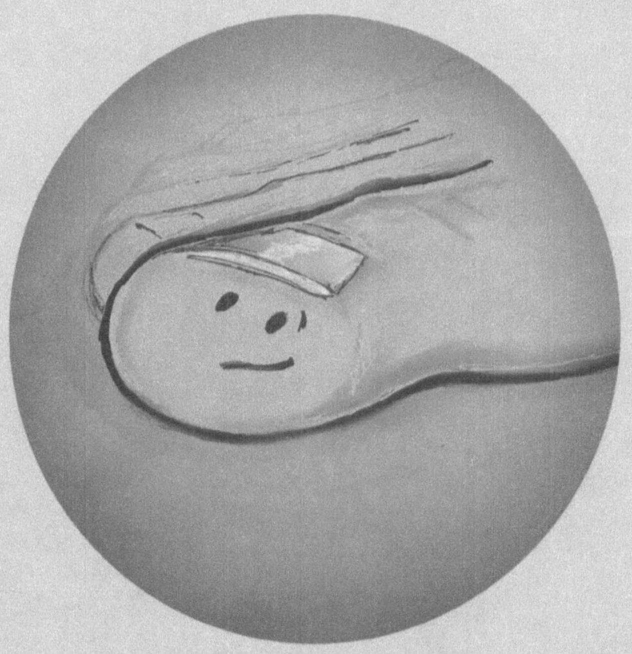

Illustrated by John Randall

This is the story of
Toe.

You may imagine that Toe is a time and a place and a people. Or, you may imagine that Toe is an individual.

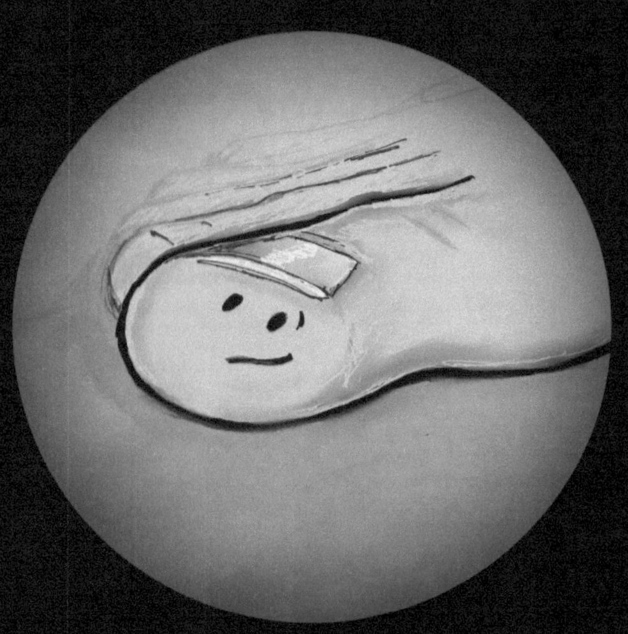

Both are true. Toe is Toe.
And this is how
Toe experiences the world
right now...

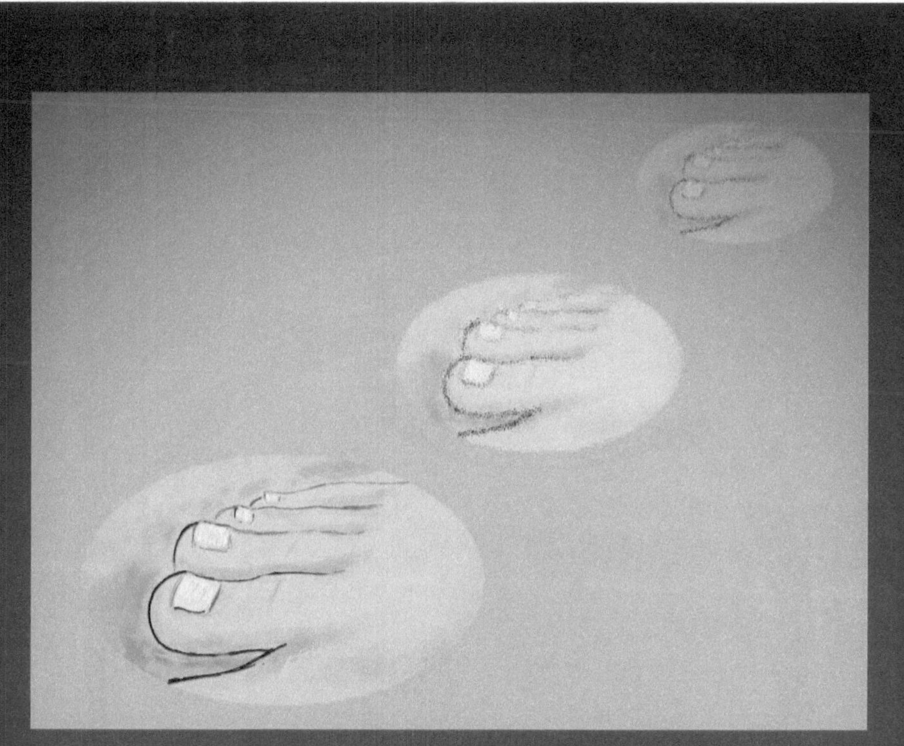

Toe experiences time moving from past to future, as if in a forward motion. When Toe looks to the future, the vision grows dimmer and dimmer, harder to see and predict.

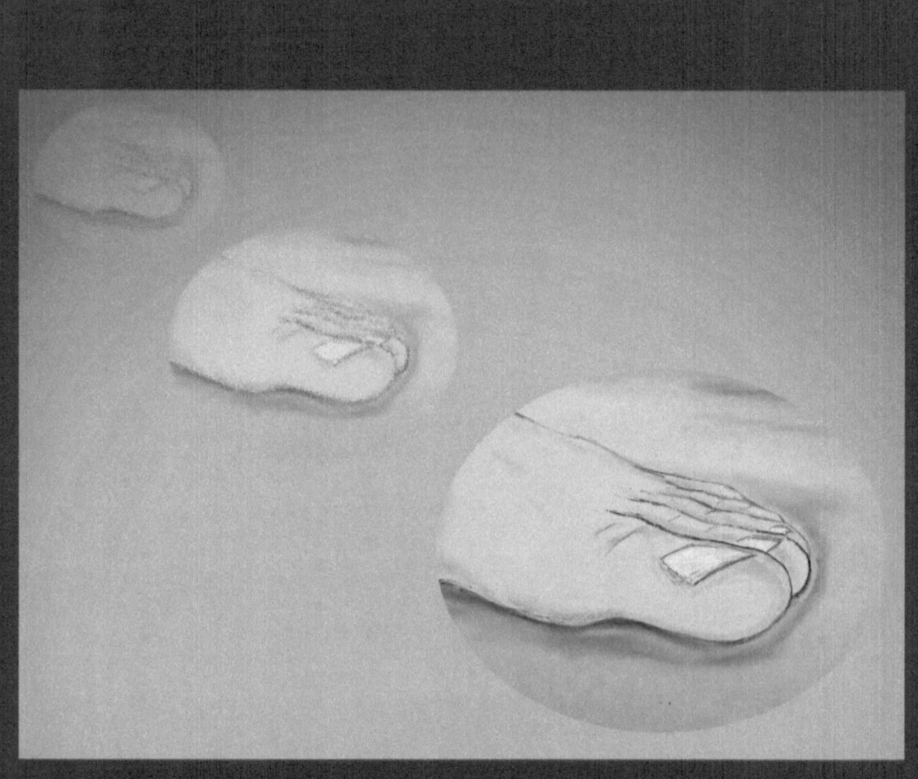

And when Toe looks backward,
the immediate past looms
large in Toe's mind.
However, the further back
Toe looks, the dimmer the
memory--just like looking forward.

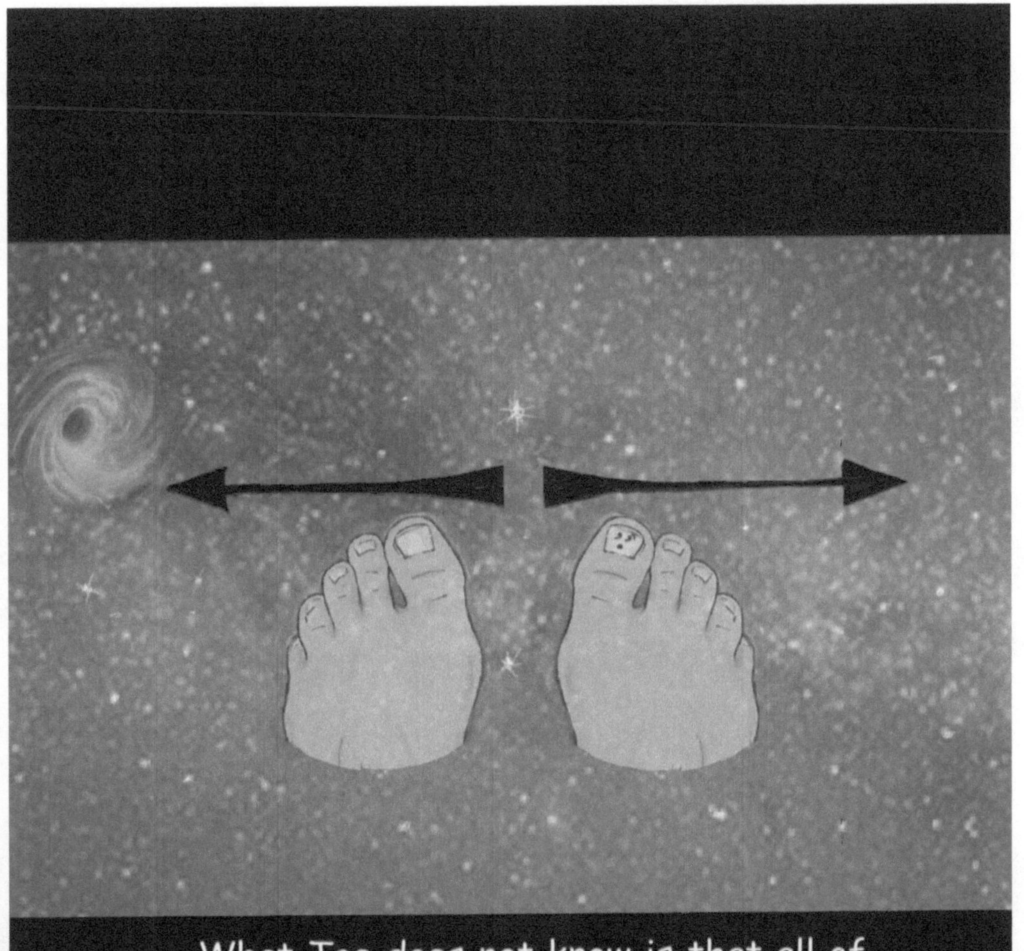

What Toe does not know is that all of the other toes are not shooting through existence like arrows.

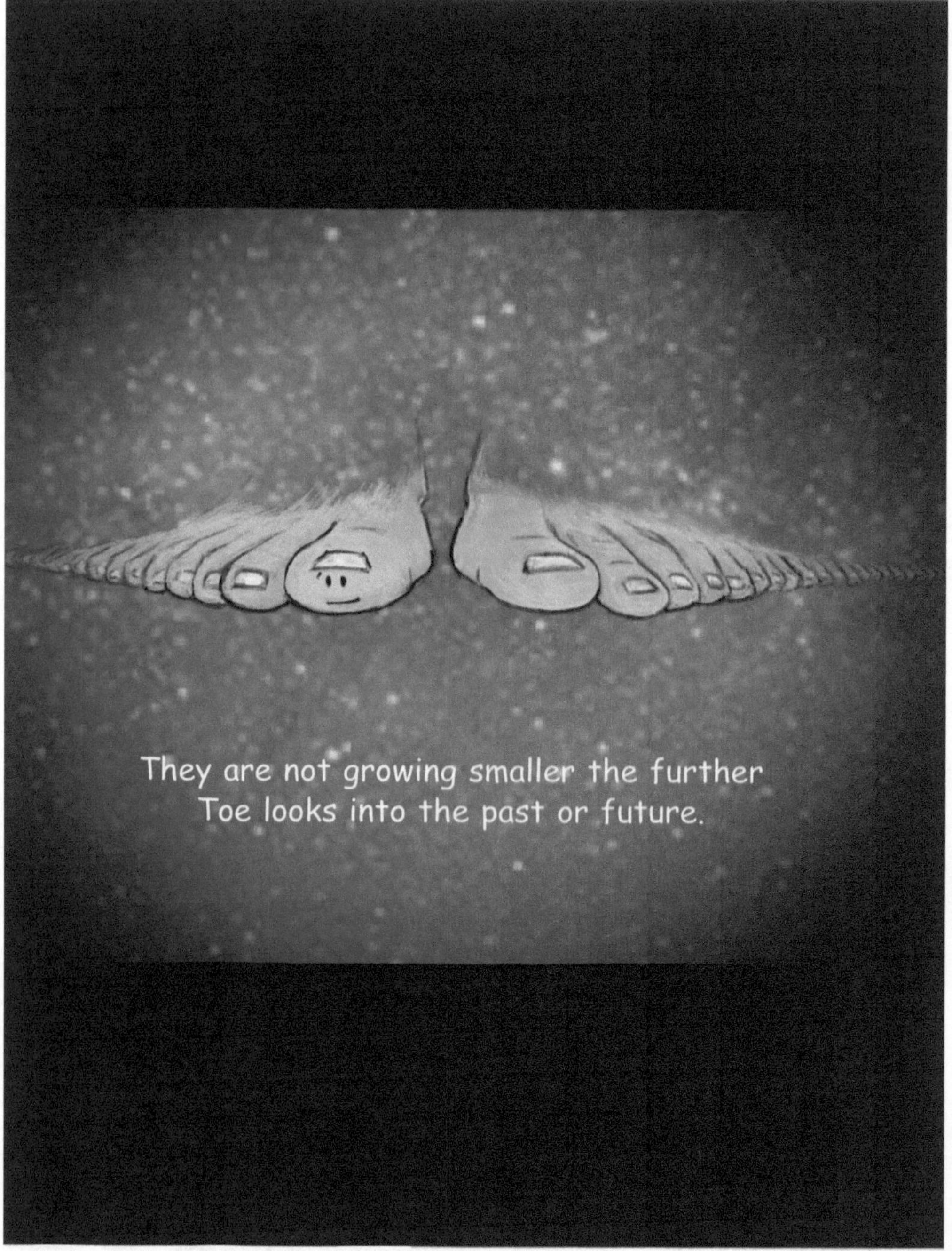
They are not growing smaller the further
Toe looks into the past or future.

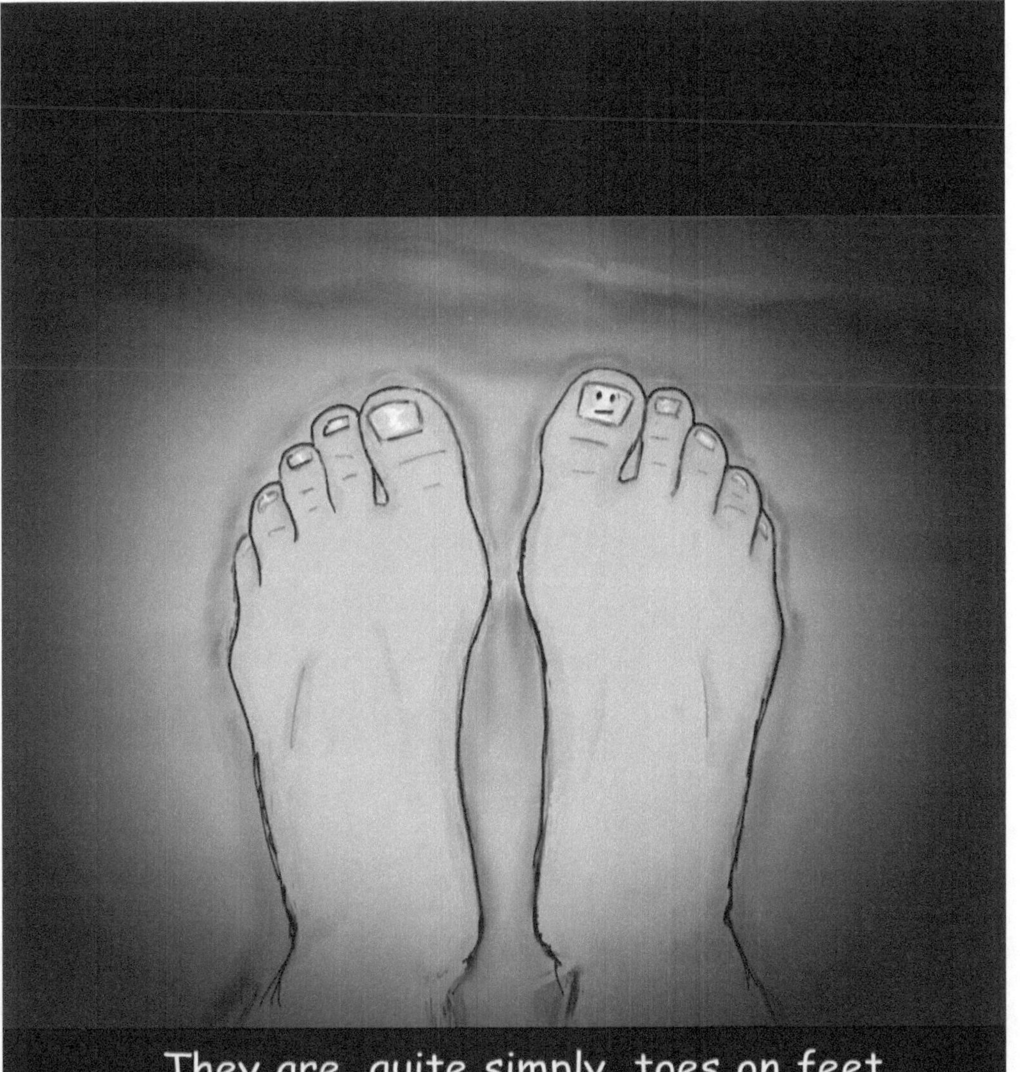

They are, quite simply, toes on feet.
Feet that are invisible to Toe.

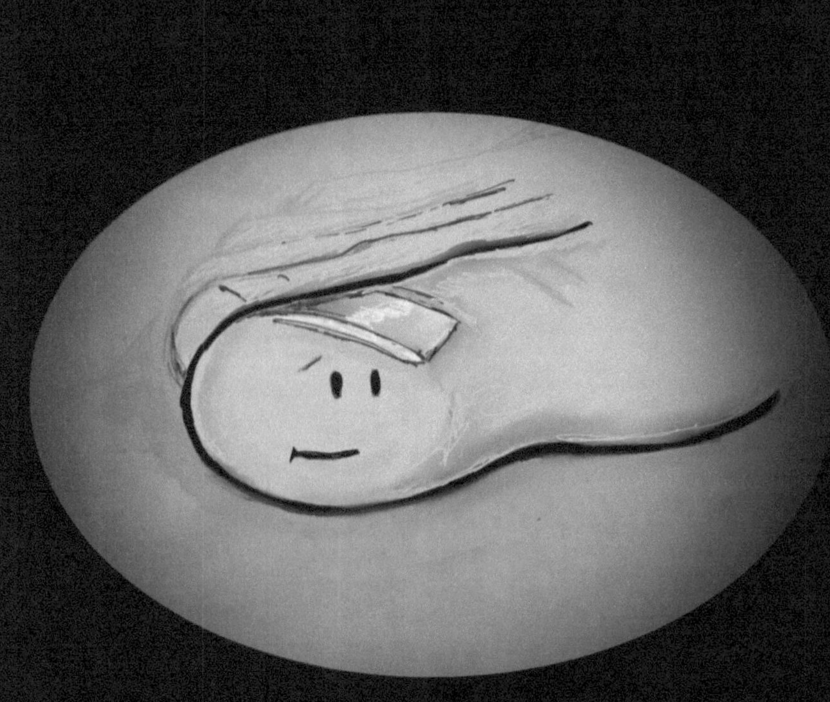

And there Toe is.
Existing.
Just like all other toes.
Part of a great, invisible foot.

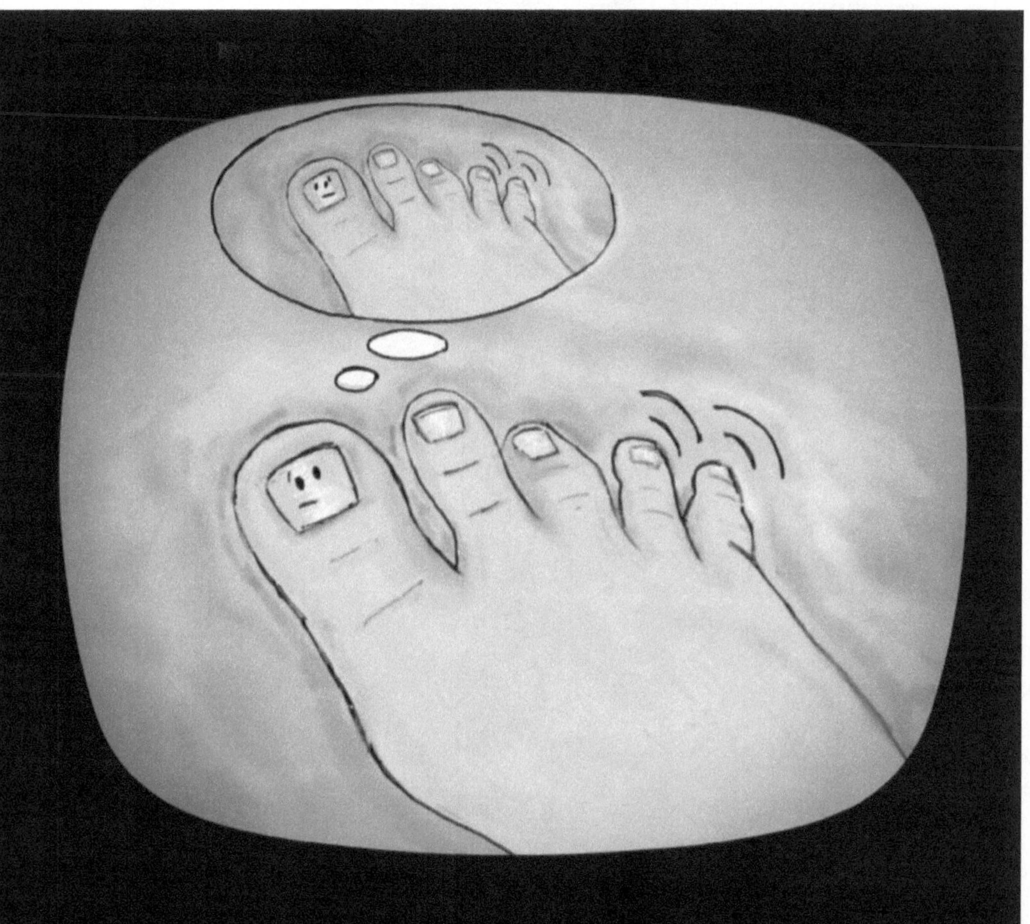

Sometimes other toes on Toe's foot wiggle, which makes Toe wiggle a bit, too. Toe calls this funny feeling, "déjà vu."

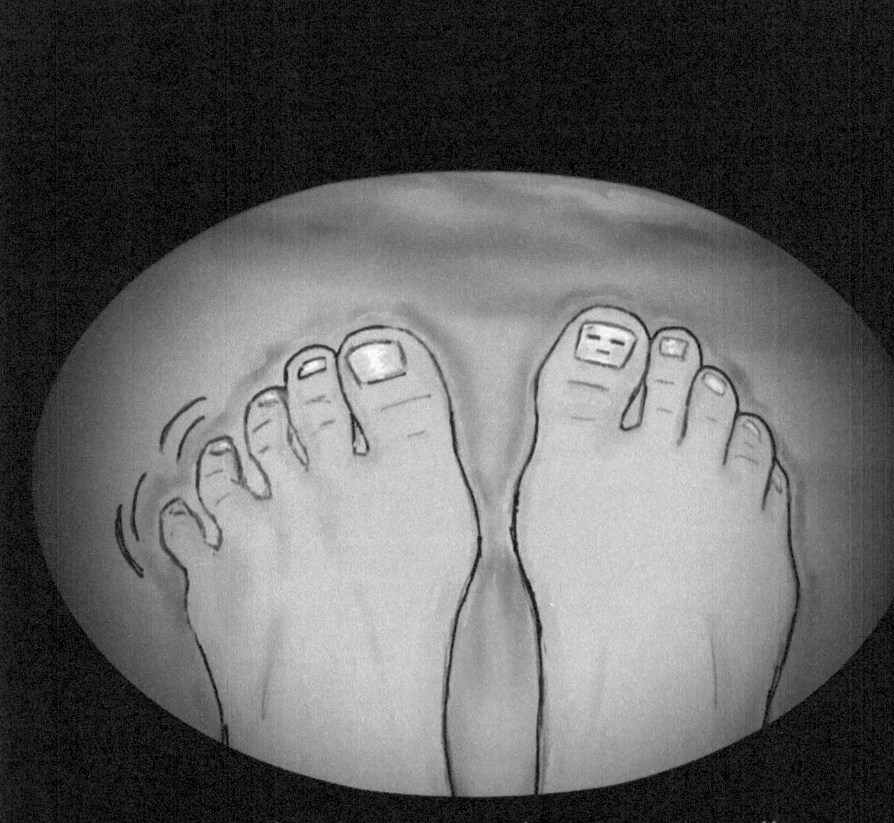

And sometimes, when Toe is still,
Toe can feel other toes on Toe's left
foot wiggling just a little bit.
Toe was taught that these are Toe's past lives.

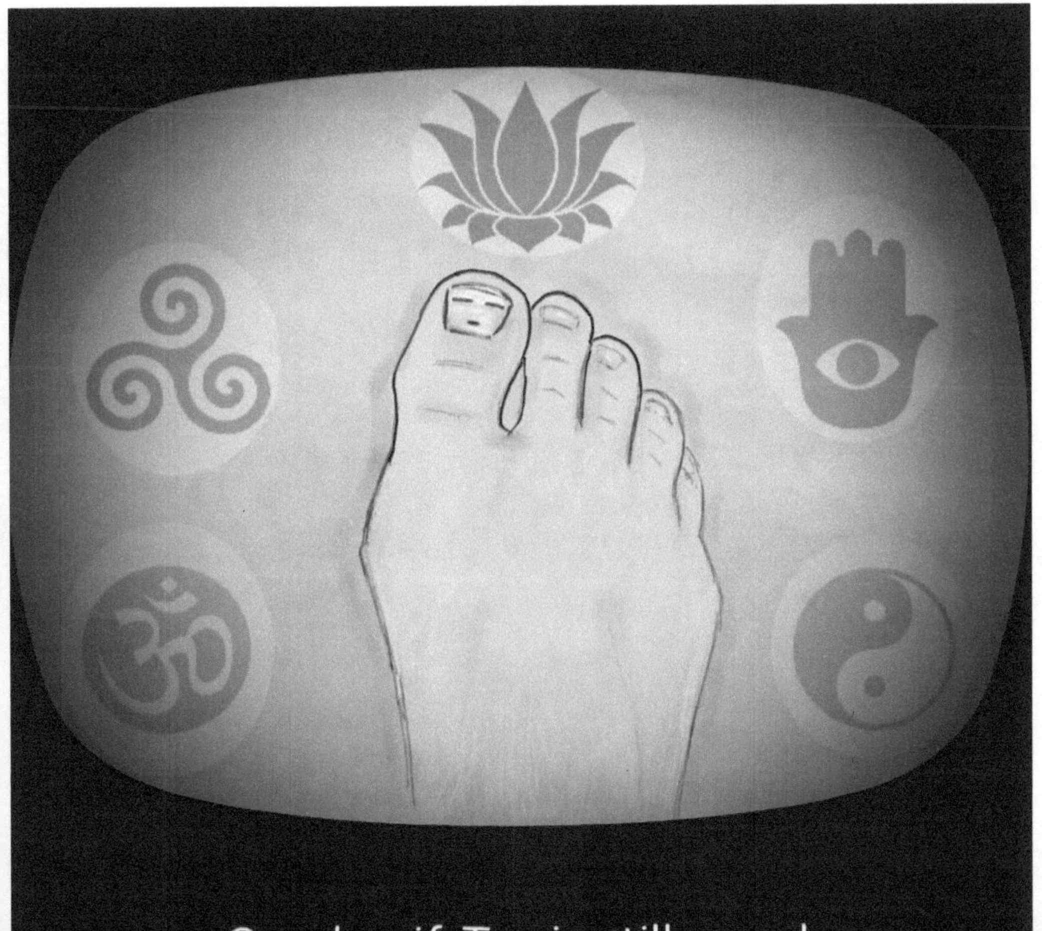

One day, if Toe is still enough,
quiet enough, listening just right,
Toe will perceive the invisible feet
of which all toes are a part and the
truth of the matter will come clear.

Until then, Toe will mistake certain mysteries
in life for Mystery with a capital "M."
That is to say, Toe will mistake the unknown
for the unknowable.
Take, for example, those long, gangly
other toes zipping around in the sky.

What are they?
Who are they?

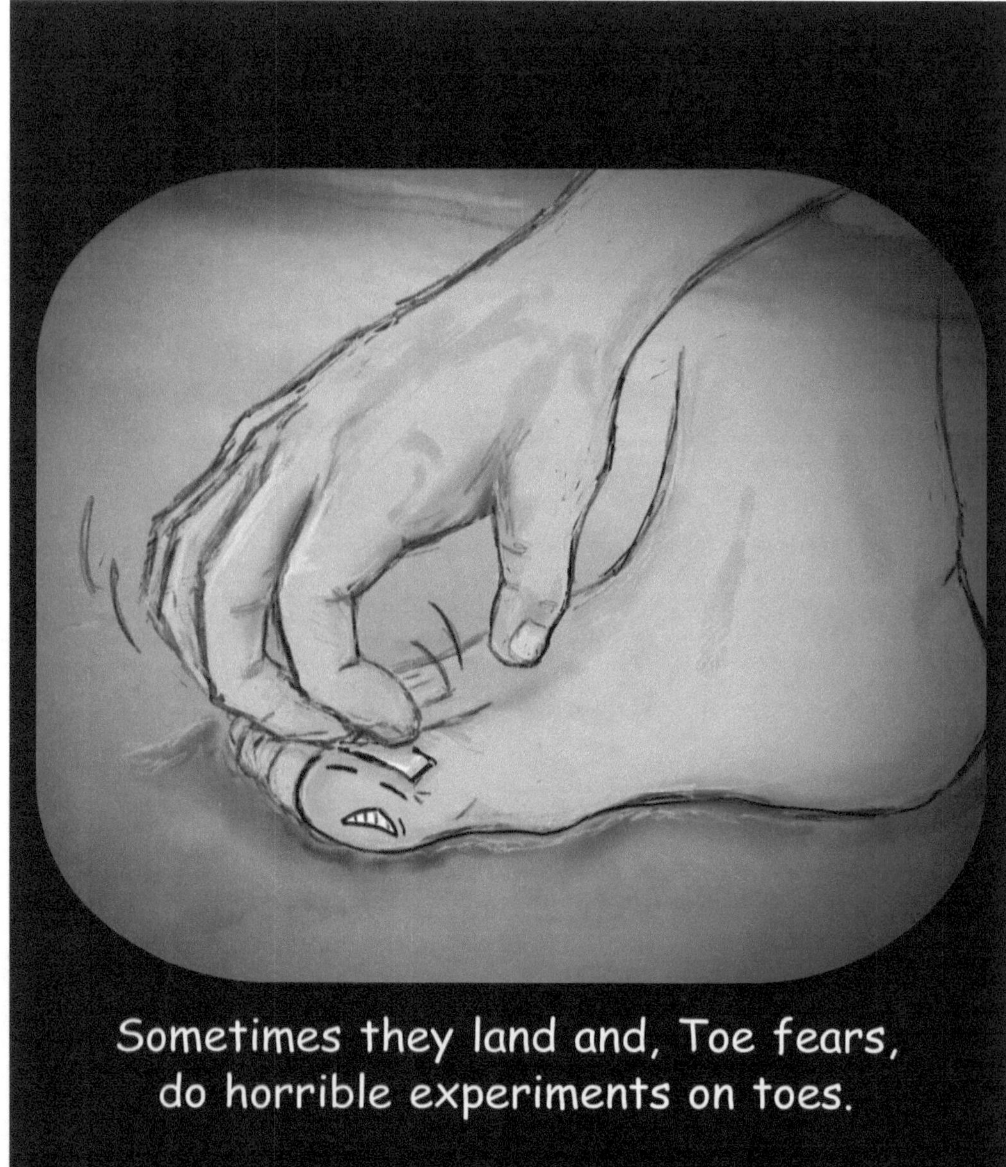
Sometimes they land and, Toe fears,
do horrible experiments on toes.

And they never speak out loud, but sometimes
communicate with Toe as if from within.

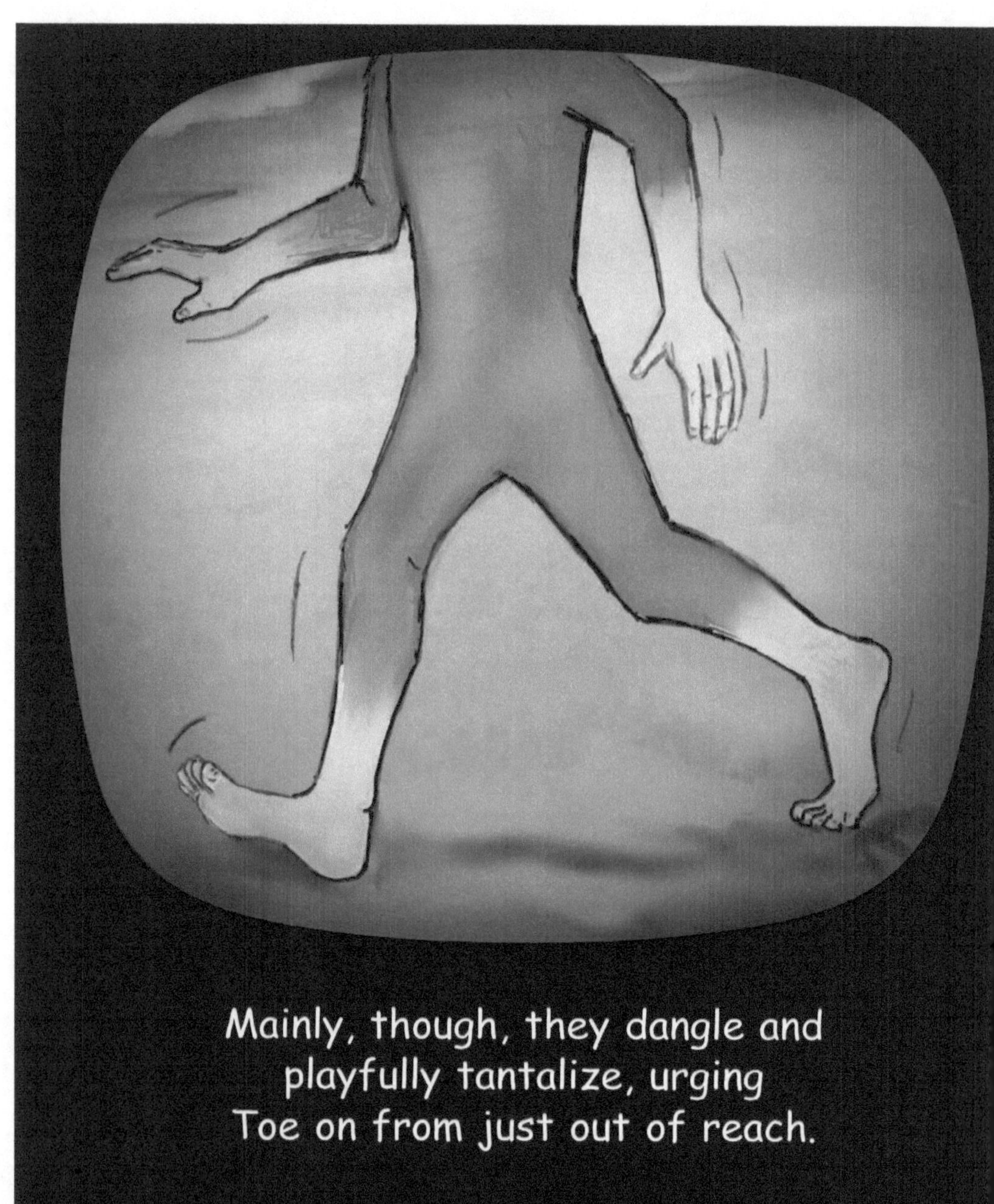
Mainly, though, they dangle and
playfully tantalize, urging
Toe on from just out of reach.

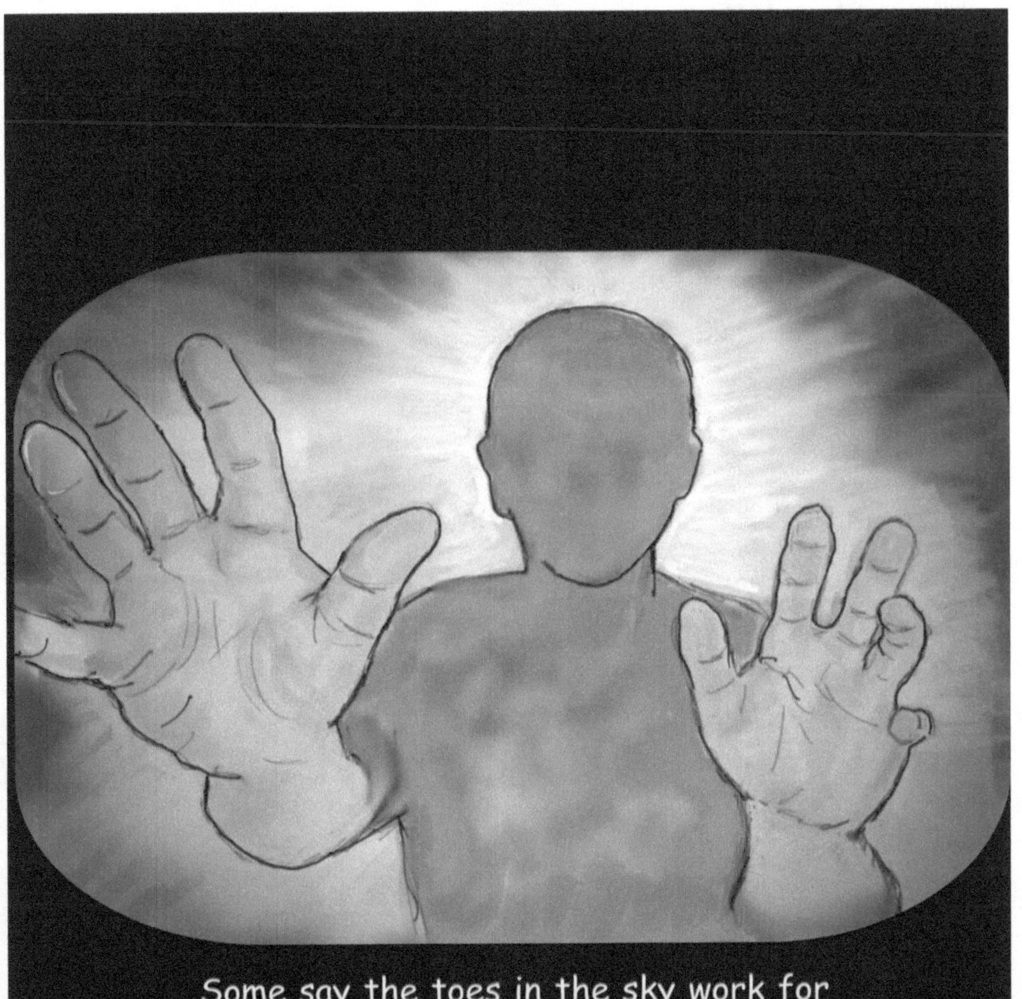

Some say the toes in the sky work for
The Grand Toe Above.

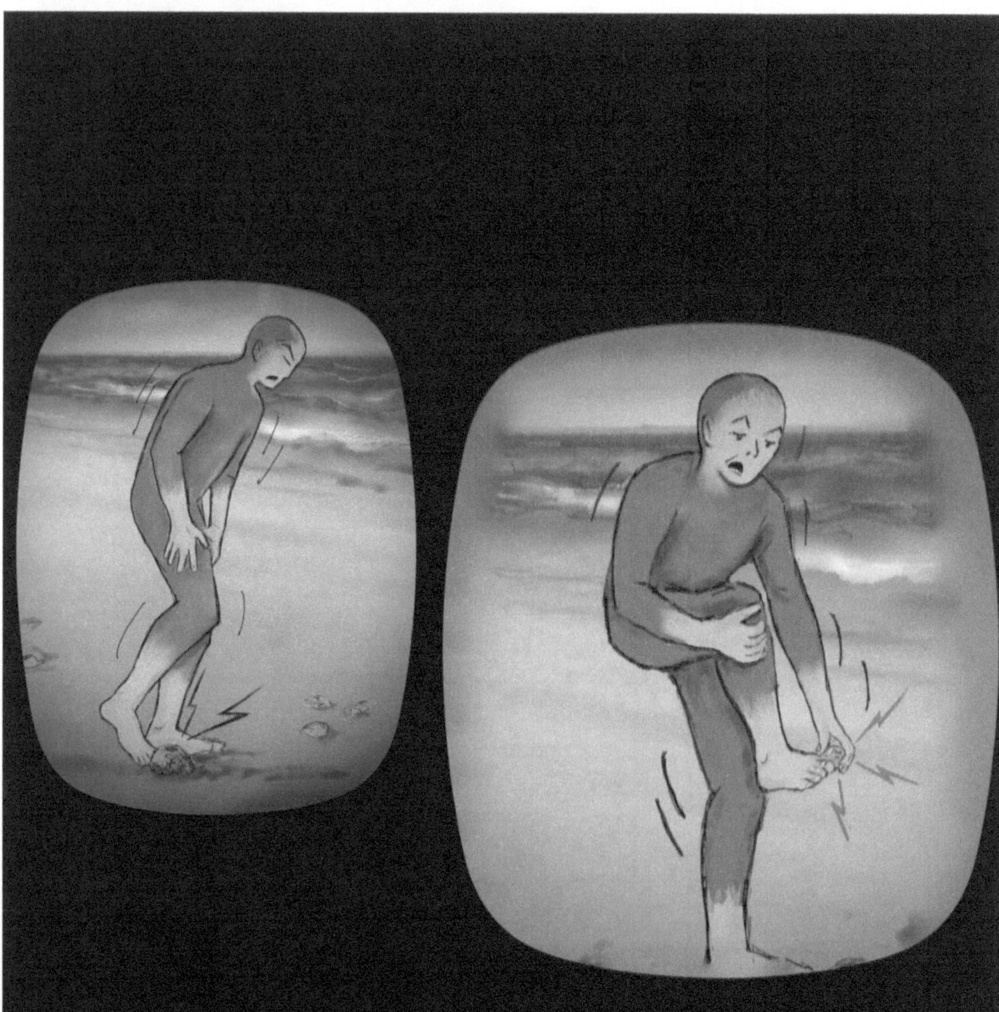

Some believe The Grand Toe Above is angry.

Others believe The Grand Toe Above
is benevolent.

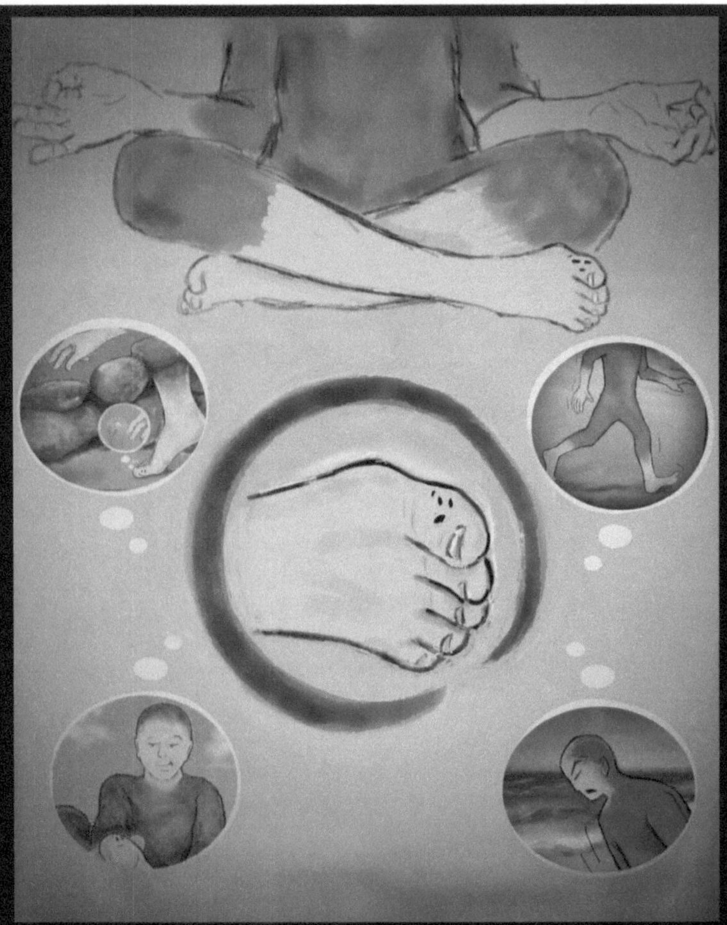

But one day, when Toe is stiller than the stillest stillness, quieter than the quietest quiet--when Toe is silence itself--
Toe will immediately understand that
The Grand Toe Above is a head who wears both of those faces and is an extension of Toe.

And Toe will see that they are working in unison
by the grace of the heart pumping life force
through all that is, for Love is
what excites and moves Toe's body.

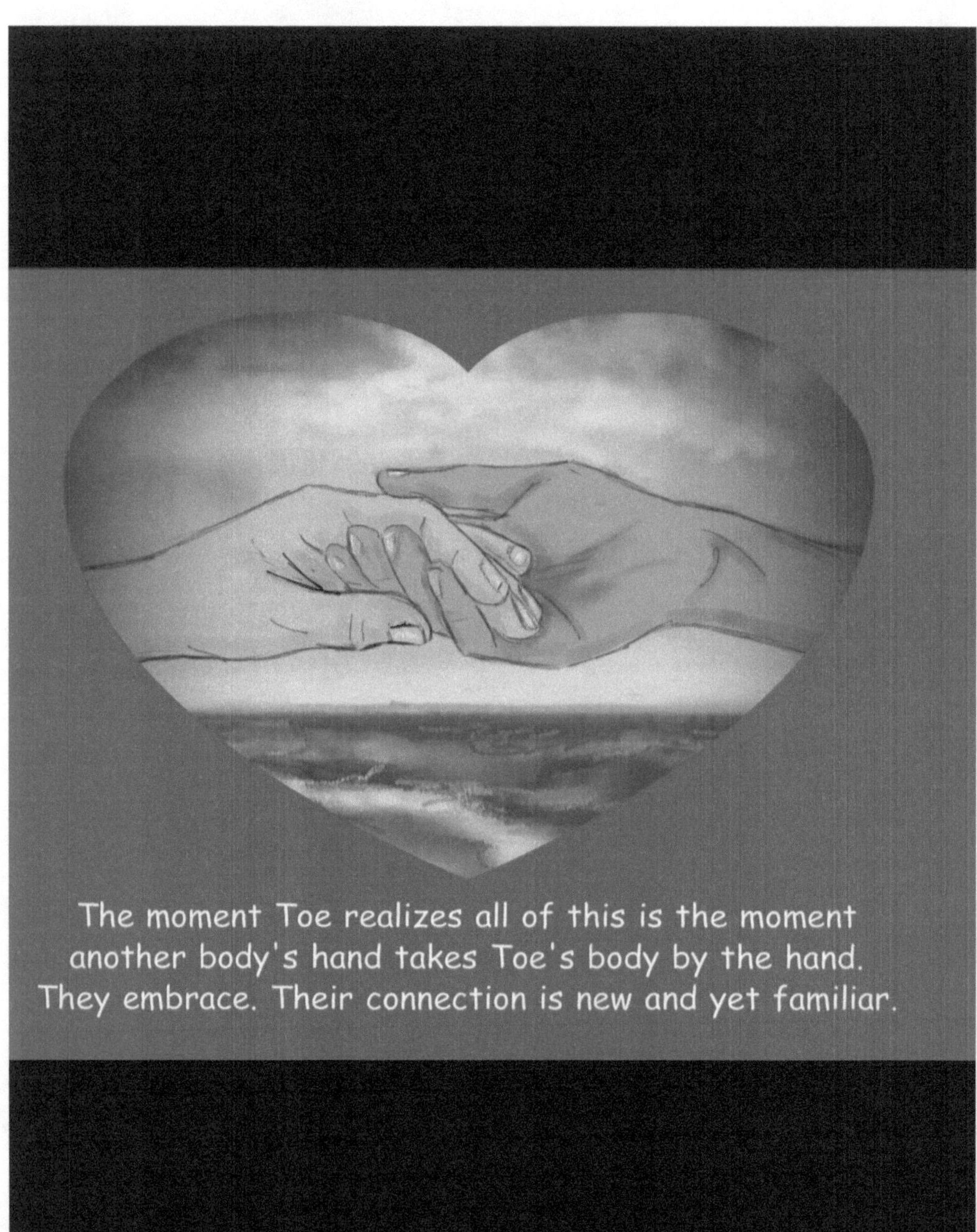
The moment Toe realizes all of this is the moment
another body's hand takes Toe's body by the hand.
They embrace. Their connection is new and yet familiar.

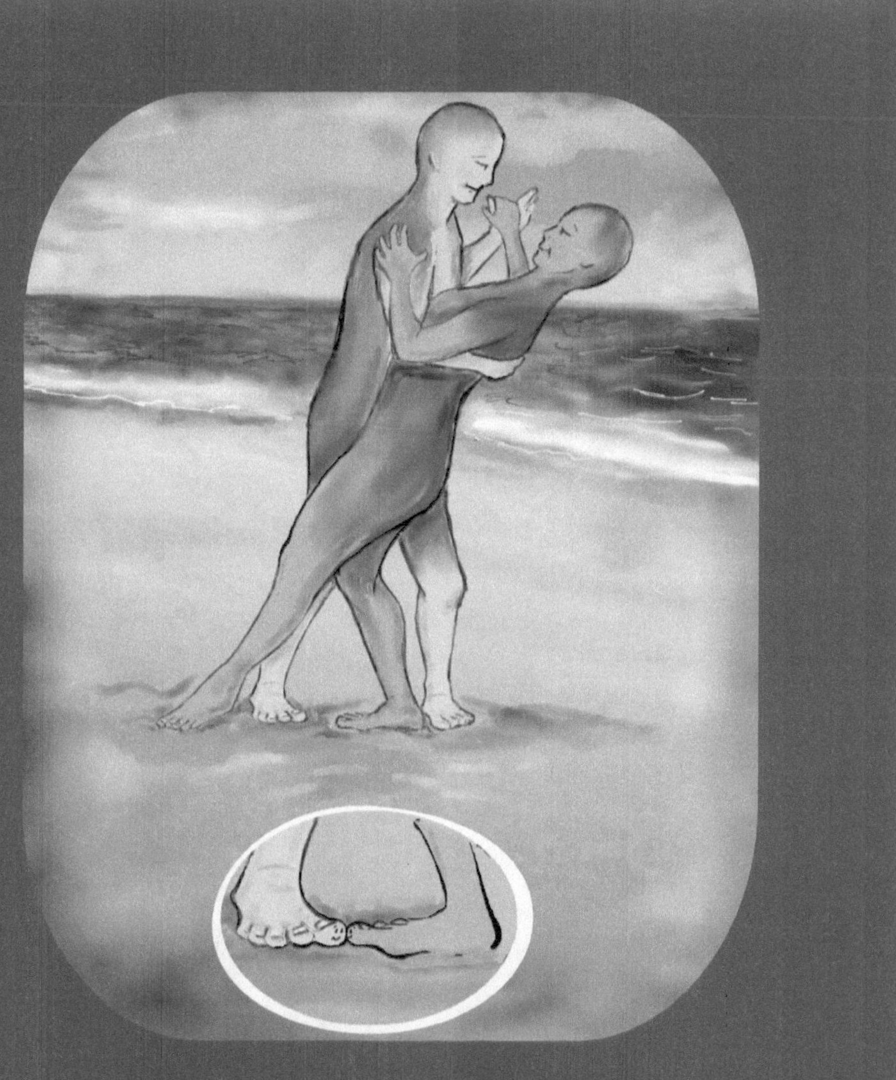

The feet, now visible to toe, dance.
Toe dances!

And the heads kiss.
How they kiss!

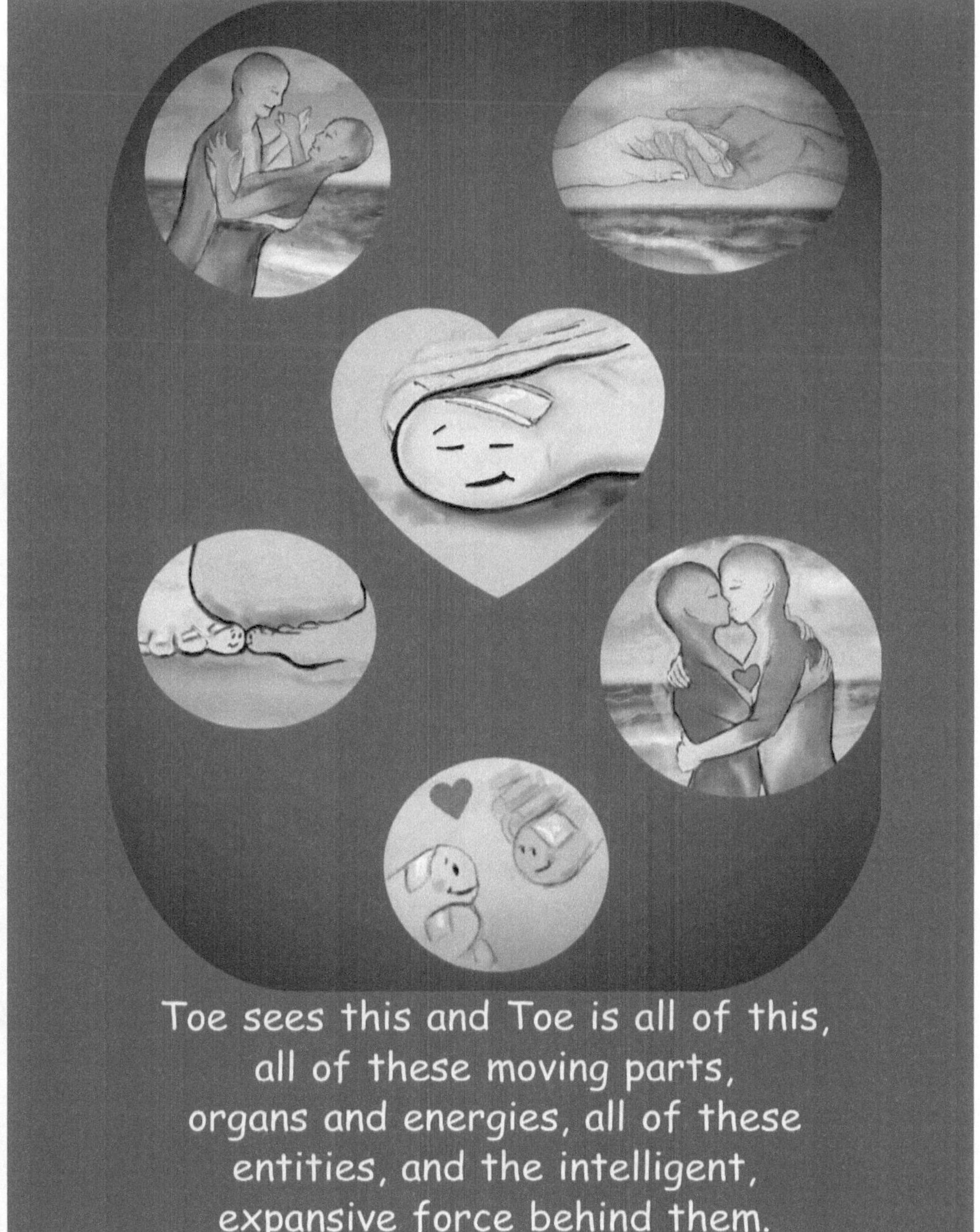
Toe sees this and Toe is all of this,
all of these moving parts,
organs and energies, all of these
entities, and the intelligent,
expansive force behind them.

Toe is Mystery with a capital "M."

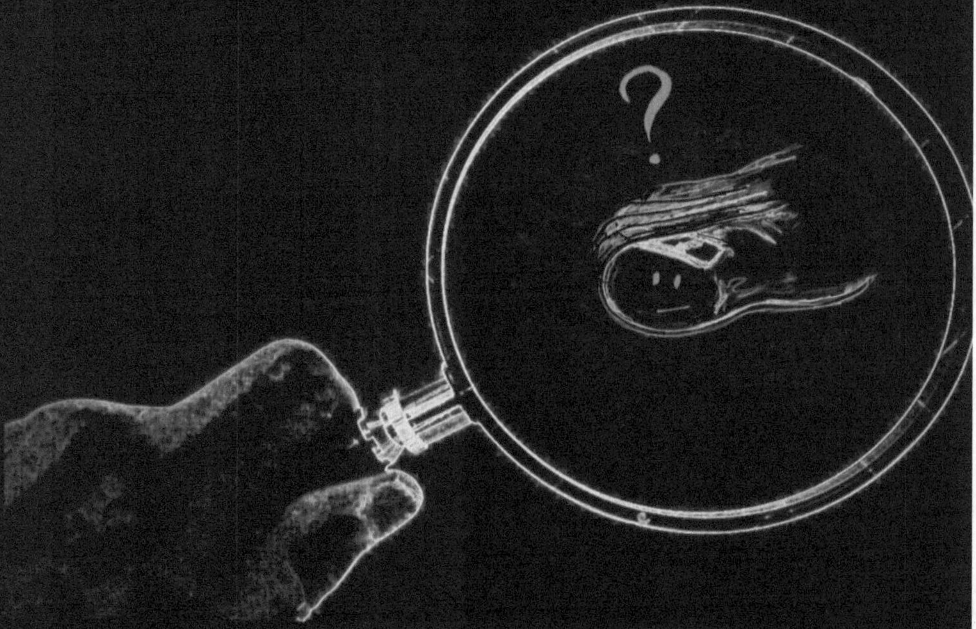

Toe is Love and in love.

And as ever, Toe is just Toe.

31.

www.ingramcontent.com/pod-product-compliance
Lightning Source LLC
Chambersburg PA
CBHW030920260626
47169CB00002B/344